P9-CDS-377

"A fine novel...Percy is a seductive writer, attentive to sensuous detail, and such a skillful architect of fiction that the very discursiveness of his story informs it with energy and tension."

Newsweek

"A funny and scarifying jeremiad on the modern age. *Lancelot* is easy to read and hard to forget."

Time

"*Lancelot* does what masterful fiction must: it tells a story that commands our attention, it introduces us to people whose struggles concern us, it touches our hearts and nettles our minds. We could not ask for more."

Miami Herald

"A complete living and breathing novel...An absolute piece of art."

Saturday Review

LANCELOT

Walker Percy

IVY BOOKS • NEW YORK

Sale of this book without a front cover may be unauthorized. If this book is coverless, it may have been reported to the publisher as "unsold or destroyed" and neither the author nor the publisher may have received payment for it.

Ivy Books
Published by Ballantine Books
Copyright © 1977 by Walker Percy

All rights reserved under International and Pan-American Copyright Conventions. Published in the United States by Ballantine Books, a division of Random House, Inc., New York, and simultaneously in Canada by Random House of Canada Limited, Toronto.

Library of Congress Catalog Card Number: 76-57197

ISBN 0-8041-0380-1

This edition published by arrangement with Farrar, Straus & Giroux, Inc.

Printed in Canada

First Ballantine Books Edition: July 1989
Sixth Printing: November 1993

Tanto giù cadde, che tutti argomenti
alla salute sua eran già corti
fuor che mostrargli le perdute genti.
Per questo visitai l'uscio dei morti . . .

PURGATORIO

He sank so low that all means
for his salvation were gone,
except showing him the lost people.
For this I visited the region of the dead . . .

Though the setting of this novel appears to be New Orleans and the River Road, this city and this famous road are used here as place names of an imaginary terrain. The River Road does not really run into "Feliciana Parish." In fact there is no Feliciana Parish now. There is no "English Coast" that I know of. There is an English Turn, but it is downriver not upriver from New Orleans. Felicity Street does cross Annunciation Street in New Orleans, but not near Lafayette Cemetery. Lafayette Cemetery does exist, but there is no jail or hospital or levee next to it. Murders and house burnings have occurred on River Road, but none, as far as I know, like those herein depicted. There never was a house named Belle Isle. There was a house named Northumberland in Spanish West Florida but it no longer stands. Nor do the characters bear any intentional relation to real persons living or dead.

LANCELOT

1

COME INTO MY CELL. MAKE YOURSELF AT HOME. TAKE the chair; I'll sit on the cot. No? You prefer to stand by the window? I understand. You like my little view. Have you noticed that the narrower the view the more you can see? For the first time I understand how old ladies can sit on their porches for years.

Don't I know you? You look very familiar. I've been feeling rather depressed and I don't remember things very well. I think I am here because of that or because I committed a crime. Perhaps both. Is this a prison or a hospital or a prison hospital? A Center for Aberrant Behavior? So that's it. I have behaved aberrantly. In short, I'm in the nuthouse.

I feel certain that I know you and know you well. It's not that I'm crazy and can't remember things but rather that the past doesn't seem worth remembering. It takes such an effort. Everything takes a tremendous effort and it's hardly worth the trouble—everything except staying in my little cell and looking at my little view.

A cell like this, whether prison or not, is not a bad place to spend a year, believe it or not. I think I have been here a year. Perhaps two. Perhaps six months. I am not sure. A clean cell, a high ceiling, a cot, a chair, and a desk. It's not too cold or hot or damp and the food's edible. A remarkable prison! Or a remarkable hospital as the case may be. And a view, even if the view is nothing more than a patch of sky, a corner of Lafayette Cemetery, a slice of levee, and a short stretch of Annunciation Street.

Isn't that all you can see? No, look again. There's a great deal more. I know that narrow world by heart and I can tell you from here a few things you may not have noticed. For example, if you lean into the embrasure and crane to the left as far as possible, you can see part of a sign around the corner. By the utmost effort and if you press your temple against the bricks, you can make out the following letters:

Free &

Ma

B

Notice that it is impossible to see more than that. I have looked at that sign for a year. What does the sign say? Free & Easy Mac's Bowling? Free & Accepted Masons' Bar? Do Masons have bars?

My memory is coming back. I think you have something to do with it. When I saw you in the hall yesterday, I knew that we had known each other and closely. Haven't we? It's been years and you've changed a great deal, but I know you all right.

When our eyes met, there was the sense of our having gone through a great deal together, wasn't there? There was also the sense of your knowing a great deal more than I. You opened your mouth as if you were going to say something, then thought better of it. I feel like an alcoholic who knows certain people only when he is drunk. You are like a tactful "drunk" friend who is willing not be acknowledged at certain times.

Yes, I asked you to come. Are you a psychiatrist or a priest or a priest-psychiatrist? Frankly, you remind me of something in between, one of those failed priests who go into social work or "counseling," or one of those doctors who suddenly decides to go to the seminary. Neither fish nor fowl. If you're a priest, why don't you wear priest clothes instead of those phony casuals? You're as bad as the nuns. What nuns don't realize is that they look better in nun clothes than in J. C. Penney pantsuits.

You're the first person I've wanted to see. I've refused all psychiatrists, ministers, priests, group therapy, and whatnot. After all, what is there to talk about? I've nothing to say and am certainly not interested in what they say.

No, what first struck me about you was that you're the only person around here who doesn't want to talk. That and an abstracted look in which I recognize a certain kinship of spirit. That plus the fact that I knew you and saw that you knew me even better.

What? Yes, of course I remember Belle Isle and the night it burned and the tragedy, the death, the deaths of . . . But I think that was because I've been told about it and have even been shown the newspapers.

But you . . . I actually remember you. We were close, weren't we? You see, I've been rather depressed and "in the dark" and only lately have managed to be happy just living in this room and enjoying the view. But when I saw you yesterday, it was like seeing myself. I had the sense of being overtaken by something, by the past, by myself. One look at that same old sardonic expression of yours and it was as if I suddenly remembered everything and was not even surprised. I even knew what you were going to say when you shook your head and opened your mouth to say something and didn't say it. You were going to say as usual, weren't you, "For Christ's sake, Lance, what have you gone and done now?" Or something like that. Right?

Only later that night I remembered that I remembered something on my own hook, without being told. My own name. Lance. Rather remembered your liking to pronounce all of it: "Lancelot Andrewes Lamar," you used to say. "You were named after the great Anglican divine, weren't you? Shouldn't it have been Lancelot du Lac, King Ban of Benwick's son?"

It was as if I remembered everything but could not quite bring myself to focus on it.

I perceive that you're not a patient but that something is wrong with you. You're more abstracted than usual. Are you in love?

You're smiling. Smiling but not saying anything. You have to leave? Will you come tomorrow?

II

COME IN, COME IN. SIT DOWN. YOU STILL WON'T?

I have a confession to make. I was not quite honest
yesterday when I pretended not to know you. I knew you
perfectly well. There's nothing wrong with my memory.
It's just that I don't like to remember. Why shouldn't I
remember you? We were best of friends, in fact inseparable
if you recall. It's just that it was quite a shock seeing you
after all these years. No; not even that is true. I noticed you
in the cemetery day before yesterday. Still I hardly knew
what to say to you. What do you say to someone after
twenty years when you have already said everything.

It bothers you a bit too, doesn't it? You are shy with me.
But you like my window and my little view, I can see.

You still look doubtful. About my sanity? Well yes,
after all, here I am in the nuthouse. But I remember you
perfectly, everything we ever did, every name you ever
had. We knew each other by several names depending on
the oblique and obscure circumstances of our lives—and
our readings. I bet I remember your names better than you.
To begin with, you were simply Harry, when you lived at
Northumberland close to us on the River Road and we

5

went to school together. Later you were known variously as Harry Hotspur, a misnomer because though you were pugnacious you were not much of a fighter. Also as Prince Hal, because you seemed happy only in whorehouses. Also as Northumberland, after the house you lived in. Also as Percival and Parsifal, who found the Grail and brought life to a dead land. Also by several cheerful obscene nicknames in the D.K.E. fraternity of which the least objectionable was Pussy. Miss Margaret Mae McDowell of Sweet Briar, I want you to meet my friend and roommate, Pussy. Later, I understand you took a religious name when you became a priest: John, a good name. But is it John the Evangelist who loved so much or John the Baptist, a loner out in the wilderness? You were a loner.

So as you see, I remember a great deal about you. Right?

Ah, you smile your old smile.

Yet you prefer to look at the cemetery.

It makes a pretty scene today, don't you think? All Souls' Day. A pleasant feast for the dead: the women in the cemetery whitewashing the tombs, trimming the tiny lawns, setting out chrysanthemums, real and plastic, lighting candles, scrubbing the marble lintels. They remind me of Baltimore housewives on their hands and knees washing the white doorsteps of row houses.

A pretty sight, the bustling cluttered cemetery, the copper-penny-colored rain trees, the first fitful north wind blowing leaves every which way. If you listen carefully, you can hear the dry curlicues of crepe-myrtle leaves blowing up and down the paths like popcorn. When the wind shifts you catch a whiff of coffee and tar from the Tchoupitoulas docks.

In New Orleans I have noticed that people are happiest when they are going to funerals, making money, taking care of the dead, or putting on masks at Mardi Gras so nobody knows who they are.

Well, I found out who you are. Your profession, that is. A priest-physician. Which is to say, a screwed-up priest or a half-assed physician. Or both. Ah, I managed to surprise you, didn't I? Yes, someone told me yesterday. But it is more than that. It was something I observed.

You were taking a shortcut through the cemetery. One of the women scrubbing the tombs stopped you to ask you something. Obviously she recognized you. You shook your head and moved on. But what could she have asked you? Only one thing under the circumstances. To say a prayer for the dead. An old custom here, particularly on All Souls' Day. You turned her down.

So something went wrong with you too. Or you wouldn't be here serving as assistant chaplain or substitute psychiatrist or whatever it is you're doing. A non-job. Are you in trouble? Is it a woman? Are you in love?

Do you remember "falling in love," "being in love"?

There was a time when I thought that was the only thing that really mattered. No, there were two things and two times in my life.

At first I thought "being in love" was the only thing. Holding a sweet Georgia girl in your arms and dancing to the "Limelight" theme in the Carolina mountains in the summer of '52, out of doors, with the lightning bugs and the Japanese lanterns.

Later I became coarser or perhaps more realistic. I began to wonder if there was such a thing as "being in love," or whether the best things in life might not be such simple, age-old pleasures as ordinary sexual intercourse and ordinary drinking. Indeed, what could be finer than to be a grown healthy man and to meet a fine-looking woman you've never seen before and to want her on the spot and to see also that she likes you, to invite her to have a few drinks in a bar, to put your hand under her dress, to touch the deep white flesh of her thigh, to speak into her ear, "Well, now, sweetheart, what do you say?" Right? No?

But that's falling in love too, in a way, isn't it? Yet very different. I wonder which is better. To tell you the truth, I haven't quite sorted it out yet.

But certainly "love" is one or the other, no doubt the latter. Sometimes I think we were the victims of a gigantic hoax by our elders, that there was an elaborate conspiracy to conceal from us the one simple fact that the only important, certainly the best thing in life, is ordinary sexual love.

I "fell in love" with Lucy Cobb from Georgia and married her. Then she died. Then I "fell in love" with Margot and married her. She died too.

Would it surprise you if I told you that I might be falling in love again? With the girl in the next room. I've never seen her. But they tell me she was gang-raped by some sailors in the Quarter, forced to commit unnatural acts many times, then beaten up and thrown onto the batture. She won't speak to anybody. And she has to be force fed. Like me she prefers the solitude of her cell. But we communicate by tapping on the wall. It is strange. Her defilement restores her to a kind of innocence.

Communication is simple when you are "in love." Driving with Lucy Cobb through the Carolina summer night with the top down and the radio playing the "Limelight" theme, one could say to her simply:

"I like that, don't you?"

And she could say: "Yes."

With the girl in the next room it is the same. Yesterday I tapped twice.

She tapped back twice.

It might have been an accident. On the other hand, it

could have been a true communication. My heart beat as if I were falling in love for the first time.

Then you know my story? I know it too of course, but I'm not sure how much I really remember. I think of it in terms of headlines: BELLE ISLE BURNS. BODIES OF FILM STARS CHARRED BEYOND RECOGNITION. SCION OF OLD FAMILY CRAZED BY GRIEF AND RAGE. SUFFERS BURNS TRYING TO SAVE WIFE. No doubt I read such headlines. I wonder why the headlines are easier to remember than the event itself.

Now I've begun to remember some things perfectly. It was seeing you that did it.

The first thing I remembered was the exact circumstances under which I discovered that my wife was deceiving me. But what did that have to do with you? Memory is a strange thing.

The next thing I remembered made more sense. I remembered the first time I had seen you since childhood. You were sitting in the fraternity house alone, drinking and reading Verlaine. That made quite an impression on me. I remember wondering whether you were not trying to make an impression. What kind of an act is that, I wondered. (It was a bit of an act, wasn't it?)

Then this morning I remembered a great deal more. It was not as if I had really forgotten but rather that I didn't have the—the what?—the inclination to think about the past. I had got out of the trick of doing it. Seeing you was a kind of catalyst, the occasion of my remembering. It is like the first time you look through binoculars: everything is confused, blurred, unfocused, flat; then all of a sudden *click*: distance drops away and there is everything in the round, bigger than life.

I think I began to remember by remembering our likenesses and our differences: we both lived in old houses on the River Road on the English Coast, I in Belle Isle, you in Northumberland.

Though we would never have admitted it, we regarded ourselves as an enclave of the English gentry set down among hordes of good docile Negroes and comical French peasants. Our families were the original Tory English colonials who accepted Spanish hospitality in Feliciana Parish to get away from the crazy rebellious Americans. But we were united less by a common history than by our dislike of Catholics and the Longs. We were honorable families.

You and I were also classmates, fraternity brothers, and later best of friends. We went to whorehouses. I understand young men don't have to go to whorehouses any more.

There the resemblances stopped. Your family was rich so you went to prep school in the North. We were poor so I went to public high school. You were thin, withdrawn, and you drank too much, were said to be brilliant and to have the promise of a great future (did you?), yet you were obscure, almost unknown: when you graduated you didn't know six people in the entire school.

I was the opposite: the type who reaches the peak of his life in college and declines thereafter: prominent on campus, debater, second-string all-S.E.C. halfback, Rhodes scholar, even "smart," that is, a sort of second-echelon Phi Beta Kappa. Being "smart" on the football team meant that you read *Time* magazine and had heard of the Marshall Plan. ("You don't believe he can tell you about the Marshall Plan? Ask him! He's one more smart sapsucker.") They, my teammates, admired "smartness" more than anybody I've met before or since.

I achieved my single small immortality at the age of twenty-one when I caught an Alabama punt standing on the back line of the end zone and ran it out 110 yards for a touchdown. It is still on the record books as the longest punt return in history. The beauty is, it always will be—it can't be surpassed. It's like running the mile in zero minutes.

I was "smart," but never smart in your complex way of drinking and reading Verlaine (that was an act, wasn't it?)

You were also belligerent when drunk and since you were built like Pope Pius XII, six feet and about 120 pounds, many was the the time I had to save your ass from being whipped. (Yes, I was also Golden Gloves runner-up and though I weighed only 170 could take anybody on the football team, another source of astonishment to those Cajuns: "That son of a bitch beat the shit out of Durel Thibodeaux!" (defensive tackle, 265).

You were melancholy and abstracted and attractive to women but so thin I had to fix you up with big handsome motherly girls who didn't mind hugging your bones.

There was a difference in our families. The men in my family (until my father) were gregarious, politically active (anti-Long), and violent. The men in your family tended toward depression and early suicide.

Yet look who's depressed now.

You cock the same sardonic eye at me you cocked when you looked up from Verlaine.

As I say, seeing you allowed me to remember the circumstances under which I discovered that my wife had deceived me, that is, had had carnal relations with another man.

Is it this which was so difficult to remember? It is not

that I forgot it but that I found it intolerable to think about.
But why should it be intolerable? Is the sexual offense a
special category and therefore unlike other offenses, theft,
assault, even murder?

Or is it that the sexual belongs to no category at all, is
unspeakable? Isn't sexual pleasure unspeakable? Then why
shouldn't the sexual offense be unspeakable?

No, I didn't really forget anything. It was rather that
seeing you allowed me to think about it. I wonder why.
Because we were friends or because you are used to hearing the unspeakable? Or because seeing you reminded me
of the pigeonnier?

But let me ask you seriously: Why is it such an unspeakable thing for one creature to obtrude a small portion of its
body into the body of another creature? Is it not in fact a
trivial matter when one puts it that way? I don't think
women attach too much importance to it.

But suppose I put it another way. Isn't it unspeakable to
me to imagine Margot lying under another man, her head
turning to and fro in a way I knew only too well, her lips
stretched, a little mew-cry escaping her lips? Isn't that unspeakable? Yes. But why? When I imagined other things
happening to Margot, even the worst things, they were
painful but not intolerable: Margot seriously ill, Margot
hurt in an accident, Margot stealing money, even Margot
dead, murdered. The thought of Margot dead was painful
but not intolerable. But Margot under another man . . .

Hm. Do you think it is only our generation who put so
much stock in it, the sexual connection, or as the kids say,
got hung up? The ancients didn't seem to dwell on it too
much; even the Bible is rather casual. Your God seemed
much more jealous of false idols, golden calves, than his
people messing around with each other. Perhaps God's
jealousy is different from ours. I wouldn't have minded

Margot kneeling before a Buddha. Then why should I worry about a small matter like Margot taking a small part of Merlin's body into her body? As a physician, wouldn't you say that nothing more is involved than the touch of one membrane against another? Cells touching cells.

Not even your church took it very seriously until recent years. Dante was downright indulgent with sexual sinners. They occupied a rather pleasant anteroom to hell.

And the present generation! Sex doesn't even seem to rate among the Top Ten experiences. I remember once I visited my son. He got out of bed, where he and his girl friend were lying naked and twined about each other, yawned, threw a sheet over her, then proceeded to tell me what was really on his mind: a guitar. A guitar! A certain kind of guitar. Oh, Christ, if only he could afford that guitar! Maybe I was good for four hundred dollars? As I wrote him a check I remember thinking: Very well, he lusts after, loves that guitar. But once he got it, would he mind somebody else playing it? Perhaps. But he wouldn't find it unspeakable.

My son got enough of women before he was twenty. Presently he appears to be a mild homosexual. But in either case, hetero or homo, it doesn't seem to count for a great deal to him.

Is it just our generation which got hung up on it?

You shrug and cock an eye at the cemetery.

Then is it just me?

I remember where I first discovered her adultery. In the room under the pigeonnier. Do you remember that room? You and I used to sit there on weekends or in the summer and drink and read aloud—you mostly—the dirty parts of *Ulysses* and *Tropic of Cancer*. That was a discovery for me too: that there were not only bad dirty books and great clean books but also great dirty books (yes! that's the con-

13

nection: two discoveries made in the same place). When you and I went there, it was still being used by the pigeons, six inches deep in pigeon shit upstairs, and the cooing-chuckling going very well with Joyce and Miller read aloud. Downstairs was a junk room, an accumulation of the detritus of summer, crumbling hammocks and badminton nets and busted croquet balls, but dry and cool. Do you remember that summer? That was the year they drilled an oil well where the old wing of Belle Isle used to be (it too had burned mysteriously a hundred years earlier), and hit gas. For the first time since the war we had a little money. Do you remember poking around the junk in the pigeonnier and finding what looked like the original Bowie knife? Maybe it was. My ancestor did know Bowie, even had a part in the notorious Vidalia sand-bar duel in which Bowie actually carved a fellow limb from limb. At any rate, my grandfather made a good story of it when I showed him the knife, claimed it was one of the originals made by Bowie's slave blacksmith (though it wasn't: the original was made from a rasp and still showed the grooves), and displayed it as part of his spiel to the tourists whom he used to lead around Belle Isle at a dollar a head. He'd tell them Bowie stories and Eleanor Roosevelt stories.

Later Margot, discovering that the pigeonnier was an architectural gem, had it converted into a study for me. To her delight, after scraping off 150 years of pigeon shit they found the original cypress floor of two-by-twelves marvelously preserved, two-foot-thick walls of slave brick—even pigeons lived better than we do now. She found me a plantation desk and chair made by slave artisans and there I sat, feeling like Jeff Davis at Beauvoir, ready to write my memoirs. Except I had no memoirs. There was nothing to remember.

At any rate, it was there at 5:01 in the afternoon that I

discovered purely by chance that my wife had been, and probably was still, unfaithful to me.

It is a mystery which I ponder endlessly: that my life is divided into two parts, Before and After, before and after the moment I discovered that my wife had been rendered ecstatic, beside herself, by a man on top of her.

My discovery occurred purely by accident. At exactly 5:01 p.m. the Ethyl whistle had just stopped blowing.

I happened to look down at my desk and saw something. Only on second sight—and I don't even know why I looked at it again—did it begin to take on a terrific significance.

My reaction was not what you might suppose. I can only compare it, my reaction, to that of a scientist, an astronomer say, who routinely examines photographic plates of sectors of the heavens and sees the usual random scattering of dots of light. He is about to file away one such plate, has already done so, when a tiny little something clicks in his head. *Hold on. Hm. Whoa. What's this? Something is wrong. Let's have a look.* So he takes another look. Yes, sure enough, one dot, not even a bright dot, one of the lesser dots, is a bit out of place. You've seen the photos in the newspapers, random star dots and four arrows pointing to a single dot. To make sure, the astronomer compares this plate with the last he took of the same tiny sector of the heavens. Sure enough, the dot is out of place. It has moved. What of it, thinks the layman, one insignificant dot out of a billion dots slightly out of place? The astronomer knows better: the dot is one millisecond out of place, click click goes the computer, and from the most insignificant observation the astronomer calculates with absolute certainty and finality that a comet is on a collision course with the earth and will arrive in two and a half months. In eight weeks the dot will have grown to the size of the sun, the oceans risen forty feet, New York will be under water, skyscrapers toppling, U.N. meeting on Mount Washington, etc.

How can such dire and absolutely verifiable events follow upon the most insignificant of evidence?

In my case, the evidence was not the minute shift of a dot on a photographic plate but a letter on my desk. No, not a love letter; no, I mean a letter in the alphabet. The letter *O*. I'll explain, if you're interested. Christ, you don't seem to be. Are you watching that girl I hear singing? I hear her every day. You know her, don't you?

I've seen you speak to her on the levee. She's lovely, isn't she? Clean jeans, clean combed hair halfway down her back. She crosses the levee every day. I think she lives in one of the shacks on the batture. Probably a transient from the North, like one of the hundreds of goldfinches who blow in every October.

One becomes good at observing people after a year, like an old lady who has nothing better to do than peep through the blinds. I observed that you know her well. Are you in love with her?

Ah, that does surprise you, doesn't it? Listen to the girl. She's singing.

> *Freedom's just another word, Lord, for nothing*
> *left to lose*
> *Freedom was all she left for me*

Do you believe that? Maybe the girl and I come closer to believing it than you, even though you surrendered your freedom voluntarily and I didn't. Maybe the girl knows more than either of us.

But we were speaking not of astronomical categories but rather of the sexual. A horse of another color, you might say. Well, yes and no. There are certain similarities. Compare the two discoveries. The astronomer sees a dot in the wrong place, makes a calculation, and infers the indisputable: comet on collision course, tidal waves, oceans rising, forests ablaze. The cuckold sees a single letter of the alphabet in the wrong place. From such insignificant evidence he can infer with at least as much certitude as the astronomer an equally incommensurate scene: his wife's thighs spread, a cry, not recognizably hers, escaping her lips. The equivalent of the end of the world following upon the out-of-place dot is her ecstasy inferred from the *O*.

Beyond any doubt she was both beside herself and possessed by something, someone? Such considerations have led me to the conclusion that, contrary to the usual opinion, sex is not a category at all. It is not merely an item on a list of human needs like food, shelter, air, but is rather a unique ecstasy, ek-stasis, which is a kind of possession. Just as possession by Satan is not a category. You smile. You disagree? Are you then one of the new breed who believe that Satan is only a category, the category of evil?

Yet how can such portentous consequences be inferred from such trivial evidence? I will tell you if you wish to know, but first I want to report my own reaction to my discovery, which was, to say the least, the strangest of all. You would think, wouldn't you, that the new cuckold would respond with the appropriate emotion—shock, shame, humiliation, sorrow, anger, hate, vengefulness, etc. Would you believe me when I tell you that I felt none of these emotions? Can you guess what I did feel? *Hm. What's this? What have we here? Hm.* What I felt was a prickling at the base of the spine, a turning of the worm of interest.

Yes, interest! The worm of interest. Are you surprised? No? Yes? One conclusion I have reached here after a year

in my cell is that the only emotion people feel nowadays is
interest or the lack of it. Curiosity and interest and boredom have replaced the so-called emotions we used to read
about in novels or see registered on actors' faces. Even the
horrors of the age translate into interest. Did you ever
watch anybody pick up a newspaper and read the headline
PLANE CRASH KILLS THREE HUNDRED? How horrible! says
the reader. But look at him when he hands you the paper.
Is he horrified? No, he is interested. When was the last
time you saw anybody horrified?

Yet not even my sad case seems to interest you. Are you
listening? What do you see down in the cemetery? The
women getting ready for All Souls' Day? whitewashing the
tombs, trimming the tiny lawns, putting out chrysanthemums real and plastic, scrubbing the marble lintels. Cater-
cornered from the cemetery if you look close is what used
to be the Negro entrance to the old Majestic Theater, now
Adult Cinema 16. Remember going there when we came to
New Orleans? We used to see movies like *The 49ers* with
—who? Vera Hruba Ralston (the hubba hubba girl) and
Charles Starrett, or was it Veronica Lake and Preston Fos-
ter? Or Robert Preston and Virginia Mayo? Now they're
showing something called *The 69ers*. From here all you
can make out of the poster is a kind of vague yinyang,
showing, I guess, a couple, as if Charles and Vera Hruba
had got caught in the vortex of time and gone whirling
yinyanged down the years.

Across the street you can make out the blackboard of La
Branche's Bar. What's the specialty today? Gumbo? Oyster
po' boys, shrimp soup? And Dixie draught.

New Orleans! Not a bad place to spend a year in prison
—except in summer. Imagine being locked up in Birming-
ham or Memphis. What is it I can smell, even from here,
as if the city had a soul and the soul exhaled an effluvium

18

all its own? I can't quite name it. A certain vital decay? A lively fetor? Whenever I think of New Orleans away from New Orleans, I think of rotting fish on the sidewalk and good times inside. A Catholic city in a sense, but that's not it. Providence, Rhode Island, is a Catholic city, but my God who would want to live in Providence, Rhode Island? It's not it, your religion, that informs this city, but rather some special local accommodation to it or relaxation from it. This city's soul I think of as neither damned nor saved but eased rather, existing in a kind of comfortable Catholic limbo somewhere between the outer circle of hell, where sexual sinners don't have it all that bad, and the inner circle of purgatory, where things are even better. Add to that a flavor of Marseilles vice leavened by Southern U.S.A. good nature. Death and sex treated unseriously and money seriously. The Whitney Bank is as solemn as the cemetery is lively. Protestants started Mardi Gras, you know. Presbyterians take siestas or play gin at the Boston Club. Jews ride on carnival floats celebrating the onset of Christ's forty-day fast.

I like your banal little cathedral in the Vieux Carré. It is set down squarely in the midst of the greatest single concentration of drunks, drugheads, whores, pimps, queers, sodomists in the hemisphere. But isn't that where cathedrals are supposed to be? It, like the city, has something else even more comforting to me, a kind of triumphant mediocrity. The most important event which occurred here in all of history was the John L. Sullivan–Jim Corbett fight. Three hundred years of history and it has never produced a single significant historical event, one single genius, or even a first-class talent—except a chess player, the world's greatest. But genius makes people nervous, including the genius, so he quit playing chess and began worrying about money like everyone else. It is altogether in keeping that the famous Battle of New Orleans was fought after the war was over and was without significance.

After the terrible events at Belle Isle, a year of non-events in a place like this is a relief. There is a sense here of people seriously occupied with small tasks. We, you and I, our families, were different from the Creoles. We lived from one great event to another, tragic events, triumphant events, with years of melancholy in between. We lost Vicksburg, got slaughtered at Shiloh, fought duels, defied Huey Long, and were bored to death between times. The Creoles have the secret of living ordinary lives well. A hundred years from now I don't doubt that women like those out there will be scrubbing the tombs on All Souls' Day, a La Branche will be polishing his bar, and a dirty movie will be playing across the street.

But in order for you to understand what happened at Belle Isle and why I am here, you must understand exactly how it was that day a year ago. I was sitting in my pigeonnier as snug as could be, the day very much like today, the same Northern tang in the air, but utterly still, sun shining, sky as blue as Nebraska cornflowers, not a cloud in the sky. I was reading a book. Yet even before I glanced down at my desk and discovered my wife's infidelity, there was something odd about the day. You will understand this because we, you and I, used to have a taste for the odd and the whimsical.

For now that I've thought about it, things were a little odd even before my interesting discovery. There I sat in my pigeonnier, happy as could be, master of Belle Isle, the loveliest house on the River Road, gentleman and even bit of a scholar (Civil war, of course), married to a beautiful rich loving (I thought) wife, and father (I thought) to a lovely little girl; a moderate reader, moderate liberal, moderate drinker (I thought), moderate music lover, moderate hunter and fisherman, and past president of the United Way. I moderately opposed segregation. I was moderately happy. At least at the moment I was happy. But not for the reasons given above. The reason I was happy was that I was reading for perhaps the fourth or fifth time a Raymond Chandler novel. It gave me pleasure, (no, I'll put it more strongly: it didn't just give me pleasure, it was the only way I could stand my life) to sit there in old goldgreen Louisiana under the levee and read, not about General Beauregard, but about Philip Marlowe taking a bottle out of his desk drawer in his crummy office in seedy Los Angeles in 1933 and drinking alone and all those from-nowhere people living in stucco bungalows perched in Laurel Canyon. The only way I could stand my life in Louisiana, where I had everything, was to read about crummy lonesome Los Angeles in the 1930's. Maybe that should have told me something. If I was happy, it was an odd sort of happiness.

But it was odder even than that. Things were split. I was physically in Louisiana but spiritually in Los Angeles. The day was split too. One window let onto this kind of October day, blue sky, sun shining, children already building Christmas bonfires on the levee from willows their fathers had cut on the batture. The other window let onto a thunderstorm. My wife's friend's film company had set up a thunderstorm machine in the tourist parking lot where ordinarily cars from Michigan, Indiana, Ohio would be parked while rumpled amiable bemused Midwesterners paid their five dollars and went gawking through the great rooms as foreign to them as Castel Gandolfo (never, surely, in history were there ever a stranger pair than those victors and us vanquished). A propeller on a tower blew rain on the south wing of Belle Isle, whitening the live oaks, and the thunder machine thundered, a huge stretch of sheet metal

21

with a motor and a padded eccentric cam. They were trying it out. A scene in the movie required a hurricane. The propeller roared like a B-29, wind and rain lashed Belle Isle, the live oaks turned inside out, Spanish moss tore loose, the sheet metal thundered. But on the other side of the pigeonnier the sun shone serenely.

Margot had told me about it but I didn't pay much attention. The movie was about some people who seek shelter in the great house during a hurricane, a young Cajun trapper, a black sharecropper, a white sharecropper, A Christlike hippy, a Klan type, a beautiful half-caste but also half-wit swamp girl, a degenerate river rat, the son and daughter of the house, even though there are no sharecroppers or Cajuns or even a swamp hereabouts and river rats disappeared with the fish in the Mississippi years ago. And I don't even know what a "half-caste swamp girl" is. I am still unclear about the plot. The Negro sharecropper and the redneck's father, who seem at first to hate each other, form an unlikely alliance to protect the women of the house against rapists of both races. With the help of the Christlike hippy, white and black discover their common humanity. There was something too about the master of the house trying to steal the sharecropper's land, which has oil under it. My only contribution to the story discussions was to point out that the land could not belong to the sharecropper if he was a sharecropper.

The five o'clock whistle at Ethyl blew. I put the book down face up on my desk. It was the plantation desk Margot had given me, built high so a planter in a hurry could write a check standing up. I don't think those fellows ever sat down and wrote a letter or read a book. She had the legs cut off to make an ordinary desk. My eyes fell off the print to a piece of paper beside the book. I remember everything! I even remember the passage in the Chandler novel. Marlowe was looking for a man named Goodwin. He walked into a house in a canyon between Glendale and Pasadena. An *English* bungalow! in Pasadena! Don't you like that? A pleasant incongruity absolutely congruous in Los Angeles. Goodwin was living there alone. Where could Goodwin have come from? I was trying to imagine Goodwin's childhood, Goodwin twelve years old in Fort Wayne before his parents moved to California. Try to imagine someone in Los Angeles with a childhood. Inside the house Goodwin was dead, a bullet through his forehead. My eye slid off his name—I remember it because his first name was Lancelot like mine—onto the paper next to it. It was my daughter's application to a horse camp in West Texas. Margot had filled it in and left it for me to sign. Siobhan I thought was too young for a horse camp— yes, my daughter is named Siobhan. My wife Margot was born Mary Margaret Reilly of Odessa, Texas, so our daughter was named Siobhan. This was a special Montessori horse camp and Margot insisted ("I was raised on a ranch in West Texas and I am not about to have her miss it"). I didn't like the idea of her fooling with horses, great stupid iron-headed beasts, but I always gave in to Margot. I reached for the pen to sign the application and the medical waiver and my eye slid over the page to the letter *O*. No, it was not the letter *O* but the number *0*, cipher, zero. It was her blood type, I-0. I read the medical examination. At the least the camp people were careful. In case a child got kicked in an artery, they had her blood type. I-0.

I was looking at it idly. The thunder machine stopped. My head felt a little giddy but not unpleasant, as if I were dislocated and weightless in space—sliding instantaneously from an English bungalow in a Los Angeles canyon to an artificial hurricane to an absolutely still cool clear day in Louisiana. Once in a while an empty sugar-cane truck rumbled down the River Road.

Then it was that the worm of interest turned somewhere near the base of my spine. Curious. What was curious? The star dot was slightly out of place. But what was out of place here? I didn't know yet. Or did I? At any rate, I found myself climbing the iron staircase to the pigeon roost proper. There I kept my regular office equipment, file cabinets, typewriter, and so forth, which Margot didn't like downstairs where she liked to think of me as Jeff Davis writing his memoirs. Not having much to do over the years, I'd kept perfect records of what little I had done. Would you believe that I became meticulous? I'd have made a good C.P.A. Better a good C.P.A. than a half-assed lawyer. There in the file cabinet I found what I had not until that moment quite realized I was looking for: my medical discharge from the army. Sir Lancelot, as you called me, Percival, discharged from the army not bloody and victorious and battered by Sir Turquine but with persistent diarrhea. The army gave me the shits and couldn't cure me. Three months in Walter Reed, the best doctors in the world, twenty thousand dollars worth of medical care, and they couldn't cure the simple shits. So I came home to Louisiana, in August, sat in the rocking chair on the gallery of Belle Isle, downed a great slug of bourbon, and watched the river boats. Sweat popped out on my head and I felt fine.

Ah, here it was. My blood type. IV-AB. Again the worm of interest turned in my spine. I sat down in my metal swivel chair at my metal desk in the pigeon roost. It took Fluker two weeks to shovel out 150 years of pigeon shit, scrape the walls, and reveal what Margot was after, the slave brick of the walls and the three-inch cypress floor, not only not rotted but preserved, waxed by guano.

The sun was setting behind the levee and shafts of rosy light from the glazed pigeonholes pierced the dim roost like laser beams.

I began writing formulae on a pad of yellow legal foolscap. Isn't it a fact that blood types are hereditary and that when the genes or chromosomes split, the A goes one way, the B the other, but never the A and B together?

There was an unknown in the equation. I did not know Margot's blood type, but did I have to? Let Margot's gene equal X. My gene had to be A or B. Two equations were possible.

$$X + A = O$$
$$X + B = O$$

The equations do not solve. X does not have a value. My blood type and Siobhan's blood type did not compute.

So I telephoned my cousin Royal in New Orleans. You remember him, Royal Bonderman Lamar? No? You know, Raw Raw, little bitty towheaded sapsucker from Clinton, Kappa Sig, trip manager for the team the last year? Used to stand around at dances, hands in his gabardines, grinning like an idiot, stuff between his teeth? Yes? Actually he was smart as hell, is now an excellent surgeon, makes three hundred thousand a year.

I put the question hypothetically.

"You got a paternity case?" asked Royal. "I thought all you did was look after Margot's money and help niggers."

"That's what I'm doing." The worm of interest was turning. I remember listening for something in his voice, a note of superiority. In college I was the big shot, Phi Beta Kappa and halfback, and Royal carried the water bucket. Ever since, downhill all the way for me and up for him. While I was sitting under the levee sweating in my seersuckers, musing and drinking, he invented a heart valve. So I listened for the note of superiority which God knows he was entitled to. It wasn't there. Same Royal, simply cheerful, grinning over the phone, stuff between his teeth.

"You mean you got a nigger paternity suit? I never heard of such a thing."

"Just tell me, Royal."

"Tell you what? Oh." He was still the same Royal in a way, agreeable and willing. The horsing around and even the "nigger" business was not quite as it sounded though, but part of a new broad manner he'd hit upon, found possible, just as he'd found it possible to be grave and loving at weddings in the family and even unsmiling, put his arm around a niece, and, not quite as tall as she, kiss her and wish her every happiness and mean it. Not even the "nigger" business was as it sounded because he operated on blacks and whites alike and didn't call them niggers or even by their first names and sat them down together in his waiting room and did more for them than I did. He outdid me in the race thing. He did more and talked less.

"No. A type IV-AB cannot beget a type O no matter who or what the mama is."

"I see."

"What you got is a nig—"

"I know, I know."

"—ger in the woodpile."

"I know."

The thunder machine started up again.

"My God, what's that, Lance?"

"A thunder machine."

"A what? Never mind."

"Thank you, Royal."

"Give my love to Margot."

26

"Right, right," I said and almost forgot to say, Give mine to Charlotte. "Give my love to Charlotte." I hung up.

Give my love. I thought of something and called Royal again.

"Is the period of pregnancy exactly nine months?"

"It depends on what you mean by month. Average gestation for a full-term infant is ten lunar months. Two hundred and eighty days. But why—"

"What's the average weight of a full-term infant?"

"Male or female?"

"Female."

"Seven pounds."

"Thanks, Royal."

"Okay, Tiger."

Tiger. Did he call me that in school? Or was there a note of condescension?

"Thanks."

My records were very good. In seconds I can, could— Jesus, the place burned to the ground, didn't it?—no, still can. The pigeonnier didn't burn and I guess the records are still there. I could look up any given day's receipts of the tourist take at Belle Isle.

I made calculations. This time the equations were simpler. In fact there were no equations because there were no variables. It was arithmetic. I needed four pieces of data. I had two: Siobhan's birthday, April 21, 1969, and birth weight, 7 lbs. Subtract 280 days from April 21, 1969. I looked at my feedstore calendar. The remainder is July 15, 1968. I could remember nothing. Can you remember where you were in the summer of '68? You can? Yes, you would. You didn't keep records but you always had a nose for time and places. I remember you stone drunk here in New Orleans, on the ground in the weeds, on the levee, peaceable and not quite unconscious, sniffing the soil and

27

saying "What place is this?" Is that why you chose the god you did, the time-place god?

My third and indispensable item came from a shot in the dark. The dark of the dead file where I kept old income tax data and work sheets. A shot in the dark, not really a lucky—unlucky?—shot, but rather the only shot I had. My worm of interest tingled and guided me like a magnet to a manila folder neatly lettered DEDUCTIONS, 1968. I'm sure you don't have to worry about deductions but it's a good way to remember where you were and what you did ten years ago. A hundred years from now histories will be written from the stubs of Exxon bills. Bastardy will be proved by Master Charge. There was a chance I could find out where I spent the summer or at least hit on enough clues to remember the summer. Suppose Margot and I had gone to Williamsburg to talk to the National Heritage people about Belle Isle (we did one summer). A possible deductible. It would show: Coach-and-Four motel bill, Delta Air Lines carbon. Suppose I had spent two weeks in Washington with the Civil Rights Commission (I did that in the 1960's). A deductible: receipted Shoreham Hotel bill. Suppose I spent a month in England buying antiques to show and sell at Belle Isle (I did that in the bad years). A clear deductible: Pan Am or Amex card. But where was I in the summer of 1968?

I found out. Not where I was but where Margot was. Was that the significance of the tingling of the worm of interest? that actually I already knew but did not know that I knew or would not admit it, had even suppressed the knowledge so that it might then be properly discovered, just as the astronomer already knows in his heart of hearts that that dot will have moved but won't even think about it until the photographic plate is in his hand and he can see the dot in the right-wrong place—all this in order to do what? In his case savor the superiority of the real over the imaginary? In my case to do what? postpone the interesting horror the way a person will turn an unopened telegram over and over in his hand?

Here it was. Amex stub and customer's copy and receipted bill from the Arlington, Texas, Roundtower Motor Lodge for $1,325.27. A clear deductible. Not for me but for Margot, who at the time was still technically an actress, never a very good one but an Equity-card-carrying one and clearly engaged in the practice of her profession, that was why we deducted it, not acting but attending Robert Merlin's workshop at the famous Dallas-Arlington Playhouse. The entire month of July. Eastern Airlines tickets for June 30 and return August 1. She had not come home and I had not visited her. I knew because all at once I remembered the summer of '68. The courts had just caught up with Feliciana Parish and a few of us moderate and peace-loving persons of good will of both races had our own workshops, with the schoolboard and teachers and PTA's, so people wouldn't get killed when school opened. We succeeded. Nobody got killed. On the contrary. New life was conceived.

Siobhan then was conceived on or about July 15, 1968, give or take a few days. How many days? a week? ten days? two weeks? As Royal said, biology is not an exact science but a matter of averages and probabilities. So put July 15 at the summit of a probability curve and add or subtract two weeks in either direction along the x axis and, as I discovered later, the curve is so flat and close to the axis that breathing under it is difficult and conception damn near impossible.

A fact then: Siobhan was fathered in Texas in July 1968 and not by me.

The thunder machine started and stopped again. Someone was tinkering with it. A door slammed, the heavy front door of Belle Isle. I looked down through a pigeonhole. Margot and Jacoby and Merlin got in the station wagon and drove away. I'd have known it was Margot by the way she drove. Her hand made an arc through the green windshield. She turned the car like a man, or a Texas girl, not push-pulling with two hands but palming the wheel around with one hand. Looking down into the car from the pigeon roost, I could see her bare knees. When she got into a car she hiked up her dress like a man does his pants. They were headed, I knew, for the Holiday Inn on I-10 where the film company stayed and the manager let them have a conference room so Merlin could view the rushes.

The three of them sat on the front seat, Merlin in the middle next to Margot. Merlin was one of the few men I ever knew who couldn't drive. There used to be more such people when I was a child, often quite gifted, intelligent men. Especially creative people. Picasso and Einstein never learned to drive, did they?

The girl in the next room and I communicated yesterday! She has not said a word for months, not since her terrible experience, but we communicated!

At six o'clock, when they brought us coffee, I knocked once as usual: good morning! To my astonishment, after a minute or two there came a timid little knock back: good morning.

I could not believe my ears. Perhaps it was not a reply at all. Perhaps she had turned over her chair.

So I knocked again. It was a tentative knock, a knock with a question mark. In thirty seconds, it came back. Knock. No mistake.

Yet was it a communication? If so, what kind? Two chimpanzees could do as well.

Still the question: Is that communication or imitation? Monkey see, monkey do. Perhaps the girl is lying there, a hopeless idiot, her eyes vacant, her knuckles straying against the wall, like a two-year-old child lying in bed.

So I tried the simplest code of all: One knock = A, two = B, and so on.

But how to propose it to her as a code? Not as easy as you might think. I spent the morning thinking it over. It became clear that the only way to avoid imitation is to ask a question and the only way to establish a code is repetition. After all, we have all the time in the world.

It is very awkward, of course. For example, my question began with a *W*, which requires twenty-three knocks. But no matter. Once the idea of a code is established, once she catches on, we can simplify.

I sent this message: 23 knocks pause 8 pause 15 double pause 1 pause 18 pause 5 double pause 25 pause 15 pause 21.

Who are you?

I knocked at about a one-second rhythm knowing she wouldn't get it at first but thinking she might catch on and get a pencil and start counting.

No reply.

Repeat.

No reply.

Repeat.

No reply.

I tried ten times and quit.

Ah well. Tomorrow I will try again.

I must communicate with her. According to my theory, she may be a prototype of the New Woman. It is no longer possible to "fall in love." But in the future and with the New Woman it will be.

You're curious, I see. I haven't told you my sexual theory of history? You smile. No, I'm serious. It applies to both the individual and mankind.

First there was a Romantic Period when one "fell in love."

Next follows a sexual period such as we live in now where men and women cohabit as indiscriminately as in a baboon colony—or in a soap opera.

Next follows catastrophe of some sort. I can feel it in my bones. Perhaps it has already happened. Has it? Have you noticed anything unusual on the "outside"? I've noticed that the doctors and guards and attendants here who are supposed to be healthy—we're the sick ones—seem depressed, anxious, gloomy, as if something awful had already happened. Has it?

Catastrophe then—yes, I am sure of it—whether it has happened or not; whether by war, bomb, fire, or just decline and fall. Most people will die or exist as the living dead. Everything will go back to the desert.

Do you believe that dreams can foretell the future? After all, your Bible speaks of it. I used not to, but I had a dream the other night and I cannot forget it. It was not about Belle Isle or my past life at all but about my *future* life. I'm sure of it. I was living in an abandoned house in a desert place, a ghost town which looked like one of those outlying Los Angeles neighborhoods Raymond Chandler describes.

I was in a room and strangely immobilized. I don't know why but I could not move. Outside there were trees and other houses and cars but nothing moved. There was perfect quiet. Yet I was not alone in the house. There was someone else in the next room. A woman. There was the unmistakable sense of her presence. How did I know it was a woman? I cannot tell you except that I knew. Perhaps it was the way she moved around the room. Do you know the way a woman moves around a room whether she is cleaning it or just passing time? It is different from the way a man moves. She is at home in a room. The room is an extension of her.

She came out of the house. We were having a picnic, sitting on the tailgate of a truck. It was not the desert now. The land plunged almost straight down into the blue ocean. A breeze had sprung up and there was a tinkle of wind chimes. We had been working hard and were very hungry. We ate in silence, looking at each other. There was much to be done. We were making a new life. It was not the Old West and there was no frontier but we were making a new life, starting from scratch. There was no thought of "romance" or "sex" but only of making a new life. We knew what we were doing.

The New Woman is the survivor of the catastrophe and the death of old worlds—like the woman in the next room. The worst thing that can happen to her has happened. The worst thing that can happen to me has happened. We are both survivors.

What do survivors do?

Knock.

But she does not reply. Perhaps she did not survive. I'm surer of the catastrophe than I am of her survival.

33

III

YOU WERE ASKING ME HOW I FELT WHEN I DISCOVERED Margot had been unfaithful to me. Yes, that is very important if you are to understand what happened later.

First, you must understand that the usual emotions which one might consider appropriate—shock, anger, shame—do not apply. True, there is a kind of dread at the discovery but there is also a curious sense of expectancy, a secret sweetness at the core of the dread.

I can only compare it to the time I discovered my father was a crook. It was a long time ago. I was a child. My mother was going shopping and had sent me up to swipe some of his pocket money from his sock drawer. For a couple of years he had had a political appointment with the insurance commission with a "reform" administration. He had been accused of being in charge of parceling out the state's insurance business and taking kickbacks from local agencies. Of course we knew that could not be true. We were an honorable family. We had nothing to do with the Longs. We may have lost our money, Belle Isle was half in ruins, but we were an honorable family with an honorable name. Much talk of dirty politics. The honor of the family won out and even the opposition gave up. So I opened the sock drawer and found not ten dollars but ten thousand dollars stuck carelessly under some argyle socks.

What I can still remember is the sight of the money and the fact that my eye could not get enough of it. There was a secret savoring of it as if the eye were exploring it with its tongue. When there is something to see, some thing, a new thing, there is no end to the seeing. Have you ever watched onlookers at the scene of violence, an accident, a killing, a dead or dying body in the street? Their eyes shift to and fro ever so slightly, scanning, trying to take it all in. There is no end to the feast.

At the sight of the money, a new world opened up for me. The old world fell to pieces—not necessarily a bad thing. *Ah, then, things are not so nice*, I said to myself. But you see, that was an important discovery. For if there is one thing harder to bear than dishonor, it is honor, being brought up in a family where everything is so nice, perfect in fact, except of course oneself.

You nod. But no, wait. The discovery about Margot involved something quite different. There was a sense of astonishment, of discovery, of a new world opening up, but the new world was totally unknown. Where does one go from here? I felt like those two scientists—what were their names?—who did the experiment on the speed of light and kept getting the *wrong* result. It just would not come out right. The *wrong* result was unthinkable. Because if it were true, all physics went out the window and one had to start from scratch. It took Einstein to comprehend that the *wrong* answer might be right.

One has first to accept and believe what one knows theoretically. One must see for oneself. Einstein had to be sure about those other two fellows before he took the trouble to take the next logical step.

One has to know for sure before doing anything. I had to be sure about Margot, about what she had done and was doing now. I had to be absolutely certain.

It was getting dark. The movie crew had gone. Margot, Merlin, Jacoby, and Raine would be back for supper. Elgin came with my toddy on a silver tray. Toddy! We never drank toddies or juleps as you recall, just bourbon straight or maybe with water, but with Margot it was toddies and juleps. She came from West Texas, where God knows what they drank, but she figured at Belle Isle and for Merlin it was toddies and juleps. No, even before Merlin.

I sat behind my plantation desk. Elgin sat in the slave chair, made by slaves for slaves. Margot claimed, I guess correctly enough, that the work of some slave artisans had the simplicity and beauty of Shaker furniture.

"Elgin," I said. I had been thinking. "Did you happen to hear what time they got in last night? The reason I ask is I heard somebody, maybe a prowler, around two."

Elgin looked at me. "They didn't come in till after three."

He knew who "they" were. After supper, Margot, Merlin, and the rest would usually go back to the Holiday Inn to view rushes from the past week's shooting. It took a week because the film had to be flown to Burbank for developing. You have to use the same chemical bath, you can't just drop it off at the local Fotomat. I invited, rather Margot invited, Merlin and Jacoby and Raine and Dana to stay at Belle Isle. They made so much noise coming in late with all their laughter and film talk that I took to sleeping in the corner bedroom. Then Margot suggested that I would sleep better in the pigeonnier. She fixed it up and I moved in, finally staying in the pigeonnier altogether.

Even when the film folk moved back to the Holiday Inn, I stayed in the pigeonnier. Why? I looked around. What was I doing living in a pigeon roost?

"Elgin, there is something I want you to do."

"Yes, sir."

Elgin is, was, the only man, woman, or child I would trust completely outside of you, the more credit to him because it's required of you, isn't it? (Christ, what are you looking for down there? the girl?)

"Is the house empty?"

"Yes, sir. Mama's done gone home and there were some late tourists. But they've gone. At five-thirty I had to ax them to leave."

Elgin, age twenty-two, is a well-set-up youth, slim, café-au-lait, and smart—he went to St. Augustine, the elite Black Catholic school in New Orleans, knew more about chemistry than you and I learned in college. Then got a scholarship to M.I.T. He is well-spoken but to save his life he can't say *ask* any more than a Japanese can say an *r* or a German *thank you*. If he becomes U.S. Senator or wins the Nobel Prize, which he is more apt to do than you or I, he'll sure as hell say *ax* in his acceptance speech.

"Elgin, there's something I want you to do for me."

"Yes, sir." He looked at me. It was then that I realized that for a long time I hadn't asked him or anybody to do anything, because I hadn't anything to do.

"You know the 'hiding hole' next to the chimney?"

"Yes, sir." He relaxed: it is something to do with the house, he thinks, and the tourists.

The hiding hole was part of Elgin's spiel to the tourists. That summer Elgin and his sister Doreen took turns leading the tourists through the house. They tell them the usual stuff—that though Belle Isle is indeed a small island now, surrounded by Ethyl pipery, in 1859 it had 3,500 arpents of land, harvested 2,000 hogsheads of sugar, had its own race track and fifty racing horses in the stable.

—that—and this is the sort of thing Peoria housewives *oh* and *ah* at: the marble mantelpiece was delivered from Carrara accompanied by two marble cutters, a right-handed one and a left-handed one, so they could carve the fresh-cut marble at the same time before the marble "hardened" (something marble does).

—that the solid silver hardware of the doors, locks, hinges, keyholes, taken for steel by the Yankee soldiers, no, not even taken, the metal not even considered, for what Yankee or for that matter who else in the world but Louis XIV would think of a sterling-silver door hinge?

—that all the rest, brick, column flutings, wavy window glass, woodwork, even iron cookery was made by slave artisans on the place.

—that finally, the most important to my plan, the hiding hole, no more than a warming oven let into the brick next to the fireplace but actually used as a hiding hole one day when nineteen-year-old Private Clayton Laughlin Lamar home on leave in 1862 hid from a Yankee patrol. This compartment, at any rate, was discovered to run the length of the chimney on both sides for three stories and so was fitted out later by an enterprising Lamar as a dumbwaiter to raise warm food to ailing Aunt Clarisse confined twenty years to a second-story bedroom for complaints real and imaginary, the same bedroom shared until recently by Margot and me and slept in now by her alone. Or did she sleep alone?

Elgin's father, Ellis Buell, and I used to play in the dumbwaiter, letting each other up and down from living room to bedroom to attic. If there is something about a concealed hole in the wall which fascinates Ohio tourists, there is something about traveling in it from one room to another by a magic and unprovided route which astounds children. Children believe that a wall is a wall, that the word says what is and what is not, and that if there is something else there the word doesn't say, reality itself is tricked and a new magic and unnamed world opens.

"Does that dumbwaiter still work?"

"That old rope rotten." Elgin was excited. Not excited. Mystified. What am I up to? What he gon do next? He doesn't know, but he'll go along.

Late supper as usual. Margot, Merlin, Dana, Raine, and my daughter Lucy. Tex Reilly, Margot's father, and Siobhan up on the third floor watching *Mannix*. A happy arrangement for all concerned because it got Tex and Siobhan out of the way without banishing them. Tex made his money by inventing a new kind of drilling "mud" but Margot thought he wouldn't fit in with this company. She was ashamed of him. The other night they were blasting Hollywood as usual and the grossness of Hollywood types like Chill Wills. Fair enough. Chill may indeed be gross. The trouble is, Tex looks and talks a lot like Chill Wills.

It was after nine. Nothing was changed, except me. My "discovery" changed everything. I've become watchful, like a man who hears a footstep behind him. And sober. For some reason or other, since my "discovery" at 5:01 p.m., more than four hours ago, it had not been necessary to drink.

Merlin as usual went out of his way to be nice to me. He liked me and I him. His charm was genuine. He deferred to me as his local expert on the Southern upper class and asked good questions: "Was there much socializing between the English plantation society on this side of the river and the French-Catholic on the other?" (Yes, there was. They'd row back and forth across the river and dance all night.) His ear was sharp: "I notice people here, not necessarily the lower classes, saying something like: 'Why you do me that?' instead of 'Why do you do that to me?' Is that Black, French, or Anglo-Saxon?" (I didn't know.)

His blue gaze engaged me with a lively intimacy, establishing a bond between us and excluding the others. Somehow his offense against me was also an occasion of intimacy between us. I felt it too. Things were understood and unspoken between us. It went without saying for example that actors are dumbbells. Not even Margot followed us when he spoke of Tate's "Ode to the Confederate Dead" and Hemingway's nastiness to Fitzgerald.

It was as if we were old hands at something or other. But at what? Why should there be a bond between us? But he listened with total attentiveness, leaning across to me over his folded brown arms. He was lean and fit and old, muscular, thick-chested, heavy shock of yellowed gray hair curling over one eye. He had emphysema, I think: his neck ligaments held his chest up like a barrel. No sign of considerable age except the white hairs sprouting over the zipper of his jump suit and the white fiber around his blue iris.

Margot had a triumphant night, I remember. They were worried about the "second unit" falling behind schedule. The second unit was supposed to shoot a scene, the opening scene of the film in fact, a flashback where the young son comes home from Heidelberg, steps off the steamboat at the plantation landing. They had rented a steamboat (a New Orleans excursion boat), found a landing in Grand Gulf, but the current was wrong and the boat could not warp into a landing. Days had been wasted, thousands spent.

"The board is four days out," said Margot severely. The "board" was actually a board with paper chits stuck onto it like a calendar, showing the exact sequence of scenes to be shot. About Margot there was very much the sense of being a team member. She was in fact Merlin's "executive assistant."

What to do? Build another landing in a place with less current? More time, more money. Raine and Dana couldn't care less. Lucy, my daughter, didn't even hear. She was looking at Raine as usual, mouth slightly open.

Margot knitted her brows and drummed all ten fingers furiously on the table. "Jesus, we can't lose another day." She even enjoyed the hassles.

Margot saved the day. In fact her triumph was complete.

She snapped her fingers. "Hold it!" she said to no one in particular. "Just hold it. I may have an idea. Let me make one phone call."

When she returned, she was flushed with pleasure and excitement, but she kept her voice offhand. "What about this, Bobby?" she asked Merlin, stretching up her arms and yawning. When she stretched up her arms like that, her completely smooth axillae flattened and showed two wavelets of muscle.

She had remembered there was a steamboat on False River, a cut-off backwater of the Mississippi. "It's small, almost a miniature, but so are the landings there. And there's no current. What we could do is a long shot of the boat coming into the Dernier landing, which is tiny, of a scale with the boat. I know the Derniers well. What's more, the Dernier house even looks like a miniature Belle Isle. You could cut to the roofline over the levee and no one could tell the difference."

Merlin thought about it. He nodded. "We'll go with that," he said casually, almost curtly, without looking at her. She could have been a pool secretary. "Okay. Call Jacoby."

It was the businesslikeness of course which pleased her so much. Now she was not only one of them but a valued one.

When she was happy or excited, her freckles turned plum-colored. Her pigment darkened with the moon. I could gauge her sexual desire by her freckles.

Then surely my "discovery" was wrong. She was as happy as a child, so happy she reached over and hugged me, not Merlin. Merlin paid no attention to her. His white-rimmed blue eye engaged mine as usual. He wanted to talk about an article of mine, really no more than a note, about an obscure Civil War skirmish in these parts, published in the *Louisiana Historical Journal*. He had taken the trouble to look it up.

As usual I was first to leave the table. It was my custom (all of a sudden I realized how much of my life had become a custom) to leave them to their movie talk, pay a visit to Siobhan and Tex, and arrive at my pigeonnier in time for the ten o'clock news. It had become important to me in recent years to hear the news every hour—though nothing of importance had happened for years. What did I expect to happen?

But this time I did something different. I left the worn path of my life. Once out of sight, instead of crossing to the stairs, I turned left into the dark parlor next to the dining room, from which it was separated by sliding oak doors. A few minutes earlier I had noticed that the door was open some six inches. It was possible, standing with my back against the door, to hear the diners and by moving from side to side to see their reflection in the dim pier mirror on the opposite wall. The images traveled some fifty feet, thirty feet from diner to mirror, twenty feet back to me. Lucy, my daughter, was at one end of the table. Even from this distance it was possible to see in the small blur of her face how like and unlike her mother she is, Lucy, my first wife. There is the same little lift and lilt when she moves her head but the features are both grosser and more gorgeous, like a Carolina wildflower transplanted to the Louisiana tropics. For her, Lucy, Belle Isle was no more than a place to stay. We were not close. She and Margot didn't like each other much. My son? I had not seen my son since he quit college and went to live in a streetcar behind the car barn.

Presently Lucy left.

Margot, Merlin, and Dana talked. There was the sound in their voices of my not being there.

Two small events occurred.

Margot leaned over Merlin to say something to Raine I could not hear, her hair brushing past his face. When Margot spoke, she had a way of swaying against her listener, so that her shoulder and arm touched him. He leaned back, absently, politely, to make room, but as her shoulder rose —is her hand propped on his knee? he took a mock bite of the bare brown flesh at his mouth, not really a bite; he set his teeth on the skin. So perfunctory an act it was, he hardly seemed aware of doing it. His fixed blue gaze did not shift.

"Okay," said Merlin presently. "So we'll use the pigeonnier for Raine and Dana's fight. I agree. The checkerboard lighting pattern would be much more effective than a slave cabin. Still, I like—"

"What about Rudy?" Dana asked, I think he asked. Rudy? What was Rudy? Did he say Rudy? I don't think he said Rudy.

No one seemed to be listening.

"What?" said Merlin after a minute.

Raine bobbed her head to and fro, propping and unpropping her cheek with her finger, hair falling away. She was humming a tune.

Again Margot leaned across Merlin to answer. I could not hear.

I could hear my absence in Raine's voice. She was different. There had grown up between us a kind of joking flirtation. She was Dana's girl, of course. But I could tell her how beautiful she was (she was) and unbend enough to kiss her when we met, kiss on the mouth the way they all do. She could tell me how beautiful I was (am I?). When we were in a room with people, there existed a joking agreement between us that she would be attentive to me, would not turn her back even if she is talking to someone else. It was as if we pretended to be married and jealous of each other. But now without me she was different.

Rudy? Who is Rudy? Me? Why Rudy?

Raine was humming a tune, or rather making as if she were humming a tune, a child's head-bobbing tune, as if it were a signal.

Was the tune "Rudolph the Red-Nosed Reindeer"?

Is that because I drink and sometimes have a red nose?

Is it because Rudolph had antlers?

Did Dana say Rudy? Actually I do not really think he did.

How strange it is that a discovery like this, of evil, of a kinsman's dishonesty, a wife's infidelity, can shake you up, knock you out of your rut, be the occasion of a new way of looking at things!

In the space of one evening I had made the two most important discoveries of my life. I discovered my wife's infidelity and five hours later I discovered my own life. I saw it and myself clearly for the first time.

Can good come from evil? Have you ever considered the possibility that one might undertake a search not for God but for evil? You people may have been on the wrong track all these years with all that talk about God and signs of his existence, the order and beauty of the universe— that's all washed up and you know it. The more we know about the beauty and order of the universe, the less God has to do with it. I mean, who cares about such things as the Great Watchmaker?

But what if you could show me a *sin*? a purely evil deed, an intolerable deed for which there is no explanation? Now there's a mystery. People would sit up and take notice. I would be impressed. You could almost make a believer out of me.

In times when nobody is interested in God, what would happen if you could prove the existence of sin, pure and simple? Wouldn't that be a windfall for you? A new proof of God's existence! If there is such a thing as sin, evil, a living malignant force, there must be a God!

I'm serious. When was the last time you saw a *sin*? Oh, you've seen quite a few? Well, I haven't, not lately. I mean a pure unadulterated sin. You're not going to tell me that some poor miserable slob of a man who beats up his own child has committed a *sin*?

You don't look impressed. Yes, you know me too well. I was only joking. Well, half joking.

But joking aside, I must explain my second discovery. After I walked out of the dark parlor, where no one ever sat, and quietly out the front door, I took a different route to my pigeonnier. A tiny event but significant. Because it was only when I did this that I realized that I had taken exactly the same route for months, even years. I had actually made a path. My life had fallen into such a rut that it was possible to set one's watch (Suellen told me this) when

45

I walked out the front door at night. It must be two minutes to ten because he likes to get there just in time to turn on the ten o'clock news. News of what? What did I expect to happen? What did I want to happen?

No. First, I paid a visit to Siobhan and Tex, who talked about runny babbits.

"I liked the bunny rabbits," said Siobhan, hugging my neck.

"You like those runny babbits!" cried Tex, still holding out his hands for her, and, thinking he'd made a joke, kept on repeating it: "I told you you'd like those runny babbits!"

Tex got on her nerves, in fact bored the hell out of her. It was almost as if he knew it and wanted to, enjoyed the mindlessness of runny babbits.

Siobhan escaped both of us, squatted under the TV livid in the phosphorescent light, her cloudy blue eyes not even then quite focused on the big-eyed cartoon animals.

Tex, of course, got on his next favorite subject, not chivvying Siobhan with his bad jokes but chivvying me for my neglectful ways. He couldn't get over the fact that I had allowed Margot to rebuild the old burned wing of Belle Isle over a gas well even though it had been capped.

For the tenth time he upbraided me in his fond jabbing inattentive way. Was it his wealth, I often wondered, which gave him license to be such a pain, a prodding tunnel-visioned unheeding bore, or had he gotten rich because he was such a pain?

Yet he was a friendly-seeming pleasant-looking fellow with his big-nosed Indian-brown face, slicked-down black-dyed hair, liver-spotted muscular arms. At first sight one might take him for a golf pro, an old seasoned, whiskey-cured sun-drenched Sam Snead—until one noticed that he was not, that his way of standing around hands on hips was not like a golfer at all but the way an oilfield roughneck stands slouched at his alert ease, waits his moment while great machinery hums, heavy pipes swing, chains clank. Yes, that was it, that was his happiness and unhappiness: idleness can be happy only if the machinery is running and one looks on with a presiding interest, comforted as only machinery, one's own machinery, can comfort. His sudden riches had stunned him. In the silence of wealth he felt deprived, deafened, and so he must reach out, grab, poke, drive Siobhan crazy.

"When are you going to cement that well in?"

"There's nothing left down there but a little marsh gas, Tex."

"How you get by with having a Christmas tree under your house beats me." He can't or won't listen.

"It was put there before the state law was passed. Anyhow, it's only a small shallow well."

"It still has two hundred pounds of pressure."

"Christ, no. Thirty pounds at the outside."

"—two hundred pounds in rotten wartime black pipe."

Christ, you stupid Texas bastard, why don't you listen?

"It's got to be sealed," Tex droned on. "A Christmas tree won't do it. The only way to seal a well is to cement it."

"I know."

"How in hell can Maggie seal a producing well and build a house over it?"

On he went, poking me like poking Siobhan, poking and not listening, not even listening to himself. His fond unhappy eyes drifted away. Even his expert opinion was nutty. In the same breath he complained about the well producing and not producing and didn't listen long enough to hear the contradiction. Getting rich had made him so miserable he must make everyone miserable.

Why didn't I do something about Siobhan, not about the

well, which I couldn't have cared less about, whether it produced or not, went dry or blew up, but why didn't I do something about Siobhan? Either throw Tex out or give her back to Suellen or both. They'd both be better off. Christ, for all I knew Tex was fooling with her. Doesn't it happen sometimes with fine fond upstanding grandfathers? You nod. You mean they're penitent afterwards? Good for them. Suellen was good to Siobhan before and would be again. She had raised me, thousands of Suellens had raised thousands like me, kept us warm in the kitchen, saved us from our fond bemused batty parents, my father screwed up by poesy, dreaming of Robert E. Lee and Lancelot Andrewes and Episcopal chapels in the wildwood, and my poor stranded mother going out for joyrides with Uncle Harry.

Why didn't I do something about Siobhan earlier? Here's a confession, Father. Because I didn't really care, and that had nothing to do with her not being my daughter (that made me feel better, gave me an excuse). We are supposed to "love" our children. But what does that mean?

Yet, and here's the strangest thing of all, it was only after my discovery, after I found out that Siobhan was not my child, that I was able to do something about it. Since Siobhan was not my child, I could help her! It was simple after all: (1) Tex was bad for the child, (2) something should be done, (3) nobody was doing anything or even noticing, (4) therefore I would tell Tex to move back to New Orleans and let Suellen take care of Siobhan.

Why couldn't I take care of her? To tell you the truth, she got on my nerves.

Why didn't I love Siobhan when I thought she was my own child? Well, I suppose I "loved" her. What is love? Why this dread coldness toward those closest to you and most innocent? Have families ever loved each other except when some dread thing happens to somebody?

Oh, yes, you speak of love. That is easy to do. But do you wish to know my theory? That sort of love is impossible now if it ever was. The only way it will ever be possible again is if the world should end.

Siobhan turned fretfully to the TV to watch the animated cartoon.

"What a coinkidinki!" Tex cried, hugging Siobhan. "Just when you asked about runny babbits, Tex turned on the TV and there they were."

"Say coincidence," I told Tex.

"What's that?" he asked quickly, cupping his ear, listening for the first time.

"I said, don't say coinkidinki to her, for Christ's sake. Say coincidence."

"All right, Lance," said Tex. He listened! Maybe he hadn't listened to me before because I hadn't told him anything.

I pondered. Could it be true all one needs to know nowadays is what one wants?

Leaving the pleached alley of oaks, my usual route, I cut across the meadowlike front yard, took the gardener's gate through the iron fence, and climbed the levee.

Believe it or not, I had not seen the river for years. A diesel towboat was pushing an acre of barges against the current. It sounded like a freight engine spinning its wheels. I turned around. Belle Isle looked like an isle, a small dark islet hemmed in by Ethyl pipery, Dow towers, Kaiser stacks, all humming away. Farther away, near the highway, gas burnoffs flared in the night as if giant hunters still stalked the old swamp.

The stars were dim but by following the handle of the dipper I recognized Arcturus, which my father showed me years ago. My father: a failed man who missed the boat all around but who knew how far away Arcturus was. He was editor of a local weekly, where he published his own poems and historical vignettes about this region on such subjects as St. Andrew's Chapel: the First Non-Roman Church in the Parish (I remember thinking that my ancestors must have arrived here to find the swamp teeming not with wild Indians but with Romans). The Kiwanis Club gave him a certificate officially entitling him the Poet Laureate of Feliciana Parish. He was an ordinary newspaper poet, an ordinary newspaper historian, and he had an ordinary newspaperman's wonder about science.

"Think of it," he said, standing in this spot and showing me Arcturus. "The light you are seeing started thirty years ago!"

I thought about it. In those days we thought about such things.

But what I was thinking that night a year ago was not how strange it was that light from Arcturus started out thirty years ago (when we were listening to Parkyakarkus and Frank Munn, the Golden Voice of Radio) but how strangely one's own life had turned out during these same thirty years while Arcturus' light went booming down the long, lonesome corridors of space.

Then for the first time I saw myself and my life just as surely as if I were standing in the dark parlor and watching myself sitting at the table with Margot.

Do you know what happened to me during the past twenty years? A gradual, ever so gradual, slipping away of my life into a kind of dream state in which finally I could not be sure that anything was happening at all. Perhaps nothing happened.

That, after all, is quite a discovery for the man you knew, president of the student body, all-conference halfback. Most Likely to Succeed, Rhodes scholar, Golden Glover, holder of the record of the Longest Punt Return in the entire U.S.A.

Clearly you haven't done too well either. You know what our trouble was? We liked to go to school too much. And into the service. I managed to stay in school or the service until I was thirty-two. And you with your M.D., D.D. In fact, aren't you taking some courses at Tulane now?

I practiced law in a small town on the River Road. I say practice in quotes, so to speak, because I found that I was doing less and less law as time went on. True, times got harder, business was slow. In the end I was doing a couple of hours of title work a day and that was it.

One good thing about small towns: it was convenient to come home for lunch. Margot was usually there at first. We'd have a drink or two or three before lunch—something she was used to doing with her lady friends in New Orleans. That was a pleasure. After Suellen's lovely lunch, we often made love. Not a bad life! drink well, eat well, and make love to Margot. I fell into the custom of taking a nap. The naps grew longer. Then one day, I did not go back to the office in the afternoon. Instead, and as an excuse because it was said to be good for one, I took up golf. The three other members of the foursome were Cahill Clayton Lamar, cousin and failed gentry like me, bad dentist, good golfer; and two successful newcomers, the undertaker and the chiropractor.

But golf is a bore. I quit.

During the sixties I was a liberal. In those days one could say "I was such and such." Categories made sense—now it is impossible to complete the sentence: I am a—what? Certainly not a liberal. A conservative? What is that? But then it was a pleasure to take the blacks' side: one

had the best of two worlds: the blacks were right and I
wanted to be unpopular with the whites. It was a question
of boredom. Nothing had happened since I ran 110 yards
against Alabama—we lived for great deeds, you remember, unlike the Creoles, who have a gift for the trivial,
for making money, for scrubbing tombs, for Mardi Gras.
The sixties were a godsend to me. The blacks after all were
right, the whites were wrong, and it was a pleasure to tell
them so. I became unpopular. There are worse things than
being disliked: it keeps one alive and alert. But in the seventies the liberals had nothing more to do. They were finished. I can't decide whether we won or lost. In any case,
in the seventies ordinary whites and blacks both turned
against the liberals. Perhaps they were right. In the end,
liberals become a pain in the ass even to themselves. At
any rate, the happy strife of the sixties was all over. The
other day I ran into a black man with whom I had once
stood shoulder to shoulder defying angry whites. We
hardly recognized each other. We eyed each other uneasily.
There was nothing to say. He told me had had a slight
stroke, nothing serious. We had won. So he bought a color
TV, took up golf, and developed hypertension. I became an
idler.

I gave up golf and stayed home to do a bit of reading
and even some research and writing: the Civil War of
course: nobody knew much about what happened in these
parts. I even wrote a learned article or two. Sometimes I
took the tourists around Belle Isle, like my grandfather before me. But instead of telling them Eleanor Roosevelt
jokes as he did, I gave them scholarly disquisitions on the
beauty of plantation life, somewhat tongue-in-cheek—to
see how far I could go without getting a rise from these
good Midwestern folk—hell, I found out it's impossible to
get a rise from them, they hate the niggers worse than we

ever did. Things are not so simple as they seem, I told them. There is something to be said for the master-slave relation: the strong, self-reliant, even piratical master who carves a regular barony in the wilderness and lives like Louis XIV, yet who treats his slaves well, and so help me they weren't so bad off on Belle Isle. They became first-class artisans, often were given their freedom, and looked down on the white trash. "Now take a look at this slave cabin, ladies and gentlemen. Is it so bad? Nice high ceilings, cool rooms, front porch, brick chimney, cypress floors. Great arching oaks back yard and front. Do you prefer your little brick bungalow in Lansing?" They watched me carefully to catch the drift and either nodded seriously or laughed. It's impossible to insult anybody from Michigan.

On winter afternoons it began to get dark early—five o'clock. Elgin would build us a fire and Margot and I would have several drinks before supper.

During the day I found myself looking forward to radio news on the hour. At night we watched TV and drank brandies. After the ten o'clock news I had usually grown sleepy enough to go to bed.

So what was my discovery? that for the last few years I had done nothing but fiddle at law, fiddle at history, keep up with the news (why?), watch Mary Tyler Moore, and drink myself into unconsciousness every night.

Now I remember almost everything, except—Every event in the past, the most trivial imaginable, comes back with crystal clarity. It's that one night I blank out on—no, not blank out, but somehow can't make the effort to remember. It seems to require a tremendous effort to focus on. What I remember is that miserable Janos Jacoby looking up at me,

the firelight in the trees... The headlines come back.
SCION CRAZED BY GRIEF. RESTRAINED FROM ENTERING
HOUSE. HANDS BURNED.

That night. I can't get hold of it. Oh, I try to, but my
mind slides back to the past or forward to the future.

I can remember perfectly what happened years ago, like
the time we, you and I, were riding down the river on a
fraternity-sorority party and were passing Jefferson Island,
which lies between Mississippi and Louisiana, was
claimed by both states, and in a sense belonged to neither,
a kind of desert island in the middle of the U.S., so you,
drinking and solitary as usual, said to no one in particular:
"I think it would be nice to spend a few days in such a
place," pulled off your coat, and dove off the *Tennessee
Belle* (that was an "act" too, wasn't it?); I, of course, having to go after you as usual, taking just time enough to
wrap some matches in a tobacco pouch, and even so it took
me three hours to find you huddled shivering under a log,
looking bluer than Nigger Jim and more emaciated than
usual; you, ever the one to do the ultimate uncalled-for
thing—I never really knew whether it was a real thing or a
show-off thing. And do you know, I've often wondered
whether your going off to the seminary out of a clear sky
was not more of the same—the ultimate reckless lifetime
thing. Hell, you were not Christian let alone Catholic as far
as anyone could notice. So wasn't it just like your diving
off the *Tennessee Belle* to go from unbeliever to priest,
leapfrogging on the way some eight hundred million ordinary Catholics? Was that too an act, the ultimate show-off
thing or the ultimate splendid thing? You shrug and smile.
And as if that weren't enough, you weren't content to be
an ordinary priest. Father John from New Orleans; no, you
had to take off for Uganda or was it Biafra? You had to go
to medical school and outdo Albert Schweitzer, because of

course that was outdoing even him, wasn't it, because you had the True Faith and he didn't, being only a Protestant.

And it didn't turn out too well, did it? Else why are you here?

Something is wrong, isn't it? Have you lost your faith? or is it a woman?

Is that all you can do, look at me with that same old hooded look? You smile and shrug. Christ, you don't even know the answer yourself.

But you left, you see. And you might have stayed. Maybe you were needed here. Maybe I needed you worse than the Biafrans. If you'd been around all those years . . . Christ, why is it that I could never talk to anybody but you? Well, you're here now and I can use you. I've discovered that I can talk to you and get closer to *it*, the secret I know yet don't know. So I'll start behind it and work up to it, or I'll start ahead of it and work back.

My mind slides forward, to the future, to the person next door. I have an idea even crazier than one of yours. It is that somehow the future, my future, is tied up with her, that we, she and I, must start all over. Did I tell you that I saw her yesterday? Just a glimpse as I ventured out on one of my infrequent forays, this time for my monthly physical and mental examination. Her door was open. She was thin and black-haired but I couldn't see her face; it was turned to the wall, that wall, her knees drawn up. Her calves were slim but well-developed and still surprisingly suntanned. Had she been a dancer? a tennis player? She reminded me of Lucy.

Here's my crazy plan for the future. When I leave here, having served my time or been "cured," I don't want to go back to Belle Isle. I don't want to go back to any place. The only thing I'm sure of is that the past is absolutely dead. The future must be absolutely new. This is true not only of me but of you and of everyone. A new beginning must be made. People must begin all over again, as tentatively as strangers meeting on Jefferson Island (didn't you have something like that in mind when you spoke of the "peculiar possibilities" of Jefferson Island?). I want to go with her, a mute, psychotic, totally ravaged and defiled woman, take her to a little cottage over there—close to the river beyond Magazine Street—a little Negro shotgun cottage, and there take care of her. We could speak simply. "Are you hungry?" "Are you cold?" Perhaps we could take a walk on the levee. In the new world it will be possible to enjoy simple things once again.

But first I must communicate with her. I realize that. Have you tried talking with her? She won't talk? She's turned her face to the wall and that's that.

A new life. I began a new life over a year ago when I walked out of that dark parlor after leaving the supper table. Or rather walked into that dark parlor. Now I believe there will be a third new life, just as there are three worlds, the old dead past world, the hopeless screwed-up now world, and the unknown world of the future.

So anyhow I began my new life then when I stepped out of my life routine worn bare and deep as a cowpath across a meadow, climbed out of my rut, stopped listening to the news and Mary Tyler Moore. And strangely, stopped drinking and smoking. The second I left my old life's cowpath, I discovered I didn't need a drink. It became possible to stand still in the dark under the oaks, hands at my sides, and watch and wait.

I forgot to tell you another thing that happened in the parlor, a small but perhaps significant thing. As I stepped into the parlor with its smell of lemon wax and damp horsehair, I stopped and shut my eyes a moment to get used to the darkness. Then as I crossed the room to the sliding doors, something moved in the corner of my eye. It was a man at the far end of the room. He was watching me. He did not look familiar. There was something wary and poised about the way he stood, shoulders angled, knees slightly bent as if he were prepared for anything. He was mostly silhouette but white on black like a reversed negative. His arms were long, one hanging lower and lemur-like from dropped shoulder. His head was cocked, turned enough so I could see the curve at the back. There was a sense about him of a vulnerability guarded against, an overcome gawkiness, a conquered frailty. Seeing such a man one thought first: Big-headed smart-boy type; then thought again: But he's big too. If he hadn't developed his body, worked out, he'd have a frail neck, two tendons, and a hollow between, balancing that big head. He looked like a long-distance runner who has conquered polio. He looked like a smart sissy rich boy who has devoted his life to getting over it.

Then I realized it was myself reflected in the dim pier mirror.

When I returned to the pigeonnier cold sober, I took a good look at myself in the mirror, something I hadn't done for a long time. It was as if I had been avoiding my own eye for the past few years.

Looking at oneself in a mirror is a self-canceling phenomenon. Eyes looking into eyes make a hole which spreads out and renders one invisible. I had seen more of myself in that single glimpse of a ghostly image in the pier mirror, not knowing it was I.

What did I see? It is hard to say, but it appeared to be a

describing himself.

man gone to seed. Do you remember the picture of Lancelot disgraced, discovered in adultery with the queen, banished, living in the woods, stretched out on a rock, chin cupped in both hands, bloodshot eyes staring straight ahead, yellow hair growing down over his brows? But it's a bad comparison. My bloodshot eyes were staring too but it was not so much the case of my screwing the queen as the queen getting screwed by somebody else.

I moved closer. The cheek showed the razor track of the morning's shave; above it, the demarcated swatch of light fuzz on the knoll of the cheekbone. Capillaries were rising to the surface but had not yet turned into spiders. The nose was not broken, despite football and boxing, not red, blackheaded. The eyes showed a broken vessel and a blood spot like a fertile egg. There were grains in the lashes. The hair roots were not quite clean and were dandruff-flaked. The lips were cracked. The fingernails were black. The chin showed patches of beard missed by the razor. I shaved carelessly and washed seldom. More like Ben Gunn than Lancelot.

Five, six, seven years of unacknowledged idleness (it takes work to be idle and not acknowledge it), drinking and watching TV, working at play, playing at work—what does it do to a man? My hands were open in front of my face. The fingers closed and opened. I felt like Rip van Winkle waking up and testing his bones. Was anything broken? Was I still in one piece?

Was I still strong? How much abuse will a body take? I looked at my fist. I looked at the plantation desk. Raised chest-high originally so that the busy planter (busy with what?) could write his checks standing up, it had been lowered by Margot to make a regular desk. Good solid inch-thick walnut. I put my fist through the middle of the backboard. It went through. I looked at my fist. The knuckles were bleeding. The pain came through tentatively as if it were not sure it had permission. I thought: It has been a long time since I felt pain. I did ten pushups. My arms trembled; it left me sweating. I tried the Bowie knife test, do you remember? With my right hand I stuck the knife into the soft pecky cypress wall with all my strength. With my left hand I tried to withdraw it without working it to and fro. I could not. Then was my right arm strong or my left arm weak?

For the first time in years I bathed very carefully, scrubbing every inch of my body, washing my hair, cleaning and paring my nails, shaving every hair on my face. The bathwater was gray-black. I took a cold shower, scrubbed myself with a towel till the skin hurt, combed my hair, put on shorts. I lay down on the bricks and took a deep breath. The cold of the bricks penetrated the skin of my thighs. For years, I realized, I had lived in a state of comfort and abstraction, waiting for the ten o'clock news, and had not allowed myself to feel anything. When the base of my lungs filled with air and my viscera moved, I realized that I had been breathing shallowly for years. Lowering my chin, I could see the wide V-shaped flare of my ribs; the abdomen fell away out of sight. There was a cherry mole on my breastbone I had never noticed before. I had not looked at myself for years.

Raising my chin as far as it would go, I could see Margot's painting of Belle Isle upside down. There was a year when Margot painted bayous, Spanish moss, and plantation houses.

I stood up. Can a man stand alone, naked, and at his ease, wrist flexed at his side like Michelangelo's David, without assistance, without diversion, without drink, without friends, without a woman, in silence? Yes. It was possible to stand. Nothing happened. I listened. There was no sound: no boats on the river, no trucks on the road, not even cicadas. What if I didn't listen to the news? I didn't. Nothing happened. I realized I had been afraid of silence.

For the past year or so, I had been walking carefully, eyes straight ahead, like a man favoring a secret wound. There was a secret wound which I had not been able to admit, even to myself. Now I could. It was that lately I had trouble making love to Margot. It was the last thing I expected. For the best thing we'd always had between us was a joyous and instant sex. We also drank and ate a lot as well and it was very good between us. Once we were at a banquet at the Governor's mansion, a meeting of the Landmark Preservation Society, Margot the president at the speaker's table and in a gold lamé gown without underwear (because underwear made lines). She was eating green peas and in a few minutes would make a speech. I caught her eye. In thirty seconds we were in the Governor's bathroom, which wouldn't lock, but her bare ass was against the door, no lock required. Two minutes later husband and wife took their places, wife gave speech, husband ate apple pie.

IV

THE FIRST TIME I EVER SAW HER WAS SOMETHING LIKE that. Belle Isle was poor. As a liberal lawyer I wasn't making much money taking N.A.A.C.P. cases. We depended on the tourist dollar. That year we came into a little bonus: we were chosen for the Azalea Trail, ten thousand good middle-class white folks, mostly women, tramped through the house shepherded by belles in hoop skirts. It brought in over five thousand dollars and we needed the money and so put up with the inconvenience: being put out of the house, carpets trampled, plates missing.

Margot was a belle. Her father, Tex Reilly, who had made ten million dollars in mud, had moved to New Orleans to make still more in offshore rigs and so arrived in the Garden District, rich, widowed, and with a debutante-age daughter. He bought a house. What he didn't know was that New Orleans society takes as much pleasure ignoring Texas money as New York money, which was all right with Tex, except that his daughter couldn't be queen of Comus or queen of anything or even a maid—or even go to the balls. He didn't even get far enough to find out that guests don't go to the Mardi Gras balls to dance but only to watch the maskers dance. The Azalea Festival was a different matter. It was a happy marriage of rich new oil people and old broke River Road gentry. If the newcomers couldn't dance with Comus and parade through New Orleans, they could buy old country houses and parade through the rest.

The day was a fiasco. It drizzled, blew, hailed, and finally stormed. But the ladies came anyhow, at least five thousand, leaking water and grinding buckshot mud into our fragile faded Aubussons. The belles stationed on the gallery, a charming bevy, to welcome the visitors, got wet, hair fell, colors ran.

I came home from work, taking the service drive, parked and headed for the back stairs and the roped-off upstairs living quarters with no other thought in mind but to get past the tourists and the belles and the mud and watch the 5:30 news. News! Christ, what is so important about the news? Ah, I remember. We were wondering who was going to get assassinated next. Sure enough, the next one did get killed. There it was, the sweet horrid dread we had been waiting for. It was the late sixties and by then you had got used to a certain rhythm of violence so that one came home with the dread and secret expectation that the pace had quickened, so that when the final act was done, the killing, the news flash: the death watch, the funeral, the killing during the funeral, one watched as one watches a lewd act come to climax, dry-mouthed, lips parted, eyes unblinking and slightly bulging—and even had the sense in oneself of lewdness placated.

In those days I lived for the news bulletin, the interrupted program, the unrehearsed and stumbling voice of the reporter.

As I rounded the corner of the gallery, briefcase swinging out in the turn (what was in the briefcase? A fifth of

Wild Turkey and a hard-cover copy of *The Big Sleep*), one belle caught my eye. Or rather her eye caught my eye and I couldn't look away. She was as sopping wet and her colors as run together as the rest but she was not woebegone. She was backed against the plastered brick, hands behind her open to the bricks, backs of hands against her sacrum, bouncing off the wall by ducking her head and pushing with her hands. Under the muddy fringe of her hoop skirt, I could see her feet were bare. Her short hair was in wet ringlets like spitcurls on her forehead, but still springy and stiff at her temples.

"You must be the master."

"What's that? Eh?"—I must have said, or something as stupid. All I remember is standing holding my briefcase, too dumb to come out of the rain.

"Aren't you the master of Belle Isle?"

"Yes."

"You must be Lancelot Lamar."

"That's right."

"You don't look like I expected"—bouncing and ducking like a thirteen-year-old yet really she was post-debutante, post-belle, twenty-three or -four.

"What did you expect?"

"A rumpled Sid Blackmer or maybe a whining Hank Jones." They turned out to be actors and it turned out she knew them or said she did. I never heard of them and nowadays don't know one actor from another.

"Who are they?"

"You look more like an ugly Sterling Hayden, a mean Southern black-haired Sterling Hayden in seersuckers."

"Who is he?"

"Sterling Hayden gone to seed and running a sailor's bar in Macao."

"He sounds charming." It wasn't raining hard but I

stepped onto the gallery to get out of it. "And *you* are charming. But I am hot and tired and need a drink. I think I'll go through the house."

"I'm wet and cold and need a drink too."

I looked at her. She wasn't pretty and she wasn't Scarlett (the other belles were trying to be Scarlett, hoyden smile and so forth, were also unpretty, were, in fact, dogs, what is more, wet dogs . . .). Her face was shiny and foreshortened—was it the way she tilted her head back to push herself off the wall?—her mouth too wide. Dry, her coarse stiff hair invited the hand to squeeze it to test its spring (how I loved later to take hold of that hair in both hands, grab it by the roots in both fists, and rattle her skull with a surprising joking violence). Raindrops sprang away from it. Her hands were big. As she spoke her name we shook hands for some reason; her hand, coming from behind her, was plaster-pitted and big and warm. The second time we met, at the Azalea Festival reception in New Orleans (I had to go in to get my check for their use of Belle Isle), we shook hands again, and as her hand clasped mine, her forefinger tickled my palm. I was startled. "Does that mean the same thing in Texas that it does in Louisiana?" I asked her. She looked puzzled. As it turned out, it didn't. Her neck was slender, round, and vulnerable but her back was strong and runneled. I'm getting ahead of myself. But what she was or had and what I caught a glimpse of and made me swallow was a curious droll direct voluptuousness, the boyishness being just a joke after all when it came to her looking straight at me. I noticed that her freckles turned plum-colored in the damp and bruised skin under the eye. At the time I didn't know what her darkening freckles meant. Yet I sensed that her freckles were part of the joke and the voluptuousness.

How strange love is! I think I loved you for equally

curious reasons: that for all your saturninity, drinking, and horniness, there was something gracile and frail and feminine about you. Sometimes I wanted to grab you and hug those skinny bones—does that shock you? I did hold your arm a lot at first just to feel how thin you were. Later we never touched each other. Perhaps we were too close.

She hugged her bare shoulders and shivered. "I said I could use a drink too."

I thought a moment.

"My God, what a frown. What lip biting! You look like you're about to address a jury. I like the way you bite your lip when you think."

"Is that right?"

"Yes, that's right."

"Come on." I think I actually took her by the hand. I wanted to hold that warm, pitted hand again! At any rate, it came to pass that for the second or third time in my life, I left life's familiar path—I being a creature of habit even then, doing the same thing day in and day out—took her by one hand, picked up the briefcase with the other, and went back down the service drive and across to the pigeonnier, the farthest place from the tourists, servants, and family, nobody but Ellis using it to store garden tools, and invited her in. Of course it wasn't fixed up then and was dusty and cluttered but dry and pleasant.

"Warm! Dry!" She clapped her hands as I cleared a place among the tools and found an old glider mattress to sit on. "Get me out of this damn thing." I swear I think she almost said *git* but not really: she was halfway between *git* and *get*, just as she was halfway between Odessa, Texas, and New Orleans.

Damned if the hoop skirt didn't work like chaps! It hooked on behind and came right off and meanwhile she was undoing her jacketlike top and so she stepped forth in pantaloons and bodice—I guess it was a bodice—all run with violet and green dye like a harlequin. I remember wondering at the time: Was it that she looked so good in pantaloons or would any woman look that much better in pantaloons? And also wondering: What got into our ancestors later that, with such a lovely curve and depth of thigh and ass, they felt obliged not to conceal but burlesque both, hang bustle behind and hoops outside? Was it some unfathomable women's folly or a bad joke played on them by men?

She sat, muddy feet touching, knees apart, arms straight out across them, looking up at the ceiling through her eyebrows.

"This was for pigeons?"

"Upstairs. There are still a few. Listen." Down the iron staircase came the chuckle-coo but it began to rain hard again and we couldn't hear anything.

I opened the briefcase between us and took out the fifth of Wild Turkey 86 proof, as mild as spring sunshine. Margot clapped her hands again and laughed out loud, the first time I ever heard the shouting, hooting laugh she laughed when she was really tickled. "What in the world—!" she addressed the unseen pigeons above us. "Did you *plan* this?"

"No, I can't leave it in the office, the help gets into it."

"Oh, for heaven's—! My God, what luck. What great good luck. Oh, Scott—" Or something to that effect, I don't quite remember. What I do remember was that in her two or three exclamations my ear caught overtones that overlay her original out-from-Odessa holler (gollee?): a bit of her voice teacher here, a bit of New Orleans there (they were saying Oh Scott that year), a bit of Winston Churchill (great good luck), a bit of Edward VII (at long last). Or was it Ronnie Colman? I had not yet heard her cut loose and swear like an oilfield roughneck.

I took off coat and tie. I smelled of a day's work in an unair-conditioned law office (Christ, I still hate air conditioning, I'd rather sweat and stink and drink ice water. That's one reason I like it here in jail). She smelled of wet crinoline and something else, a musky nose-tickling smell.

I must have asked her what her perfume was because I remember her saying orris root and laughing again: Miss What's-Her-Name, grande dame and ramrod of the Azalea Festival, wanted everything authentic.

"I think I'll have a drink."

"From the bottle?"

"Yes. If you like I'll get you some ice water."

When I finished, she upped the bottle, looking around all the while. She swallowed, bright-eyed. "Do you do this every day?"

"I usually take a bath first, then sit on the gallery and Elgin brings me some ice water."

"Well, this is nice too."

We drank again in silence. It was raining hard and we couldn't hear the pigeons. The tour buses were turning around, cutting up the lawn, sliding in the mud, their transmissions whining.

"Do you have to go back with them?"

"I'd as soon stay. Do you live here alone?"

"Yes."

"You're not married?"

"No. I was. My wife's dead. I have a son and daughter, but they're off at school."

"I thought Mr. and Mrs. Lamar were husband and wife."

"No, son and mother. But my mother died last year."

"And you're here alone?"

"Yes."

"All by yourself?"

"Except for my son and daughter, but they're seldom here."

"I'd be here all the time!" she cried, looking around.

"I am."

"I see," she said not listening, but looking, not missing a trick. She did see, she never stopped seeing. "What a lovely studio apartment this would make. And the little iron spiral staircase. Priceless! Do you know what this would rent for in New Orleans?"

"No."

"Two fifty at least."

"I could use it."

"You mean you don't do all this"—she nodded toward the buses, now moving out in a slow caravan—"just to show your beautiful house?"

"I do it to make money. I don't like to show my beautiful house."

"Mmmm." What I didn't know at the time was how directly her mind worked. What she was thinking was: I have ten million dollars and you don't; you have a great house and I don't; you have a name and I don't; but you don't have me. You are a solitary sort and don't think much about women but now you do. "Feel how cold I am."

"All right."

She took my hand and put it on her bare shoulder. Her flesh was firm and cool but there was a warmth under the cool.

"You've got a big hand. Look how small it makes mine look." She measured our hands, palm to palm.

"It's not all that small."

"No, it's not. Hoo hoo! Haw haw!" she guffawed. "You

68

could put a bathroom there." She pointed both our hands toward a closet of flower pots. "A kitchenette there. Bedroom up there. Think of it! I saw Beauvoir last week. Jeff Davis had a place like this. Let me fix it up for you."

"All right."

"What a cunning little place!" *Cunning*. Where did she get that? Not Odessa. I hadn't heard it for years. That's what my mother's generation said, meaning cute, adorable, charming. Margot herself, not really a good actress, nevertheless had a good ear. She could have listened to my mother for five minutes, ear cocked, and made *cunning* her own. "I'd put a planter there, use an old stained-glass door, hang my Utrillos there."

"Real Utrillos?"

She nodded absently. "Those walls!" She was taking in the famous octagon angles.

We were drinking all the while. She drank from the fifth as easily as if it were a Coke, using her tongue to measure and stop the flow. It had stopped raining. The sun broke out over the levee and the room glowed with a warm rosy light from the slave bricks. Outside, little frogs began to peep in the ditches.

"Couldn't we get more comfortable? I'm totaled." She simply lay down on the glider mattress, propping her head on one hand. "No pillow?"

The nearest thing to a pillow I could find was a foam-rubber cylinder, a boat fender. We took another drink. She patted the mattress. Such was the dimension of mattress and pillow that the only way we could use them was to lie close facing each other.

The sun came out before it set. We lay together in the rosy dusk, heads propped on the boat fender, which seemed to have a thrust of its own. There was nowhere to

69

put my arm but across her waist. Below it, her pantalooned hip rose like a wave.

"You're very sexy in seersuckers," she said, absent-mindedly drumming her fingers on my hip. She was a little drunk but also a little preoccupied. It was strange, but lying with her I became conscious of myself, my own body stirring against the hot crinkled fabric.

I kissed her. Or rather our mouths came together because they had no other place to go. As we kissed, the sunny bourbon on our lips, her wide mouth opened and bade me enter, welcoming me like a new home. It was her head which came around, up and over onto mine. My hot sweated seersucker commingled with her orris root and rained-on flesh and damp crinoline. Outside in the ditches the rain frogs had found their voices and were peeping in chorus. Her fine leg, pantalooned and harlequined—not quite genuine belle was she but more Texan come to Mardi Gras—rose, levitated, and crossed over my body. There it lay sweet and heavy.

We laughed with the joy of the place and being there, and drank and kissed and I felt the deep runnel of her back above her pantaloons.

"Does the door lock?" she asked.

"It's not necessary, but if it will make you feel better." I got up and locked the door, turning an eight-inch iron key and driving a dead bolt home with a clack.

"My God, it sounds like the dungeon at Chillon. Let me see that key."

I lay down and gave her the iron key. She held it in one hand and me in the other and was equally fond of both. She liked antiques and making love. As she examined it, she imprisoned me with her sweet heavy thigh as if she had to keep me still while she calculated the value of the iron key. I had to laugh out loud. I was just getting onto her droll-

70

ness and directness. She might just as well have said: I've got something sweet for you, old boy, the sweetest something you'll ever have but hold it a minute while I look at this old key. She had a passion for old "authentic" things. Texas must have everything but old things.

She was right, she had something sweet and she knew as only a woman can know, with absolute certitude, that she had me, that through some odd coming together of time and place and circumstance and her equally odd mixture of calculation, drollness, and her cool-fleshed hot like of me—oh yes, she wanted me as well as my house—she infallibly knew where the vector of desire converged, the warm cottoned-off place between her legs, the sheer negativity and want and lack where the well-fitted cotton dipped and went away. I kissed the cotton there.

We drank and laughed at the joy of the time and the discovery: that we each had what the other wanted, not exactly "love" as the word is used, but her new ten million and my old house, her sweet West Texas self and my just as sweet Louisiana Anglo-Saxon aristocracy gone to pot, well-born English lord Sterling Hayden gone to seed in Macao. It was like a rare royal betrothal, where the betrothed like each other as well. Like? Love. Laugh and shout with joy at the happiness between them.

Her calculation and cool casting ahead delighted me. As her thigh lay across me, it seemed to be sentient of itself, assigned as it was the task of fathoming the life beneath it, and even as we kissed her eyes were agleam and not quite closed as she took in the pigeonnier, big enough for a thousand pigeons or one man. An "architectural gem" she called it.

But what is love? I thought even then. For by your dear sweet Jesus I did love her there for her droll mercinariness and between her sweet legs and in her mouth and her splendid deep strong runneled back sinking dizzily into a narrow solid waist before it flared into the loveliest ass in all West Texas, but loved as well her droll direct Texas way and even her quickness in overlaying it with Dallas acting-school lingo, New Orleans uptown talk, and God knew what else.

At heart she was a collector, preserver, restorer, transformer; even me and herself she transformed: to take an old neglected abused thing, save it, restore it, put it to new and charming use. She loved to drink, laugh, and make love, but almost as well, better maybe, and orgasmically too, she liked cleaning away a hundred years of pigeon shit and finding lovely oiled-with-guano cypress underneath, turning a dovecote into a study, me into Jefferson Davis writing his memoirs. She was a Texas magician.

It was different from being "in love." I was "in love" with Lucy Cobb, my first wife.

The first time I saw Lucy Cobb: on the tennis court at Highlands, North Carolina, I the Louisiana outlander and ill-at-ease among the easy ingrown Georgians and Carolinians, not knowing them or quite how to dress and so dressed up wrong in coat and tie in late afternoon and standing off a ways under a tree, hands in pockets watching the tennis players, and thinking despite myself: What a shame you all don't know who I am, for in Louisiana people would, Louisiana being what it is, a small American Creole republic valuing sports, fistfights, cockfights, contests, shootouts, *Gunsmoke*, winning, and above all, football, and there I was in what turned out to be the high tide of my life what with being chosen Athlete of the Year by Y.M.B.C. and Rhodes scholar besides, like Whizzer White, which latter contributed nothing to my fame except a storied exotic detail ("... and he's smart too!")—the South a very big place after all and the rough camaraderie of Louisiana not necessarily working here in the muted manners of the east South, where people seemed to come and go, meet and part by agreed-upon but unspoken rules. I was famous in Louisiana, as famous as the Governor, and for one reason alone: running 110 yards against mighty Alabama, and unknown in Carolina.

Lucy's smooth thin brown legs scissored and flashed under her white skirt. When she hit the ball, she got her body into it, shoulders, back, and even a final flex of pelvis. She must have played tennis all her life. Decorous as she stood talking, lounged at the net, laughed, spun her racket, eyes cast down, when she served, her body arched back, then in full reach stretched, then flexed and swung in mock-erotic abandon. Served to, she waited in an easy crouch, shifting her weight to and fro.

What I see even now when I think of her is the way she picked up the ball or rather did not pick it up but toed it onto her racket in a cunning little turning in of her white-shod foot. No, not thin was she but slim, because her joints, ankle, wrist, elbow did not show bone but were a simple articulation.

Her face a brown study under her parted straight brown hair done up in back, the irises so contracted in her smiling brown eyes that she seemed both blind and fond. There was a tiny straight scar on her upper lip, diamonded with sweat, which gave the effect of a slight pout. It was more of a quirk I discovered later, the lip forever atremble, trembling on the very point of joke, irony, anger, deprecation.

There was to be a dance that night out of doors under the stars and Japanese lanterns. How to ask her? Just ask her?

What did I want? Just to dance with her, to hold that quick brown body in my arms not even close but lightly

73

and away so I could see into her face and catch those brown eyes with mine.

Then what to do? Go blundering into the four of them between sets and straight out ask her? Skulk behind a tree and waylay her on her way to her cottage? Without being introduced? What arcane Georgia-Carolina rule would that break?

As it turned out, of course, yes I should have asked her, asked her any way at all, and of course there were no rules. And as it turned out, she had noticed me too, as girls do: seeing without looking and wondering who that tall boy was looking at her, hands in pockets under his tree. Why doesn't he come over and state his business? Why doesn't he ask me to the dance? She was direct: later when I showed up in her parents' cottage and stood about smiling and watching her, uncharacteristically shy (what were the cottage rules?), she would even say it: Well? State your business.

We were married, moved into Belle Isle, had two children. Then she died. I suppose her death was tragic. But to me it seemed simply curious. How curious that she should grow pale, thin, weak, and die in a few months! Her blood turned to milk—the white cells replaced the red cells. How curious to wake up one morning alone again in Belle Isle, just as I had been alone in my youth!

Jesus, come in and sit down. You look awful. You look like the patient this morning, not me. Why so pale and sad? After all, you're supposed to have the good news, not me. Knowing you, I think I know what ails you. You believe all right, but you're thinking, Christ, what's the use? Has your God turned his back on you? It was easier in Biafra, wasn't it, than in plain old Louisiana, U.S.A.?

Well, at least I have good news. The girl in the next room answered my knock! I knocked and she knocked back! She has not caught on that we might invent a new language. She just repeats the one knock, two knocks. That is a beginning, a communication of sorts, isn't it? When I tried a sentence, not *who are you* but *how are you* (because *h* has only eight knocks against *w*'s twenty-three), she fell silent.

How to simplify the code? Or what do you think of a note passed out my window and into hers? See how I've straightened out this coat hanger, but it's not enough. Two coat hangers, perhaps.

What? Why not just go around and see her?

But she will not speak to anyone. Hm. You see that is the point. To *make conversation* in the old tongue, the old wornout language. It can't be done.

On the other hand, I could go to her door and knock twice. She would know who it was and could knock or not knock.

Then do what? Talk? Talk about what? Some years ago I discovered that I had nothing to say to anybody nor anybody to me, that is, anything worth listening to. There is nothing left to say. So I stopped talking. Until you showed up. I don't know why I want to talk to you or what I need to tell you or need to hear from you. There is something . . . about that night . . . I discovered something. It's strange: I have to tell you in order to know what I already know. I talk, you don't. Perhaps you know even better than I that too much has been said already. Perhaps I talk to you because of your silence. Your silence is the only conversation I can listen to.

Then what do I want of her, the woman next door?

In some strange way she is like Lucy. Lucy was a virgin! and I did not want her otherwise. What I wanted was to dance with her on a summer night, hold her lightly and look into her eyes. I wanted Margot's sweet Texas ass and I wanted Lucy's opaque Georgia eyes.

This girl in the next cell is not a virgin. She was raped by three men in one night and then forced to perform fellatio on them.

I've learned more about her. In fact, I managed to catch a glimpse of her chart while the nurses were off in the lounge drinking coffee. She is twenty-nine and comes, like Lucy, from Georgia. She dropped out of Agnes Scott, a fine young-ladies' school, and went to live in an artists' community in La Jolla. The standard boring story of our times. Then, thinking better of it, of California and the New Life (which of course is not a new life at all but the last spasm of the old, the logical and inevitable culmination, the very caricature of the old, the new life being nothing more or less than what their parents would do if they dared), she removed to the Ninth Ward of New Orleans, lived in Desire project, offered herself up in service to mankind. Whereupon mankind took her up on her offer, raped her for her pains, and left her for dead in the Quarter.

Then how is she like Lucy? How is she the Lucy of the new world? Is it because the violation she suffered has in some sense restored her virginity, much as a person recovering from the plague is immune to the plague? I don't quite know why she is so much like Lucy except that I want the same thing of her I wanted from Lucy: to come close but keep a little distance between us, to ask the simplest questions in a new language—*How are you*—just to hear the sound of her voice, to touch the tips of her fingers, to hand her through an open door ahead of me, my hand pressed lightly against the small of her back.

* * *

The night of the day I discovered Margot's infidelity, I left my old life path, became sober for the first time in years, bathed, shaved, dressed in clean clothes, and spent the night wide awake and watchful in my plantation rocker placed at such an angle that, looking through a window and the one clear pane of glass in the stained-glass door Margot had sure enough found for me (the final camp touch which Margot said would make the pigeonnier a charming little place and it did), I could see Belle Isle and most of the private drive.

My supper companions had left for the Holiday Inn about eleven o'clock to view the week's rushes. That took no more than an hour, but afterwards they often got carried away by discussion, "more like knock-down-drag-out-argument," said Margot, which went on till one or two in the morning.

How long would the knock-down-drag-out argument last that night, I wondered and, instead of drinking myself to sleep, stayed up to see.

She did not come home at all.

Or rather her Country Squire wagon, she alone in it, turned into the driveway at 8:30 the next morning, rolling so slowly that it hardly made a crunch in the pea gravel. As punctually as Kant setting out for the university at exactly six o'clock so that shopkeepers along the way could set their watches by him, it had been my custom to arise at exactly nine o'clock, stagger to a cold shower, and, of late, take a drink. At exactly 9:37 (two minutes after the news) I would take my seat at the breakfast table at Belle Isle. At 10:15 I was at my office, helping Negroes in the sixties, handling old ladies' estates in the seventies.

That morning I sat in my plantation rocker, sober and clear-headed, and rocked for a while.

I sat down to breakfast at the usual time, Margot ate

heartily, elbows on table, wiry head bent over steaming scrambled eggs. My hand shook slightly as I drank coffee; my stomach shrank as if braced against the first hot bourbon of the day.

"How were the rushes?"

"Oh, Christ. One abortion after another. The bloody color was off again. Bob was beside himself."

Now *bloody* was the word. Merlin was not really English but lived there long enough so that everything was bloody this and bloody that.

In my new sobriety things were better and worse. My senses were acute, too acute. I became aware of the warp and woof of the tablecloth. My eyes followed one linen thread under and over, under and over. I noticed flecks of white porcelain showing through the worn gold leaf on the rim of the coffee cup where the lips touched it ninety degrees away from the handle. When Elgin touched me to see if I wanted more coffee, I nearly jumped out of my chair.

I watched Margot. She ate like a horse and looked fine, not fat but firm and full-armed. Ten years had turned her from callow coltish skittish-mustang Texas girl to assured chatelaine and mistress of Belle Isle, more Louisianian than Louisianians for they didn't know what they were like and she did. Her face was if anything more soft-eyed and voluptuous, as only a thirty-two-year-old woman can be voluptuous. There was now a fine freckling over her bare shoulders from her golfing, like a lady golf pro. In the thin clear translucent skin beside the nose bridge, the freckles had merged into a darkening and dampening which in any other woman might have looked like circles under eyes but in her was simply plum-shadow and ripeness. When she sat down she settled herself, broadening her bottom to fit exactly the shallow B-shaped scoop of her chair.

Outwardly nothing was changed. Yet when I folded the

newspaper and pushed back my chair to leave, she wiped the last crumb of bacon from her lip and said almost to herself: "I was tired afterwards—in fact I got sick as a dog so I stayed on at the Inn, barged in on Raine and just said, Sister, move over."

Nothing was changed except that when she said that, I was pushing away from the table and I stopped a second both arms outstretched to the table's edge. More than a second, for my eyes were on the second hand of my watch. A fly crawled along the gold band (gift from Margot). I waited for him to step off onto my wrist. He did. I watched him touch a hair. He did, crawling under it, everting and scrubbing his wings. As he did so, he moved the hair. The hair moved its root which moved a nerve which sent a message to my brain. I felt a tickle.

I went to my office as usual, came home for lunch as usual, returned to the pigeonnier as usual, but instead of having three drinks and taking a nap, I sent for Elgin.

Tell me something. Why did I have to know the truth about Margot and know it with absolute certainty? Or rather why, knowing the truth, did I have to know more, prove more, *see*? Does one need to know more, ever more and more, in order that one put off acting on it or maybe even not act at all?

But why? Why did it become the most important, the sole obsession of my very life, to determine whether or not Margot slept with Merlin when in fact I knew she had, or at least with somebody not me? You tell me, you being the doctor-scientist and soul expert as well, merchant of guilt and getting rid of it and of sorting out sins yet knowing as well as I that it, her fornication, anybody's fornication, amounts to no more than molecules encountering molecules and little bursts of electrons along tiny nerves—no different in kind from that housefly scrubbing his wings under my hair.

Well, for once you look very solemn and unironic. Did I love her? you ask.

Love. Hm. The older I get, the less I know about such large subjects. I can say this. There was a time just before and after we were married when I could not not touch her. There was no getting enough of her. The very behavior I used to abhor in others I carried on with her and never a second thought or care in this world; touch her in public. Neck! Go to the A & P with her, heft the cold red beef flesh in one hand and hold her warm hand with the other and in the parking lot at four o'clock in the afternoon *neck*! Spoon! We'd drive down the road like white trash in a pickup truck, heads noodled together, shoulder to shoulder, hip to hip, thigh to thigh, my right hand thrust fondly between her legs.

Even later when we drank too much together, it was good, the drinking, drunkenness, and the coming together every whichway, on the floor, across the table, under the table, standing up in a coat closet at a party. There was no other thought than to possess her, as much of her with as much of me and any way at all, all ways and it seemed for always. Drinking, laughing, and loving, it is a good life. Not even marriage spoils it. For a while.

Did I love her then, that day I speak of? Love. No, not love. Not hatred, not even jealousy. What do those old words mean? Emotions? Were there ever any such things as emotions? If so, people have fewer emotions these days. Merlin's actors could register fifteen standard emotions and not share a single real feeling between them.

No, my only "emotion" was a sense of suddenly coming alive, that peculiar wakefulness when a telephone rings in the middle of the night. That and an all-consuming curiosity. I had to know. If Merlin "knew" my wife, I had to know his knowing her.

Why? I don't know. I ask you. That's what I want with you. Not knowing why, I don't really know why I did what I did. I only knew for the first time in years exactly what to do. I sent for Elgin.

Elgin was surprised to be summoned and more surprised to see me. No bottle, no drinks, no naps, no TV, no pacing the floor hands in pockets, but standing quiet and watchful.

"Sit down, Elgin."

"Yes, sir."

We sat down in two slave chairs. Elgin, I remember, was doing tourist spiels that summer and still wore his guide jacket with the Belle Isle coat of arms on the breast pocket, a livery which no house servant had ever worn but which by my grandfather's calculation should satisfy the tourist's need for proper NBC guide and authentic Southern butler rolled into one.

Elgin's expression did not change. The only sign of his surprise was that though his face was turned slightly away, head cocked as if he were deaf, his eyes never left mine and had a wary hooded look.

"Elgin, I'm going to ask a favor of you."

"Yes, sir."

"It is not difficult. The point is, I want you to do it without further explanation on my part. Would you?"

"Yes, sir," said Elgin without a change of tone or blink of eye. "Even if it's criminal or immoral"—slight smile now. "You know I'd do anything you axed."

Elgin was a senior at M.I.T. and had what he thought were two reasons to be grateful to me, though I knew better than to rely on gratitude, a dubious state of mind if indeed there is such a thing. And in truth I had done very little for him, the kind of easy favors native liberals do and which are almost irresistible to the doer, if not to the done to, yielding as they do a return of benefit to one and a good feeling to the other all out of proportion to the effort expended. That was one of the pleasures of the sixties: it was so easy to do a little which seemed a lot. We basked in our own sense of virtue and in what we took to be *their* gratitude. Maybe that was why it didn't last very long. Who can stand gratitude?

I helped him get a scholarship, which took very little doing what with the Ivy League beating the bushes for any black who could read without using his finger and what with Elgin graduating first in his class at St. Augustine and winning the state science fair with a project demonstrating electron spin which I never quite understood.

So Elgin was smart, Elgin was well educated. Elgin could read and write better than most whites. And yet. Yet Elgin still talks muffle-mouthed, says *ax* for *ask*, *sa-urdy* for *Saturday*, *chirren* for *children*.

He was a slim but well-set-up youth with mauve brown skin, a narrow intense face, a non-Afro close clip as high off his ears and up his neck as a Young Republican's, and a lately acquired frowning finicky manner which irritated me a little just as it irritates me in a certain kind of scientist who does not know what he does not know and discredits more than he should. Elgin was one of them. It was as if he had sailed in a single jump from Louisiana pickaninny playing marbles under a chinaberry tree to a smart-ass M.I.T. senior, leapfrogging not only the entire South but all of history as well. And maybe he knew what he was doing. From cotton patch to quantum physics and glad not to have stopped along the way.

But he and his family had yet another reason to be grateful to me, a slightly bogus reason to be sure, which I in my own slightly bogus-liberal fashion was content not to have set straight. He thought I saved his family from the Klan. In a way I did. His father, Ellis, and mother, Suellen, our faithful and until recently ill-paid retainers, and his little brother, Fluker, had all been threatened by the local Kluxers because Ellis's church (he was its part-time preacher) had served as a meeting place for CORE or Snick or one of those. They burned a cross, threatened to burn the church and come "get" the Buells. It is true I went to see the Grand Kleagle and the harassment stopped. The story which I never had quite the energy or desire to correct was that in the grand mythic Lamar tradition I had confronted the Kleagle in his den, "called him out" with some such Southern Western shoot-out ultimatum as "Now listen here, you son of a bitch, I don't know which one of you is bothering Ellis but I'm holding you responsible and if one hair of a Buell head is harmed, I'm going to shoot your ass off for you," and so forth and so forth. I put a stop to it all right, but in a manner more suited to Southern complexities and realities than the simple dreams of the sixties, when there were only good people and bad people. I went to see the Grand Kleagle all right, who was none other than J. B. Jenkins, a big dumb boy who played offensive tackle with me in both high school and college. He was as big and dumb and as good a tackle as can be, managing even to flunk out of a state school later, no small achievement in those days, and had ever since operated not a Gulf Oil service station but a Gulf Coast Oil service station. He was a good family man, believed in Jesus Christ, America, the Southern way of life, hated Communists and liberals, and was not altogether wrong on any count. At any rate, all I said to him in the sweltering galvanized tin shack of his Gulf Coast Oil station was: "Now, J.B., I want you to do me a favor." "What's that, Lance, old buddy?"

"You know what I want. I want you to lay off Ellis and his church." "Now, goddamn, Lance, you know as well as I do ain't nothing but a bunch of Jew Communists out there stirring up the niggers." "Will you take my word for something, J.B.?" "You know I will." "I swear to you there's no Jews or Communists out there and I will swear to you that Ellis is a good Godfearing Baptist like you and you have nothing to fear from him." "Yeah, but he is one more uppity nigger." "Yeah, but he's *my* nigger, J.B. He's been working for us for forty years and you know that." "Well, that's true. Well, all right, Lance. Don't worry about nothing. Lets us have a drink." So we had a drink of straight three-dollar whiskey in that 110-degree iron shack. Sweat sprang off our heads like halos. And that was that.

Ah well. Like I told you, real life is more complicated and ambiguous than in the movies. Ellis Buell was grateful. Ellis Buell had seen too much TV and *Gunsmoke*. "You should have seen Mr. Lance call that white trash out." And so forth.

His son Elgin was a different matter. Actually Elgin was the only one who didn't care much one way or the other about such matters. Like Archimedes he was more interested, exclusively interested, in writing out his formulae and would not have cared or even noticed whether it was a Kluxer or a Roman soldier who lifted his hand against him.

Elgin, I do believe, would do what I asked, not out of gratitude (a very bad emotion as both he and I knew), but because he liked me and felt sorry for me. Unlike him I had been unable to escape into the simple complexities of science. All he had to do was solve the mystery of the universe, which may be difficult but is not as difficult as living an ordinary life.

I had counted too on my request intriguing him as a kind of mathematical game, which it was. It did.

Did it ever occur to you that after we went to college we never *touched* each other? Do you remember walking down Bourbon Street behind two Russian sailors who were holding hands? Do you remember sleeping in a motel bed in Jackson, Mississippi, with a whore between us? Why was it all right for us to simultaneously assault the poor whore between us but never once touch each other? Who is crazy, we or the Russians?

Ah, you touch my shoulder. Do you know that I am embarrassed?

Oh, Christ, there is something wrong with my mind. I've drawn a blank again. It's a little frightening. I could use a drink. Everybody talks about the horrors of drink, which are real enough, but not about its beauties. Your God gave us wine, didn't he, and threw good parties? Half-drunk, I can remember everything, see everything as it is and was, the beauty in it rather than the sadness. I could remember everything we ever did. There was a lovely looseness then and a letting go and a magical transformation of those sad Southern afternoons into a garden of delights. Wasn't there? We had a good time, you and I. Then youth ended and you left for God. I joined the A.C.L.U. and became a liberal. Then a drunk. Sober, I could not bear to look at Belle Isle and the great oaks; they seemed so sad and used up and self-canceling. Five good drinks and they seemed themselves.

It's not that I can't remember. It's all there, what happened, spread out like a map, but I have trouble collecting my thoughts, focusing. Perhaps I remember too well like memorizing a speech, reciting it a dozen times before the mirror, then when the time comes to speak, you can't come up with the first word.

Once my father told me he had a recurring waking nightmare. What if one should simply fail in what one set out to do in life, fail utterly, cannot remember the first word, have the first thought, carry out the simplest action, complete the simplest task? Like an actor forgetting his lines and bringing the whole play to an awful embarrassing halt. What if one should rise to address the jury and forget? (My father had a Harvard law degree but never practiced.) Secretly I believe he was afraid that of all the people on earth he alone would fail and the world would come to an end out of shame for him.

With such a fear, what happens to a man? Nothing. He didn't, couldn't, try anything for fear the world would come to an end if he failed. So he became editor of the second best of the two weekly newspapers in a country parish, suffered from "weak lungs" whatever that is, not tuberculosis but a "tendency" toward it, and was a semi-invalid, spending his days writing poems and little historical vignettes. The high point of his life came when he was elected Poet Laureate of Feliciana Parish by the Kiwanis Club.

Let me tell you the family secret which not even you know, though you know everything else. But do you know that I honestly believe that his wife, my mother, Lily, cuckolded him too? I remember Uncle Harry, also called Buster, a distant cousin of hers, a handsome beefy Schenley salesman, ex-Realsilk salesman, who was always in and out of Belle Isle when I was a child. No one was gladder to see him than I because he brought the most expensive toys, Erector sets, scout knives with twenty blades, and would throw me ten feet in the air—happiness!

squeals! Children are more easily bribed than cocker spaniels. And there was my father reclining on a lounge chair under an afghan on the upper gallery looking down the oak alley and writing poems which were not as good as Longfellow's *Evangeline*, which is bad enough, but like it, and gentle historical vignettes whenever he located another old "non-Roman" church. Uncle Harry would come roaring up in his Buick convertible and holler out: I'm taking everybody joyriding to False River. My father would insist that Mother go: she needed the air: Suellen can look after me, can't you, Suellen? "Sho now, you go on ahead, Miss Lily, you ain't been anywhere all summer." And off they'd go, we'd go—I sometimes but not always—"joyriding." Christ, joyriding! Jesus, do you really imagine that—? Of course the question is not why but why not. Ha ha, what a laugh in a way. Because we were such an honorable family. And of course here is the most intriguing question of all: Did my father know all along?

You look so unhappy. Who are you unhappy for? Me? Lily? My father? Sinful suffering humanity? Your own sunk melancholy family? Are you playing the priest now?

Elgin? Yes, you're right. It was Elgin I was talking about. Yes. No. Wait. I did mention a map. It wasn't a map. It was a floor plan. I remember. I gave Elgin the floor plan of the Holiday Inn which I had gotten that very afternoon from my Uncle Lock, Bushrod Laughlin Lamar, who operated it.

"Elgin, here is a floor plan of the Holiday Inn."

"Yes, sir." He took it. It could have been his pay check for all the reaction he showed. Does anything white people do ever surprise blacks?

"Here's a problem where you might be able to help me.

You don't need to know the details. It is enough to say that I am concerned about my daughter Lucy, who is young and impressionable and may have gotten into some difficulties with drugs. But first I have to have the facts, beginning with where she goes, how she spends her time."

Elgin squinted hard at the floor plan as if he expected to see Lucy.

"What I want you to do is this. I want you to register at the Holiday Inn for the next three nights and keep a log of her comings and goings. You know, the film crew is there, and she's stagestruck and hangs around at all hours. In fact, make a complete record. Make a note of anyone you know: Merlin, Troy Dana, Janos Jacoby, Raine Robinette, even me and my wife. I want the whole picture. Do you understand?"

His single swift opaque look told me he did understand. Understood and agreed. Understood even that there was something I needed to know but didn't want to tell him, nor did he want me to.

"Now here's the problem. Think of it as a mathematical game. I want you to pick one of those rooms. I've fixed it up with Lock, you can have any room you want, he knows you're in the film."

Placing the floor plan on the plantation desk between us, I wrote names in empty rooms.

"The idea is to pick a room or any other vantage point which commands a view of the following: the inner door of the Oleander Room here—that's where they view the rushes—Dana's room here, Raine's here, Merlin's here, Jacoby's here. Here's the hitch (this should interest you—it baffles me): there would be no problem if the inner court were a simple quadrangle. You could simply sit at the window of nearly every room and see everything, even Merlin's room, which is on the second story. All you would have to do is choose a room, say here on the first floor opposite. But as you see, it is not so simple. The court is L-shaped. So if you took this room, you could not see Raine's room here. And if you took this room, you could see Raine's room but not Merlin's."

"Mm." Now Elgin was interested, transported from the inelegant mysteries of white folks' doings to the elegant simplicities of geometry. Using his thumb, he began to push his lip over his eyetooth, a new mannerism. My guess is he got it from one of his M.I.T. professors.

"Take these binoculars, Elgin. They are excellent night glasses. Don't forget your log. In your log make a note of everything you see: not only the exact time anyone enters or leaves a room, but anything else you happen to notice, what a person may carry with him, what they do, the smallest item of behavior."

Elgin was busy drawing lines across the court, angles and declinations. He frowned happily. I repeated my instructions.

"You mean all night?"

"Yes. That is, from eleven to dawn. Or rather, just before dawn. I don't want you to be seen."

"For three nights?"

"Maybe. At the outside. We'll see how it goes. You're relieved as of now from guide duty. Go home and get some sleep. I'll tell Ellis that I'm sending you to New Orleans to take a deposition."

"I wonder what this room is. Probably the alcove for Coke machine and ice maker."

"Probably. No window."

Elgin took off his glasses and rubbed his eyes. "You see, here's what it comes to." I could see him twenty years later, for his expression, his mannerisms had already begun to set; see him behind his desk, give himself to a problem, quickly take off his glasses and rub his eyes. "The problem as you pose it is insoluble—unless you want to rig up a system of mirrors, bore holes in floors, which I gather you don't."

"I don't."

"You see, if I were in 214, an upper room near the inner corner of the ell, I could see every room but Raine's on the first floor. On the other hand, if I were across the court near the outer corner of the ell, I couldn't see Merlin's room." More lines, lines crossing lines like electrons colliding.

"To see all rooms, posing the problem as you do, you'd need two observers. Me here and, say, Fluker here."

"Fluker! He'd go to sleep!"

We both laughed. The very name was funny for us, a secret joke.

Elgin smiled his old smile, his sweet white-flashing unmannered smile. "He sho would. Hm. Let's see. Let's-us-see." He gazed at the plan and tapped his pencil. Why did I feel like the student visiting the professor? "We-ull!" (How happy scientists are! Why didn't we become scientists, Percival? They confront problems which can be solved. We don't know what we confront. Does it have a name?)

Elgin put on his glasses. "The pool is here?"

"Right."

"Is it lit?"

"By underwater lights after ten. The floodlights are fixed to the balconies but the area around the pool is fairly dark."

"Lounges and chairs around here?"

"Yes."

"Scrubs—that is, shrubbery around here?"

"Yes." Ellis, his father, used to say *scrubs* for *shrubs*:

90

"You want me to cut them scrubs?" Not even Ellis says that any more.

"Then there's only one place." Elgin dropped his pencil with a clatter, picked it up, made a big X, dropped it again, sat back. He smiled. His eyelids lowered. He'd made a breakthrough!

"The middle of the court?"

"Sure. Where else?"

"But—"

"What kind of lounge chairs they got?"

"What kind?"

"I mean light aluminum or those heavy wooden ones?"

"Redwood, heavy, black webbing. Too heavy to steal, I remember. Lock is proud of them."

Again Elgin smiled his old brilliant sweet smile. In his triumph he permitted himself to be what he was: a twenty-two-year-old Southern youth who smiled and laughed a great deal. "It's dark here you say. The lounges are dark, the webbing is black. I'll wear black swim trunks and man can't nobody see nothing."

I smiled. He wasn't even burlesquing himself as black or Southern black but as TV-Hollywood-Sammy-Davis-Junior black and he knew that I knew it.

He snapped his fingers. "No. It's even better than that."

"How?"

"Don't you see? It wouldn't matter if anyone saw me at that distance. A man in trunks by the pool. Nobody would pay the slightest attention. Like Poe's *Purloined Letter*."

Poe's *Purloined Letter*. I thought about J. B. Jenkins, bad man, good man, bad good man, Kluxer, Christian, tackle, and comrade at arms against Alabama's mighty Crimson Tide. The only Poe he knew was Alcide "Coon-ass" Poe, tailback from De Ridder. J. B. and I, sunk in life, soaked in old Louisiana blood and tears and three hundred years of Christian sin and broadsword Bowie-knife Sharps-rifle bloodshed and victory-defeat. And Elgin leapfrogging us all, transformed overnight into snotty-cool Yankee professor.

Poe's *Purloined Letter* indeed. Poe. He too had got onto Elgin's secret: Find happiness in problems and puzzles and mathematical gold bugs. But he let go of it. Went nutty like me. Elgin wouldn't.

"How are you going to get the binoculars out there?"

"Wrapped in my towel."

"Okay. Then the location of the room doesn't matter. Go on out there now and register. Keep your log tonight. When you get back, get some sleep and meet me here about this time tomorrow. I'll put Fluker on guide duty."

"Fluker." Again we laughed. "No telling what Fluker gon say."

"He'll do fine. Anyhow, what difference does it make?"

"Yeah." Elgin was casting ahead again. "How to see to write in the dark is the thing. White pencil on black? Pencil light? No, what I'm going to use"—clearly he was talking to himself—"is a Kiefer blacklight stylus."

"You do that."

V

JACOBY? I HAVEN'T TOLD YOU ABOUT HIM? THE HEADlines? BELLE ISLE BURNS! DIRECTOR MURDERED AND MUTILATED! EX-GRID STAR HELD FOR QUESTIONING! Yes, I remember all that. Belle Isle burned to the ground except for twenty snaggle-toothed Doric columns. My hands burned trying to save Margot.

It is difficult to think about all that.

You must believe me when I tell you that it is the banality of the past which puts me off. There is only one reason I am telling you about these old sad things, or rather trying to remember them, and it has nothing to do with not being able to remember. I can remember. I can remember every word Elgin said to me in the pigeonnier. It is because the past, any past, is intolerable, not because it is violent or terrible or doomstruck or any such thing, but just because it is so goddamn banal and feckless and useless. And violence is the most banal and boring of all. It is horrible not because it is bloody but because it is meaningless. It does not signify.

Then why bother to tell you? Because something is bothering me and I won't know what it is until I say it.

93

Presently I'm going to ask you a question. Not that you will be able to answer it. But it is important that I ask it. That was always the best thing about you, that you were the only person I could ever talk to.

Why did you leave twenty years ago? Wasn't Louisiana good enough for you? Do you think the U.S.A. needs you less than Biafra? I sometimes think that if you'd been around to talk to . . .

You are silent. Christ, you don't know yourself.

I have to tell you what happened in my own way—so I can know what happened. I won't know for sure until I say it. And there is only one way I can endure the horrible banality of it: and that is that I sense there is a clue I've missed and that you might pick it up.

It is as if I knew that the clue was buried somewhere in the rubble of Belle Isle and that I have to spend days kicking through the ashes to find it. I couldn't do that alone. But we could do it.

A clue to what? To the "mystery" of Belle Isle? No. To hell with that. Belle Isle is gone and I couldn't care less. If it were intact it would be the last place on earth I'd choose to live. I'd rather live in Brooklyn. As gone with the wind as Tara and as good riddance.

No, that's not the mystery. The mystery lies in the here and now. The mystery is: What is one to do with oneself? As you get older you begin to realize the trick time is playing, and that unless you do something about it, the passage of time is nothing but the encroachment of the horrible banality of the past on the pure future. The past devours the future like a tape recorder, converting pure possibility into banality. The present is the tape head, the mouth of time.

Then where is the mystery and why bother kicking through the ashes?

Because there is a clue in the past.

Start with the present moment. Look out there. A fall afternoon in New Orleans with the peculiar gold light that fills the sky when the first wedge of Canadian cold air slides like a crystal prism under the Gulf steambath. Look at the gold light. It radiates in the crystal and filters down into the same shabby streets with the same neighborhood sounds of housewives switching on their Hoovers, TV, voices through kitchen doorways, the same smell of the Tchoupitoulas docks.

Consider the past. Imagine a man sitting in Feliciana Parish for twenty years practicing law (yes! "practicing"), playing at being a "moderate" or "liberal" whatever that is, all under the illusion that he was living his life and was not even aware that he was not.

But something happens. There is a difference. The difference between then and now is that now I've been alerted. I am aware of being the tape head. I am aware of this room being a tape head. That is why it is so simple and empty: so I can be aware. As you can see, it consists of nothing but a small empty space with time running through it and a single tiny opening on the world. I'm staying here until I can decide what the tape head is doing and whether I have anything to say about it. It is simply a devourer of time and does it necessarily turn the pure empty future into the shabby past?

A year ago (was it a year?) I made my two great discoveries: one, Margot's infidelity; two, my freedom. I can't tell you why, but the second followed directly upon the first. The moment I knew for a fact that Margot had been fucked by another man, it was as if I had been waked from a twenty-year dream. I was Rip van Winkle rubbing his eyes. In an instant I became sober, alert, watchful. I could act.

Yet something went wrong. I am glad you are simply listening, looking at me and saying nothing. Because I was afraid you might suggest either that I had done nothing wrong—like the psychologist here: no matter what I tell him, even if I break wind, he gives me the same quick congratulatory look—either that I had done nothing wrong or that I had "sinned"—and I don't know which is worse. Because it isn't that. I don't know what that means. Yet obviously something went wrong, because here I am, in a nuthouse—or is it a prison?—recovering from shock, psychosis, disorientation.

From a state of freedom and the ability to act (that night I told you about, the world was open! I was free! I could do anything, devise any plan), I now find myself closeted in a single small cell and glad to be here.

A fox doesn't crawl into a hole for a year unless he is wounded. But after a while he begins to feel good, pokes his nose out, takes a look around.

I still have the resolve to make a new life, an absolutely new beginning. But I know that one must start from scratch.

Begin with a burrow, a small clean well-swept place such as this, with one tiny window on the world and another creature in the next room. That is all you need. In fact, that is all you can stand. Add more creatures, more world, books, talk, TV, news—and we'll all be as crazy as we were before. There is too much feeding into the tape head—the new tape is too empty—too many possibilities —but the recorded tape is too full.

But what went wrong with the other new life last year? I must find out so I won't make the same mistake twice. Therefore I must go back and kick through the ashes of Belle Isle. There is something I don't understand. And you are both my leverage point and my companion. Because you knew Belle Isle and you know me and I can't tell anyone else.

In a month or so I shall be leaving here. At least that is my opinion, even though the doctors have not committed themselves. Perhaps Anna will be well enough to leave too.

Who is Anna? The woman next door. I didn't tell you I had paid her a visit and she told me her name? She also ate something for the first time. Soon they won't have to force feed her. How did that happen? Very simple. I just got tired of all that wall tapping. Yesterday I simply got up, went to my door, opened it, and went out in the hall—the first time I had ever done so voluntarily—and walked ten feet and there was her door. I knocked on it and went in. (Sometimes life is simple!) She was lying on her cot as usual, curled up, face to the wall, a tangle of hair on her cheek, thin hip upthrust in her hospital gown. Her brown boylike arms made a perfect V, hands pressed palms together between her thighs.

I stood looking down at her. She stirred.

"What's your name?" I asked her.

"Anna," she said. That was all she said.

I decided to sit beside her. She stirred again, tucking her chin in her throat so she could see me past her cheekbone. I could see the gleam between her eyelids.

Her thin brown face reminded me of Lucy, except she didn't have Lucy's funny quirky expression and the tiny scar on her lip. Her face was blank, lips slightly parted and dry, like a woman asleep. She had a scar all right, not like Lucy's, but a big white raised scar curving from forehead to cheek where she had been cut in the rape and beating. Her scar was like a whore's. Do you remember our both making the observation that all whores have scars, belly scars from hysterectomies and abortions, face scars from beatings, leg scars from car wrecks?

"Here," I told her. "Eat this." In my pocket I had half a dozen Hershey kisses Malcolm (the guard—or is he a nurse?) had given me. I unwrapped the silver foil of one and offered it to her. She made no response. I put it into her mouth.

Do you know what she did?

She raised one hand from between her thighs, took the candy out, tucked her chin again, frowned, and looked at it exactly the way a child would, then closed her eyes, put it back in her mouth, and began sucking it.

Yes. Jacoby. He was there, I think, the night of the day I talked to Elgin. At any rate, there was one night I remember.

Janos Jacoby was full of himself. Youngish, short, black forelock which he kept whipping off his eyes with a toss of his head. He was either volatile fiery French-Polish or he knew how to act volatile fiery French-Polish or maybe both. Maybe he was from the Bronx. His accent varied— he had been an actor too and so didn't know what he was. Sitting next to Margot, he gave all his attention to her, turning so far around in his chair that, his back to me, he was almost facing her. He had also gotten onto the foreigner's knack of using his accent and even his mistakes to his advantage. Searching for a word, lips tensed European style, he would hold both hands under Margot's face as if the word were there for both to examine. Though he ignored Raine and Dana—I wondered if all directors ignored all actors—he used his head, face, hands, lips like an actor, for an effect. An effect on Margot. She was charmed. Her eyes sparkled. Color rose in her cheeks. Her freckles darkened. His eyes swept past me, through me, as if I weren't there. When she spoke, her shoulder swayed jokingly toward him, touching him.

Merlin, on the other side of Margot, seemed inattentive and bored. Using his spoon handle, he made long straight marks in the tablecloth. Once in a while Margot would sway the other way and touch him as if to draw him into the conversation, but he only nodded.

Earlier Merlin and Jacoby had been in an argument, Merlin talking about the indispensability of action and story in a film, Jacoby talking in a much fancier way about "cinematographic language," "the semiotics of film," "Griffith as master of denotative language," "Metz as the only critic who understands the connotative film," and so forth. What junk. I refused to pay attention.

Merlin finally shrugged and fell silent. I couldn't tell whether Jacoby was trying to (1) upstage Merlin, (2) impress Margot, (3) do both, or (4) was speaking honestly.

Nor could I be sure whether Merlin was withdrawn because (1) Jacoby was paying too much attention to Margot, (2) he was bored by Jacoby's fancy "cinematographic semiotics."

Raine and Dana listened glumly. My daughter Lucy had managed to get herself between them and was in a transport of happiness, happy to be next to Troy Dana, whom she said she was in love with, but maybe even happier to be next to Raine, whom she worshipped as the casual possessor of those qualities most prized by Lucy and therefore, it seemed to her, most unattainable: beauty, fame, and that special "niceness" which Lucy could scarcely believe, Raine's way of remembering the film crews' names, the film crews' wives' names, servants' names, and even the servants' children's names, taking time with her, Lucy's friends. Raine's ability to "act like anybody else, a real person" seemed to Lucy to surpass the most miraculous deeds of the saints. "She is the most wonderful person I have ever known," Lucy told me.

I didn't think Raine was wonderful. She was amazingly pretty, with a pure heart-shaped face and violet-cobalt eyes which seemed to look from her depths into yours, a trick I came to learn, that steady violet gaze, chin resting on the back of her bent hand. Her depths were vacant. But she flirted with me and that was pleasant. Her single enthusiasm, beside her niceness, was her absorption with a California cult called I.P.D., or something like that— Ideo-Personal-Dynamics maybe. She told me of it at length. I remember very little except that she said it was more scientific than astrology, being based not merely on the influence of the stars but on evidence of magnetic fields surrounding people. The existence of these fields or auras had been proved, she said, by special photography.

Cobalt eyes gazing straight into mine one foot away: "Did you know your magnetic field is as unique as your fingerprints?"

"No."

"It is more exact than astrology because though we are both Capricorns, we are different."

"Yes?"

"Many people are skeptical of astrology but there is scientific proof of this."

"I understand."

"Don't you see the possibilities?"

"Possibilities?"

"For the future, for mankind, for preventing wars."

"How's that?"

"Everyone could have his ideogram, which is a scientific reading of his magnetic field. Some ideograms are clearly stronger than others or incompatible with others. If the President of the United States has a weak ideogram, it would be stupid to send him to a summit meeting. It's the ultimate weapon against Communism."

"I can see how it would be."

The actors, I noticed, took a light passing interest in everything, current events, scientology, politics. They were hardly here at all, in Louisiana that is, but were blown about this way and that, like puffballs, in and out of their roles, "into" Christian Science, back out again.

"I find it a tremendous help in both my personal and professional life. Wouldn't you like to have a reading? You know, I think you underrate yourself." She said it all in a single breath.

"Well, no, that is, yes, sure. Will you give me a reading?"

"Will I ever give you a reading!"

The trouble was that even when she was on this, her favorite subject, her voice went flat and trailed off. Her eyes were steady but unfocused. I had the feeling she wasn't listening to herself. Could it be that her I.P.D. was a trick too, not a trick she played on me but on herself, a way of filling up time?

Merlin and Jacoby argued about the movies they were making, or rather Jacoby seemed to be making, because although Merlin was the producer-director and Jacoby co-director, it was Jacoby who ran the set, yelling at actors and grips, even ordering local residents out of their own houses. It amazed me how meekly, even joyfully, the locals received these bad manners. Anything to be in a movie, or somehow connected with a movie. Then I thought: Listen who's talking and who's been kicked out of his own house.

They were arguing about the scene where the poor white sharecropper rapes the aristocratic girl in the loft of the pigeonnier.

"Of course you must realize"—said Jacoby, leaning over Margot, drawling and moving his lips muscularly—"that at this point something very important happens, Bob. Because what starts out to be a rape, an act of violence which comes from his own—how do you say, being caught—"

"Trapped," said Margot, pulling back slightly from Jacoby's face.

"Yes! Trapped by being a sharecropper and so hitting out at those people, his—"

"Oppressors."

"Right! But a moment occurs when all this disappears and the girl through her own femaleness, feminineness, what? turns this moment into something else, that is, a man and a woman—"

"Don't you mean, Jan," said Margot, her eyes glowing, "that the girl with her own gift for tenderness and caring converts a moment of violence into a moment of love? Isn't it a transformation of a political act by an erotic act?"

"Oh, Margot, you are right!" She made him happy. "Exactly. It is a transforming of the political into the erotic."

Merlin roused slightly. "It is true, I agree. Margot speaks of love. Very well. Love is great. Love conquers all. But here we are content with the erotic—this pair hardly know each other. But the point is that violence, rape or murder, or whatever, is always death-dealing whereas the erotic, in any form at all, is always life-enhancing."

"Yes! That's the nice swing, what you say, switch, don't you see, Margot?" Jacoby turned his black eyes on her. "It is the aristocrat in this case who has the life-enhancing principle and not the sharecropper, as is usually the case, since he is usually shown as coming from the dirt."

"Soil," said Margot.

Was he from the Bronx or Brno?

"Yes, and even though she comes from racism, which is equally death-dealing since it is geno—"

"Genocidal. Since a whole race is involved."

When Janos searched for a word, his eyes roamed past me, through me, to the dark corners of the room. I felt like an actor.

"And the sharecropper is always wavering between the two, the life and death principle. The girl guides him toward life through the erotic. She is his Beatrice." *Bay-ah-tree-chay*.

What irritated me was that despite myself I wanted to be noticed by Janos Jacoby—why for God's sake? for Margot's sake? and found myself trying to think of something impressive like "cinematographic semiotics." But when his eyes swept past me, through me, for the fifth time, I gave it up and decided to satisfy my own curiosity.

So I asked him: "What about the scene between the sheriff and the black sharecropper's daughter?"

"Eh?" Jacoby swung around as if to locate the origin of this unfamiliar voice. "Ah, I am not sure I know what you mean, ah— what about it?" I swear I don't think he knew my name.

"Well, he is both erotic and racist and therefore both life-enhancing and death-dealing. Having had intercourse with her, which was by no means rape, where does that leave him, canceled out so to speak, half bad half good, back at zero?"

Silence. Jacoby and Merlin looked at each other. Margot, between them, blushed. Was she blushing for me?

Jacoby sighed and shook his head. Merlin undertook to explain. "Wouldn't you agree, Lance, that there is such a thing as a sexist violent eroticism which is quite as exploitative as rape itself?"

103

SEX AS
LIFE ENHANCING?

"No. I don't understand that."

Again silence. Eyes averted. It was as if there was a turd, somehow mine, on the snowy tablecloth between us.

"Darling, what you don't realize," said Margot, blushing and taking my hand across the table, "is that the sheriff is performing an out-and-out sexist act of aggression and treats the black girl as a sex object."

"I see." I was looking at Ellis Buell, who was passing the crawfish étouffé. His eyes caught mine. But they were shuttered and did not signify.

After supper I paid my usual visit to Tex and Siobhan. They were in the library on the third floor where my father used to keep his books of Romantic English poetry, Southern history, Robert E. Lee biographies (Robert E. Lee was his saint; he loved him the way Catholics love St. Francis. If the South were Catholic, we'd have long since had an order of St. Robert E. Lee, a stern military Christian order like the monks of Mont-Saint-Michel—hell, I'm not sure we don't), Louisiana history, Feliciana Parish history, Episcopal Church history, the Waverley novels, *Jean Christophe*, Saint-Exupéry, Admiral Byrd's *Alone*, H. G. Wells's *the Science of Life*, the *Life of James Bowie*—a strange collection in which I could detect no common denominator except a taste for the extraordinary and marvelous, the sentimental, the extraordinary experience, the extraordinary adventure undertaken by a brave few, the extraordinary life of genius, the extraordinary stunt of H. G. Wells in taking on all of life, the extraordinary glory of a lost cause which becomes more extraordinary as it recedes in time and in fact Robert E. Lee and the Army of Northern Virginia had long since become for him as legendary and mythical as King Arthur and the Round Table. Do you think I was named Lancelot for nothing? The Andrewes was tacked on by him to give it Episcopal sanction, but what he really had in mind and in his heart wanted to be and couldn't have been more different from was that old nonexistent Catholic brawler and adulterer, Lancelot du Lac, King Ban of Benwick's son, knight of the Round Table and—here was the part he could never get over—one of only two knights to see the Grail (you, Percival, the other); and above all the extraordinariness of those chaste and incorrupt little Anglican chapels set down in this violent and corrupt land besieged on all sides by savage Indians, superstitious Romans, mealy-mouthed Baptists, howling Holy Rollers.

Siobhan was cross and nervous. She was a bright thin wiry perfect little blonde(!), her beauty spoiled only by clouded eyes and a petulant expression.

Tex fancied they were close, that she couldn't get along with her mother, that he had saved her from the niggers. Actually he got on her nerves and she'd have been better off with the niggers. He had a fond insistent yet inattentive way with her which parodied affection and didn't fool her. Indeed, it was as if he were out to irritate her.

She ran to give me a hug and a kiss. I hugged and kissed her back, feeling her thin little bones in her grown-up full-length nylon nightgown. She hugged me too hard, making her arms tremble; her clouded blue eyes didn't quite focus on me. She had learned Tex's trick of parody. They had been watching a cartoon on TV. "What do you think of that cute little fawn?" he asked several times in his mindless singsong, reaching out for her. He too liked to feel her little bones. At seven she was as sexual a creature as her mother but in a dim clouded approximation of it, as if she had forgotten something or was about to remember it. She could curve her lips richly but her eyes were as opaque as a doll's. She liked to show her body and would sit, dress pulled up, arms clasping knees, her little biscuit showing.

Did I love Margot? I'm not sure what you mean, what that word means, but it was good between us. The best times were the sudden unprovided times: leaving the office at ten o'clock, three o'clock, any time at all, going home to Belle Isle to pick her up, snatching her out over protests from her restorations, her as sweaty and plaster-powdered as the workmen restoring Belle Isle to a splendor it had never known; she frowning and fussing and reluctant at first, even then torn a little between me and Belle Isle. In the end we both lost out, the house and I, but she happy as I to be in the old Buick convertible beside me, top down, headed anywhere and nowhere, maybe up the Natchez Trace, singing through dark and bright, the perpetual twilight of the deep loess cuts smelling of earth, and out into the little bright meadows and the pine-winey sunlight, the singing cicadas keeping up with us like the Buick's shadow, she as close as close not forbearing to kiss my neck and cheek over and over again, my hand between her thighs, the radio playing Country Western, which she really liked, hell-bent though she was not to miss a single New Orleans symphony concert; cutoff on a cowpath and sit in the grass, the whiskey and Seven-Up between us, Kristofferson singing and she forgetting Ludwig Beethoven and singing too.

Freedom's just another word, Lord, for nothing left
     to lose
Nothing ain't worth nothing, Lord, but it's free
Feeling good was easy, Lord, when Bobby sang the
     blues

Feeling good was good enough for me
Good enough for me and Bobby McGee.

Bobby McGee got away, but she wasn't getting away from me. I didn't want freedom, I wanted her beside me on the grass, the sun making copper lights on her coarse springy hair, her miraculous gold skin glowing with a sunlight all its own. Pass the bottle, pass the Seven-Up, kiss her sweet lips, lie with her, both of us dry-sweated from different sweats, mine law-office seersucker Blackstone calfskin sweat, hers the clean bathed housewife's morning sweat. Kissing her mouth was kissing the day itself, the October sunlight and whiskey and Seven-Up on her lips and she herself in her mouth, her woman's inside taste yet hers alone too, the special odd astringent chemistry of Mary Margaret Reilly's own saliva.

Love her? I'm not sure what words mean any more, but I loved her if loving her is wanting her all the time, wanting even the sight of her, and being away from her was like being short of breath, and seeing her, just catching sight of her at a distance, was a homecoming to a happy home and a rising of heart. Once I even laughed and clapped my hands when I turned into Belle Isle and saw her on the gallery. I felt like my ancestor Clayton Laughlin Lamar coming home from Virginia in 1865.

Lucy I loved too, but Lucy was a dream, a slim brown dancer in a bell jar spinning round and round in the "Limelight" music of old gone Carolina long ago. Margot was life itself as if all Louisiana, its fecund oil-rich dark greens and haunted twilights, its very fakery and money-loving and comicalness, had all been gathered and fleshed out in one creature. It meant having her and not being haunted, holding all of goldgreen Louisiana in my arms. She was a big girl.

Later we lived by sexual delights and the triumphs of architectural restoration. Truthfully, at that time I don't know which she enjoyed more, a good piece in Henry Clay's bed or Henry Clay's bed. Once a couple of years ago when we were making love, I saw her arm stretch back in a way she had, but now not to grab the bedpost as a point of anchorage or leverage in the storm-tossed sea of love, to hold on for dear life—no, not at all: this time as her arm stretched up her fingers explored the fine oiled restored texture of the mahogany, her nails traced the delicate fluting of the heavy columns.

Later than that, when I took to the bottle—a different love story—and became a poor lover, once again inattentive and haunted, she came to prefer restoration to love. Certain architectural triumphs became for her like orgasms, like the time she dug up a ninety-year-old plaster craftsman in Bunkie, Louisiana, when everybody had told her they had all died, she having discovered old accurate sketches of the plaster roses in the ceilings of the burned wing of Belle Isle. Her face glowed: bringing together the two, the sketches and the long-lost craftsman, and seeing the great shallow roses take form was, I saw, as good for her as sexual love, at the time better in fact.

Then what happened between me and Margot?

If she was here, I know what she'd say and she'd be right as far as she went: Instead of loving me, you crawled into a bottle and I just decided I'd be damned if I'd crawl in with you. You made your decision.

But she'd also be partly wrong. The simple and amazing truth is that when she finished fixing up Belle Isle, she also somehow finished with me. The house Belle Isle was she herself, a Louisiana belle, and when she had done it over and done herself over just right and had finished with me, a proper Louisiana gent—after she had done us both, she was through with both. Once she'd done every conceivable bit of restoration, poring over old sketches, enlisting historians, importing Carrara marble carvers—once she was finished, we were finished—the only important thing for her was that everything had to be exactly as it was. Why? I asked her once. Why does everything have to be exactly as it was? She did me over too. She didn't restore me exactly, she created me according to some Texas-conceived image of the River Road gentry, a kind of gentleman planter without plantation, a composite, I came to understand, of Ashley Wilkes (himself a creature of another woman of course, an anemic poetic Georgia gent), Leslie Howard (another anemic poetic gent), plus Jeff Davis home from the wars and set up in style by another strongminded woman at Beauvoir, parked out in a pigeonnier much like mine, plus Gregory Peck, gentle Southern lawyer, plus a bit of Clark Gable as Rhett. She even bought my clothes. She liked me to wear linen suits.

I went along agreeably, amused by her extraordinary Texas notion that we "aristocratic" folk were somehow all of a piece. Of course we were not, not even aristocratic, and since I never felt much of a piece myself, I'd as soon dress the part. I even found myself playing up to the role, pacing up and down, stopping now and then to make a legal note at my plantation desk in her Florentine-leather notepad, stopping at the cypress cupboard-turned-into-bar to pour a whiskey from crystal decanter into silver jigger, the way Southern gents do in the movies.

Did you know that the South and for all I know the entire U.S.A. is full of demonic women who, driven by as yet unnamed furies, are desperately restoring and preserving *places*, *buildings*? women married to fond indulgent easygoing somewhat lapsed men like me, who would as soon do one thing as another as long as they can go fishing, hunting, drink a bit, horse around, watch the Dolphins and Jack Nicklaus on TV. So here's this fellow like me who maybe had a moment of glory in his youth, in football, in Phi Beta Kappa, as Grand Dragon of his fraternity, and now is managing Auto-Lec or Quik-Stop and every night comes home to a museum such as not even George Washington slept in.

So she finished the house and we found ourselves at a loss. What to do? We did what other well-off thirty-five-year-old couples did: went skiing in Aspen, house-partying, fishing and drinking on the Gulf Coast, house-partying and drinking in Highlands.

But what to do then? What to do with time? Make love. Have a child. We did that. At least I thought we did that. But after she finished Belle Isle and named her child Siobhan, there was nothing to do. Siobhan was well looked after, especially when granddaddy Tex moved in with us.

I could see her problem. Christ, what was she going to *do*? What to do with that Texas energy and her passion for making things either over or of a piece. What did God do after he finished creation? Christ, she didn't know how to rest. At least in Louisiana we knew how to take things easy. We could always drink.

That was when she revived her interest in the "performing arts" and went to Dallas-Arlington to study under Merlin.

Did I love her? Why are you always asking about love? Have you been crossed up too? Isn't your God's love enough for you? Margot's love was enough for me. I loved her sexually in such a way that I could not not touch her. My happiness was being with her. My old saturninity vanished. I hugged and kissed her in the street, necked in the

110

car like white trash in the daytime, felt her up under the table in restaurants, and laughed like a boy to see her blush and knock my hand away and, looking anxiously around, revert to her old Texasese: "Git away from here! What you think you doing, boy!"

There is no joy on this earth like falling in love with a woman and managing at the same time the trick of keeping just enough perspective to see her fall in love too, to see her begin to see you in a different way, to see her color change, eyes soften, her hand of itself reach for you. Your saints say, Yes but the love of God is even better, but Jesus how could this be so? Well? Your eyes go distant as if you were thinking of a time long ago. Does that mean that you are no longer a believer or that nowadays not even believers can understand such things? Doesn't your own Jewish Bible say there is nothing under the sun like the way of a man with a maid?

And there is no pain on this earth like seeing the same woman look at another man the way she once looked at you.

Do you know what jealousy is? Jealousy is an alteration in the very shape of time itself. Time loses its structure. Time stretches out. She isn't here. Where is she? Who is she with? There is so much time. The minutes and hours creep by. What is she doing? She could be doing anything. She was not here. Her not being here was like oxygen not being here. What am I going to do with the rest of the day? Something tightened in my chest.

Elgin came in with a clipboard and sat across my desk looking both wary and pleased. When he put on his black horn-rimmed glasses, his hand trembled slightly. He looked like a smart student facing an important examination. I noticed he was dressed unusually, in what I took to be his school clothes, neat belted-in-the-back jeans, white shirt, narrow black tie. Had it been a problem for him to decide how he would appear? as house servant? tour guide? private eye? smart student?

I had been sitting in my pigeonnier watching boys build a bonfire on the levee. They started before Thanksgiving, cutting willows in the batture to make twenty-foot-high tepees which burn all night Christmas eve, making a great flaming crescent the whole length of English Turn like the campfires of a sleeping army.

It was not Margot I was thinking about but time, what to do with time. Sober, free of smoke and nicotine for the first time in years, my body cells tingled, watchful and uneasy. What next? What's coming up? My tongue was ready to taste, my muscles were ready to contract, my liver hummed away, my genitals prickled. Then I realized why I drank and smoked. It was a way of dealing with time. What to do with time? A fearful thing: a human body of ten billion cells ready to do any one of ten billion things. But what to do?

The empty tape was spinning past the tape head.

"Ahem." Elgin cleared his throat. I gave a start. "What do you—"

"Oh. Is that the log you kept last night?"

"Yes, sir." Then he *had* felt the need to take on some guise or other. But which? house servant? private eye?

"Why don't you just read it, Elgin?"

That helped. Now he could prop clipboard against crossed knee, push his glasses up his nose with his thumb.

"One-forty a.m. Subjects left Oleander Room." He looked up. "They stood by the vending machines talking for ten minutes."

"They? Who were they?"

"Miss Lucy." *Miss Lucy?* He had never called her that. I saw that he felt a need to put a distance between himself and this business (though he was also proud of what he had done). In his nervousness he had put the greatest distance he could think of: he had retreated to being an old-time servant.

"Go ahead."

"One-fifty. Miss Lucy and Miss Margot to room 115, Miss Raine's room."

"Never mind the Misters and Misses."

"Okay. Troy Dana to room 118, his room, Merlin to 226, Jacoby to 145.

"Two-twelve a.m. Miss Margot leave 115 and go to 226." For Margot he still needed the *Miss*.

"Merlin's room?"

"Yes, sir. Two-twenty-five. Troy Dana leave 118 and go to 115."

"Raine's room. That puts Troy, Lucy, and Raine in 115."

"Yes, sir. Two-fifty-one a.m. Miss Margot leave" (leave not leaves: he was nervous) "226 and go to 145."

"Jacoby's room?"

"Yes, sir."

"Go on."

"Five-oh-four a.m. Lucy leave 115 in a hurry, running like, go out. To her car."

"Yes?"

"Five-fourteen. Troy Dana also leaves 115, goes to 118, his room." Leaves. He was calmer.

"Okay."

"Five-twenty-four. Miss Margot leaves 145, goes out. To her car. Oh, I forgot. Three-five. Jacoby went out for a glass of water." He looked up. "I think Miss Margot was sick."

113

"Yes?"

"That's all."

"That's it?"

"Yes, sir. You told me to leave at daylight." Feeling better, he shoved up the bridge of his glasses with his thumb. I could imagine his students years later, taking him off, doing a school skit imitating his doing this.

Ha. Maybe she *was* sick!

I remember thinking how odd Elgin was, switching back and forth from house nigger to young professor.

"Okay. That does it. Very good. Thanks, Elgin."

Relieved, he swiftly got to his feet.

"No, wait." I had already known what I was going to do. And how I was going to deal with it, time coming at me and ten billion cells tingling, waiting.

He sat down slowly. I picked up the telephone and called my cousin Laughlin at the Holiday Inn. Elgin, simply curious now, watched me.

"Lock, I need a favor." I could ask. I had loaned him the money, Margot's money, to build the motel.

"Sho, Lance. Just you ask."

He was too quick and ingratiating. Gratitude, as well it might, made him uneasy. I could see him sitting at his desk: his clean short-sleeved shirt, neat receding hair turning brown-gray, Masonic ring on finger, hand on socks with clocks, short body just slightly fat, a simple shape like a balloon blown up just enough to smooth the wrinkles. He looked like the president of the Optimists Club, which in fact he was. A doomed optimist. The only difference between Laughlin and me was that Laughlin had not even had his youthful moment of glory. Instead he had had twenty or thirty jobs in the past twenty or thirty years, at each of which he had not exactly failed (for he was earnest and if he was stupid it was in some mysterious self-defeating way

114

which not even he was aware of) but rather completed what he set out to do. He lost interest, the job ran out, the company went out of business, people stopped buying bicycles, sugar tripled in price and ruined his Nabisco distributorship. Now he answered too quickly. Two things made him nervous: one, that he owed me a favor; the other, that he was succeeding. Success terrified him.

"Just you ask, Lance," he said, gaining confidence from my hesitation.

"I want you to close the motel for a few days."

"What's that again?" he asked quickly.

"Just say they're going to cut your gas off temporarily as in fact they might. As you know, most of our gas has got to go to New England."

"I know but—close the motel? Why?"

"I'll pay you full occupancy even though you're only half full. It should be for two or three days."

"But tomorrow's Tuesday."

"What's that got to do with it?"

"Rotary."

"I mean the rooms. Go ahead and have Rotary."

"Why do you want to close the rooms?"

I fell silent. Four boys on the levee were tilting up a tall shorn willow like the Marines raising the flag on Iwo Jima. Elgin was watching me, the old Elgin now, big-eyed and unmindful of himself.

"I want all those film people out. They're almost finished. If they leave there, they'll have to get out."

"Oh." Oh, I see, he meant. I was counting on his misapprehension and let it stand. "I don't blame you."

"For what?"

He trod carefully. "For wanting to keep an eye on 'em. I've seen a lot of things in this business." He'd managed a motel in the French Quarter for a year. "You talk about humbug! But—"

"But what?"

"As long as they don't tear up the furniture or burn the beds or stink up the place with pot, I don't care who does what to who. You wouldn't believe some of the things—college kids are the worst."

He was either stupid or tactful and I do believe it was the latter. We talked easily, deplored college kids and the vicissitudes of the motel business.

"Okay, Lock?"

"Let's see. It's three-thirty. Too late to close today. But I'll put a notice in each box to be out by check-out time tomorrow." He warmed up to it. "As a matter of fact, they've been talking about cutting off my gas. How do you like that! New York City is going to get our gas! And that means no heat or air conditioning in the rooms. Don't worry about a thing." For once, his mournful gratitude gave way to good cheer. It was as if he had repaid his loan. "I don't even care. I'm changing to propane. Do you know what my gas bill was last month?"

"Thank you, Lock."

Elgin watched me as I hung up. Something had given him leave to relax and be himself.

"Elgin, there are some other things you and only you can do for me."

"I'll do them."

In my new freedom I remember thinking: If one knows what he wants to do, others will not only not stand in the way but will lend a hand from simple curiosity and amazement.

"Okay. You recall the other day we were speaking about the chimney hole and the dumbwaiter?"

"Yes." All ears now.

116

"All right. Look." Taking his log from the clipboard, I turned it over and began to draw a floor plan. "I'm making two assumptions. One is that they'll move back into Belle Isle when they leave the motel tomorrow. There's nowhere else to go."

"Right."

"Then I'm assuming they'll move back into the same rooms at Belle Isle they had before."

"Yes. They left their clothes there."

"Merlin here on one side of the chimney, Jacoby here on the other. But Margot's and Lucy's, Dana's and Raine's rooms are across the hall. That presents a technical problem."

"Technical problem?"

"Tell me something, Elgin. How would you like to make a movie?"

"Movie? What kind of movie?"

"A new kind of cinéma vérité." I picked up the pencil. "Here's where you can help me. There are a few technical problems."

Christ, here's my discovery. You have got hold of the wrong absolutes and infinities. God as absolute? God as infinity? I don't even understand the words. I'll tell you what's absolute and infinite. Loving a woman. But how would you know? You see, your church knows what it's doing: rule out one absolute so you have to look for another.

Do you know what it's like to be a self-centered not unhappy man who leads a tolerable finite life, works, eats, drinks, hunts, sleeps, then one fine day discovers that the great starry heavens have opened to him and that his heart is bursting with it. It? She. Her. Woman. Not a category, not a sex, not one of two sexes, a human female creature, but an infinity. $♀ = \infty$. What else is infinity but a woman become meat and drink to you, life and your heart's own music, the air you breathe? Just to be near her is to live and have your soul's own self. Just to open your mouth on the skin of her back. What joy just to wake up with her beside you in the morning. I didn't know there was such happiness.

But there is the dark converse: not having her is not breathing. I'm not kidding: I couldn't get my breath without her.

What else is man made for but this? I can see you agree about love but you look somewhat ironic. Are we talking about two different things? In any case, there's a catch. Love is infinite happiness. Losing it is infinite unhappiness.

So far so good, you say, somewhat ironically, I notice. A man falls in love with a lovely lusty woman, so what else is new? But can you imagine what it's like to love a lovely lustful woman who lusts but not for you?

Quite a discovery.

The truth is, it never crossed my mind in my entire sweet Southern life that there was such a thing as a lustful woman. Another infinite imponderable. Infinitely appalling. What hath God wrought?

On the other hand, why should not a woman, who is after all a creature like any other, be lustful? Yet to me, the sight of a lustful woman was as incredible as a fire-breathing dragon turning up at the Rotary Club.

What I really mean of course was that what horrified me was the discovery of the possibility that she might lust for someone not me.

But of course I had to make sure of it. Love and lust should not be a matter of speculation.

Margot, it turned out, was indeed sick the morning after Elgin's stakeout. Pale and feverish.

Then perhaps she had simply got sick and been cared for by Merlin and Jacoby. Why is it so hard to make certain of a simple thing?

Margot was sick! Hurray.

Yes, but I was not Siobhan's father and Merlin could be and Merlin was here.

My God, why was I torturing myself?

"When did it come on, Margot?" I asked her, going to her room after breakfast.

"God, I damned near fainted during the rushes. I think I did faint later. Out cold. I just barely managed to drag myself home."

Can one ever be sure of anything? Did my mother go for innocent joyrides with Uncle Harry, take the air, and see the sights as they said, or did they take the lap robe and head for the woods or a tourist cabin, one of those little pre-motel miniature houses set up on four cinderblocks with a bed, linoleum, gas heater, and tin shower, the essentials.

What does that sorrowful look of yours mean? And what if they did, would it be so bad, is that what you mean? What are you mourning? Them? Me? Us?

You know the main difference between you and me? With you everything seems to get dissolved in a kind of sorrowful solution. Poor weak mankind! The trouble is that in your old tolerant Catholic world-weariness, you lose all distinctions. Love everything. Yes, but at midnight all cats are black, so what difference does anything make? It does make a difference? What? You opened your mouth and then thought better of it—

But don't you see, I had to find out. There I was in early middle age and I couldn't answer the most funda-

119

mental question of all. What question? This: Are people as nice as they make out and in fact appear to be, or is it all buggery once the door is closed?

So I meant to find out once and for all. There is something worse than knowing the worst. It is not knowing.

In the back of my mind all along was the sensation I had when I opened my father's sock drawer and found the ten thousand dollars under the argyles my mother, nice lady that she was, had knitted for him, honorable man that he was.

One has to know. There are worse things than bad news.

VI

IT WAS LUNCHTIME WHEN MY DAUGHTER LUCY CAME
down for breakfast in quilted housecoat, face voluptuous, sleepy-eyed, slightly puffy.

"Aren't you supposed to be in school?" I asked her,
remembering it was Tuesday.

"I'm not going back to school." Her pale heavy face
slanted sullenly over her food, eyes blinking regularly. Was
she crying?

"Why not?"

"I've got a job."

"Where?"

"With Raine."

"Doing what?"

"I'm going to be her social and recording secretary."

"Jesus, what's that?"

"Daddy, they are the most wonderful people in the
world."

"They?"

"She and Troy. They are the only people I've ever
known who are completely free."

"Free?"

121

"Free to make their own lives." Lucy looked up at last.

How little we know our own children! I think I had not looked at her in years. How did I size her up, this little stranger? She was not like her mother. The years would not treat her well. At sixteen she was at her prime; later her face would get heavy in the morning. She was like a child whom voluptuousness had overtaken unawares. By the time she becomes fully aware of it, she will have run to fat. Her own chemistry had played a trick on her and her face was heavy with it. This innocent voluptuousness was the sort—and here I shocked myself—to inspire lewdness in strangers.

"We sat up all night in the motel room talking."

Then perhaps life was as innocent as that: they sat up all night talking. Margot sick and Lucy talking. Why not?

"About what?"

"Everything. Raine, you know, is deep into I.P.D. Did you know she was president of the national association?"

"No."

"My job will really be to be recording secretary for I.P.D."

"What will you learn from that?"

"I've learned more in the last three weeks than I ever learned in my life."

"What?"

"About myself. What makes me tick. For example, about the lower centers."

"The *what*?"

"The four lower centers. As opposed to the three higher, consciousness, mind, spirit."

"You mean you want to go back to California with Raine?"

"I'm going to live with Troy and Raine."

"I didn't know they were married."

"They're not. And I'm glad they're not. If they were married, I'd be like a daughter or something. This way we're equals, a threesome, one for all, all for one."

Is all niceness then or is all buggery? How can a man be forty-five years old and still not know whether all is niceness or buggery? How does one know for sure?

"Have you spoken to your mother? You'll have to have our permission, you know."

"She's all for it. At least she said so this morning. I hope she's not out of her mind—she said she had a 103-degree fever."

Then she was sick and all is niceness and not buggery.

"You mean you want to live with Troy and Raine?"

"Yes. Do you want to see their house, rather Raine's house? Isn't that neat?"

From her pocket she took out photos of Raine and of the house, the first inscribed with writing: I could only read *To my little*—Little what? I couldn't make it out. The other showed an English beam-in-plaster mansion and some California plants trimmed to shapes, spheres and rhomboids. It looked like the sort of place where Philip Marlowe called on a rich client and insulted the butler.

"Look at what Raine gave me."

Opening her housecoat, she showed me a heavy gold cross nestled in the dusky cleft of her young breasts.

"She's the most wonderful person I've ever known."

She seemed to be. Everyone seemed wonderful. All the town folk thought the movie people wonderful. And in fact they seemed to be.

I think I see now what I am doing. I am reliving with you my quest. That's the only way I can bear to think about it.

Something went wrong. If you listen I think I can figure out what it was.

It was a quest all right and a very peculiar one. But peculiar times require peculiar quests.

We've spoken of the Knights of the Holy Grail, Percival. Do you know what I was? The Knight of the Unholy Grail.

In times like these when everyone is wonderful, what is needed is a quest for evil.

You should be interested! Such a quest serves God's cause! How? Because the Good proves nothing. When everyone is wonderful, nobody bothers with God. If you had ten thousand Albert Schweitzers giving their lives for their fellow men, do you think anyone would have a second thought about God?

Or suppose the Lowell Professor of Religion at Harvard should actually find the Holy Grail, dig it up in an Israeli wadi, properly authenticate it, carbon date it, and present it to the Metropolitan Museum. Millions of visitors! I would be as curious as the next person and would stand in line for hours to see it. But what difference would it make in the end? People would be interested for a while, yes. This is an age of interest.

But suppose you could show me one "sin," one pure act of malevolence. A different cup of tea! That would bring matters to a screeching halt. But we have plenty of evil around you say. What about Hitler, the gas ovens and so forth? What about them? As everyone knows and says, Hitler was a madman. And it seems nobody else was responsible. Everyone was following orders. It is even possible that there was no such order, that it was all a bureaucratic mistake.

Show me a single "sin."

One hundred and twenty thousand dead at Hiroshima?

Where was the evil of that? Was Harry Truman evil? As for the pilot and bombardier, they were by all accounts wonderful fellows, good fathers and family men.

"Evil" is surely the clue to this age, the only quest appropriate to the age. For everything and everyone's either wonderful or sick and nothing is evil.

God may be absent, but what if one should find the devil? Do you think I wouldn't be pleased to meet the devil? Ha, ha, I'd shake his hand like a long-lost friend.

The mark of the age is that terrible things happen but there is no "evil" involved. People are either crazy, miserable, or wonderful, so where does the "evil" come in?

There I was forty-five years old and I didn't know whether there was "evil" in the world.

A small corollary to the above: Is evil to be sought in violence or in sexual behavior? Or is all violence bad and all sexual behavior good, or as Jacoby and Merlin would say, life-enhancing?

If one is looking for evil, why not study war or child-battering? Could anything be more evil? Yet, as everyone knows, mothers and fathers who beat and kill their children have psychological problems and are as bad off as the children. It has been proved that every battered child has battered parents, battered grandparents, and so on. No one is to blame.

As for war, the only time members of my family have ever been happy, brave, successful, was in time of war. What's wrong with war?

Look across the street. Do you see that girl's Volkswagen's bumper sticker: Make Love Not War. That is certainly the motto of the age. Is anything wrong with it?

Yes. Could it be possible that since the greatest good is

to be found in love, so is the greatest evil. Evil, sin, if it exists, must be incommensurate with anything else. Didn't one of your saints say that the entire universe in all its goodness is not worth the cost of a single sin? Sin is incommensurate, right? There is only one kind of behavior which is incommensurate with anything whatever, in both its infinite good and its infinite evil. That is sexual behavior. The orgasm is the only earthly infinity. Therefore it is either an infinite good or an infinite evil.

My quest was for a true sin—was there such a thing? Sexual sin was the unholy grail I sought.

It is possible of course that there is no such thing and that a true sin, like the Grail, probably does not exist.

Yet I had the feeling I was on to something, perhaps for the first time in my life. Or at least for twenty years. I was like Robinson Crusoe seeing a footprint on his island after twenty years: Not a footprint but my daughter's blood type. Aha, there is something going on!

So overnight I became sober, clear-eyed, clean, fit, alert, watchful as a tiger at a water hole.

Something was stirring. So Sir Lancelot set out, looking for something rarer than the Grail. A sin.

"Elgin, how would you like to make a movie?"

Elgin smiled. "Merlin axed me already."

"To be in one. I'm asking about making a movie, not Merlin's. Mine. I'm going to make a movie."

"You are?"

"And you're going to help me."

"I am?"

"Elgin, listen." I walked around the plantation desk and stood hands in pockets looking down at him. He sat perfectly symmetrical, arms resting at an angle across chair

126

arms, fingers laced, gazing straight ahead, a slight smile on his lips. "I'm asking a favor of you. I need someone to help me and only you can do it. There are two reasons for this. One is that only you have the technical ability to help me. The other is that you are one of the two or three people in the world I trust. The others are probably your mother and father. I must tell you that it is a large favor because you will be doing it without knowing why. Although what I'm asking you to do is not illegal, it is just as well you don't know the reasons. Do you understand?"

"Yes."

"Well?"

"Okay." Still avoiding my eye, he answered immediately. It was as if he already knew what I wanted.

"Here's the technical problem. To tell you the truth, I don't know whether it can be solved. Certainly I have no idea of how to go about it." I took out my floor plan of Belle Isle's second story. "You see these five rooms? Margot's and Raine's on one side of the hall, separated by the chimney and dumb-waiter. On the other side of the hall are these three rooms, Troy Dana's here, Merlin's here, Janos Jacoby's here. They'll be moving back to the house tomorrow as I had anticipated."

Elgin's eyelids flickered once, when I mentioned Margot's name. Otherwise his expression did not change.

Elgin didn't move, but his eyes went out of focus.

"Now here's what I want. I want a hidden camera mounted in each room and the events which occur in the room between midnight and five o'clock recorded. For one, perhaps two nights. Three nights at the most."

"No way," he said at last.

But even as he said it, shaking his head and smiling, he was casting about in his mind—happily. Happy the man who can live with problems! It was this I had counted on of course, that the problem, its sheer impossibility, would engage him immediately so that he would not think two seconds about what I was asking him to do.

Even as he smiled and shook his head, he was casting about. It was the challenge of the thing. He was like a mountain climber, pitoned, rappeled, looking straight up a sheer cliff. It couldn't be climbed. On the other hand, perhaps—

"No way." He repeated the impossibility, savored it.

"Why not?"

"At least three reasons. Not enough light. Camera noise. And no camera will run five hours."

"I see." I waited, watching him thumb his glasses up his nose bridge, scratch his head.

An odd thought: I remember thinking at the time that nothing really changes, not even Elgin going from pickaninny to M.I.T. smart boy. For you see, even in doing that and not in casting about for the technical solution, he was still in a sense "my nigger"; and my watching him, waiting for him, was piece and part of the old way we had of ascribing wondrous powers to "them," if they were "ours." Don't you remember how my grandfather used to say of old Fluker, Ellis's father, that with Fluker along on a quail hunt you didn't need bird dogs, that Fluker *knew* where the birds were?

That was part of it sure enough—not that Elgin was like a bird dog but that in being smart and through some special dispensation, perhaps by reason of our very need and helplessness, we could depend on them for anything, not just to smell out quail, but to be M.I.T. smart, smarter than we, Jew-smart, no, smarter than Jews. I could hear my grandfather: I'll put that Elgin up against a Jew anytime, any Jew. Go pick your Jew.

"Does it have to be a film?" Elgin looked up at me; his

tongue went sideways. I knew he had thought of something.

"What else—"

"How about a tape?"

"I want sight not sound."

"Videotape."

"How does that work?"

"Just like the closed-circuit TV camera you see in stores. Only—"

"Only?"

"Okay, look. How about this?" He swung round to the desk, picked up my pencil. His black eyes danced. It had come to him, the solution! "We use five mini-compact cameras here and here." He put X's in the dumbwaiter outlets to Margot's and Raine's rooms.

"I thought of that. But what about the three across the hall?"

"We'll use the A/C vents."

"The air conditioning?"

"Sure. We'll use mini-compacts with twenty-five milli-meter lenses—small enough to see through a slot in the grill."

"What about camera noise?"

"No noise. No film. It's a TV camera."

"What about the dark?"

"We'll use a Vidicon pickup tube, a Philips two-stage light intensifier—you know, it works on the fiber-optics principle, can pick up a single quantum of light."

"Then we'll need some light."

"Moonlight will help."

I looked at my feed-store calendar. "There's a half moon."

He picked up his glasses. "I might use infrared."

"Good."

"All I need is a control room. That could be anywhere."

"How about my father's library, here?"

"Don't Mr. Tex and Siobhan use that? We have to have a completely undisturbed place."

"All I have to do is move the TV set. I'll put it in Siobhan's room here."

"That's fine. I could bring in lead-in cables from the dumbwaiter and the A/C ducts by way of the third floor."

"And what will you be doing in there?"

"Recording five tapes. I'll need a Conrac monitor."

"How long will it take you to rig up all that?"

"Well, I'll have to go to New Orleans to get the equipment." He looked at his watch. "Tomorrow. Then it would take the next day to rig it—if nobody was around."

"They won't be. They're shooting in town the next two days. A courthouse scene and a love scene at the library."

"Okay. I guess the best we can do is day-after-tomorrow night—and that's only if everything goes well and I can get the equipment. But I'm sure I can get it."

"I hope so. Because they'll be shooting at Belle Isle in two or three days. Then it will be too late."

"We can do it. All you got to do is clear the house tomorrow and the day after and clear the library at night."

"How much will all that stuff cost?"

"The light intensifier is expensive, maybe four thousand. The whole works shouldn't run over eight or ten at the outside."

"Ten thousand," I said. "I have that in the house account. I think I'd better get cash for you. The bank opens at nine. You could be on your way by nine-thirty."

"Okay."

"Okay. Then what will you end up with?"

"Five tapes. Something like this." He picked up an eight-track cartridge of Beethoven's last quartets. During the last months I found that I could be moderately happy if I simultaneously (1) drank, (2) read Raymond Chandler, and (3) listened to Beethoven.

"There's only one problem," said Elgin, turning the tape over and over.

"What's that?"

"Time. Not even this will record five hours. *Ah.*" He had it, the solution. For him now in a kind of exaltation of inventiveness, it was enough to put the problem into words. Saying it was solving it. He even snapped his fingers.

"We'll have to use the new Subiru motion activator."

"What is that?" In the very offhandedness of his voice I could catch the excitement, the exhilaration of his knowledge and skill.

He shrugged. "You know, the voice-activated sound tape recorder? It only goes on when there is a noise."

"Like the President had?"

"Yeah." He was too happy to notice irony. "Same principle. Transferred to light. The tape only moves when something or someone in front of the camera moves."

"Something or someone. You mean it wouldn't just record a sleeping person?"

"Only when he or she turned over. All he got to do is move—or talk."

When something or someone moved. Yes, that was it. That was what I wanted. Who moved, toward whom, with whom.

It was necessary to visit the set, something I never did, in order to see how long the shooting would take and to warn Elgin should my houseguests decide to return to Belle Isle early. He must have time to arrange his own "set," place and wire his cameras.

I needn't have worried. They spent all day on one short scene between Margot and Dana. Fifteen or twenty times he had her up against the library stacks performing "simulated intercourse." He was filmed from the rear doing something to Margot quickly and easily. He was clothed.

Merlin was surprised to see me, but pleasant and talkative as usual. I told him I had come to make him welcome at Belle Isle and to be sure they had removed from the motel. Though the danger from the hurricane was slight, the motel was built in a swamp and could be flooded.

"You're a beautiful guy!" Merlin came close and took my arm. He had a way of making any encounter between us exclude the others. His blue eyes were fond; the white fiber made the iris spin with dizzy affection. "How extraordinary that a real hurricane should be approaching the same time as our make-believe hurricane. Actually though, this scene has nothing to do with the hurricane."

"I want to hear the zipper," Janos Jacoby told Dana.

The set was the small public library in town. Town folk watched, standing, arms folded, sitting on aluminum chairs, on the sidewalk, on the grass, in the doorway. Inside, the library was a mess; it looked as if the hurricane had already hit, everything moved out of the way to shoot Margot and Dana in the stacks. The blue-white lights were brighter and hotter than the sun outside. Heavy cables snaked over the trodden grass like a carnival ground. Between shots Dana zipped his pants, fell back, and cleaned his nails, listened inattentively to Jacoby. As the librarian in the movie, Margot wore glasses around her neck, white blouse, cashmere cardigan, sleeves pushed up. She was not at ease. Her face was cheeky and her movements wooden. She was, I saw instantly, not a good actress. What she was

132

doing was not acting, that is, imitating someone else, but acting like an actress imitating-someone-else. She was once removed from acting.

Dana was something to see: barefoot, tight jeans with silver conch belt, some kind of pullover homespun shirt, necklace with single jade stone, perfect helmet of yellow hair, perfect regular features, perfect straight brows flaring like wings. He moved well and had grace. He was an idiot but he had grace. He was a blank space filled in by somebody else's idea. He was a good actor. His eyes had somehow been made up so they seemed to gather light and glow of themselves. The town folk gaped at him as if he were another species. Perhaps he was. Perhaps somewhere on the golden sands of California had come into being a new breed of perfect creatures, young and golden.

Margot couldn't see me. The lights were too bright.

"This is a very short scene but a very critical one," Merlin explained. "It is the sexual liberation of Sarah."

"Sexual liberation?"

"Yeah. You remember. Dana is the stranger who wanders into town from nowhere and is so extraordinarily gifted—everyone is immediately aware of it. Thank God for the movies. Dana gifted? He barely had sense not to drown when he fell off his surfboard in *Beach Blanket Bingo*. But look at him, isn't he something? We can create him from the beginning like a doll. I created Dana—Dana himself is nothing, a perfect cipher. This character, this stranger is immediately perceived by everybody as somehow different—for one thing his eyes, there's an inner light, he's a creature of light. Look at him. His normal temperature is around 101. He actually glows. Most important, he is free. Everybody else is hung up—as in fact everybody is, you're hung up, I'm hung up. Right? Sarah is a Joanne Woodward type—though Margot is actually a bit too young and good-looking—but she has never known what it is to be a woman. You know. Her husband, Lipscomb, is out of it too. He sits wringing his hands while the plantation goes to pot. She holds things together, makes a pittance at the library. He's hung up. Everyone is hung up. The sharecroppers, black and white, are hung up in poverty and ignorance. The townies are hung up in bigotry and so forth. Not only is the stranger free, he is also able to free others. There is the sense about him of having come from far away, perhaps the East, perhaps farther. Perhaps he is a god. At least he is a kind of Christ type.

"He fulfills people. He fulfills the longing of the sharecroppers for their own land—he discovers that Raine's, Ella's, family owns the land. He reconciles black and white—who discover their own common humanity during the hurricane. He even gets to the sheriff (God, I wish we could have got Pat Hingle), who despite himself is tremendously moved by this glowing nonviolent vibrant creature —actually there's a strong hint here of Southern sheriff homosexuality, right? He almost reaches Lipscomb, who has lost his ties with the land, nature, his own sexuality. He does reach Sarah. He walks into the library and while her mouth falls open, he simply goes to the bookshelf, takes down the *Rig-Veda*, and reads the great passage beginning: 'Desire entered the One in the beginning.' Then, again without saying a word, he takes her hand and leads her back into the stacks, where he takes her standing against the old musty books—Thackeray and Dickens and so forth —representing the drying up of Western juices. There's a lovely tight shot of her face while she's making love against a dusty set of the Waverley novels. Great? The stranger is the life-giving principle, the books are dead, everyone is dead, Thackeray is dead, Scott is dead, the town is dead, Lipscomb is dead, she is dead, or rather she has never lived. So what we are trying to get across is that it is not just screwing, though there is nothing wrong with that either, but a kind of sacrament and celebration of life. He could be a high priest of Mithras. You see what we're getting at?"

Something went wrong. Jacoby called for an Arriflex hand-held camera and his assistant Lionel couldn't locate it. Jacoby came over to talk to Merlin. More or less automatically I held out my hand—not that I wanted to shake hands with him, but we know in the South that the real purpose of manners is to make life easier for everyone, easier both to keep to oneself and to avoid the uneasy commerce of offense and even insult. Either one shakes hands with someone or one ignores him or one kills him. What else is there? Jacoby ignored me. His bemused eye looked through me and past me. I do believe that he did not insult me but rather did not see me. In his absorption I was part of the town decor, one of them. Merlin noticed the oversight and was embarrassed, cleared his throat, did not know what to do. There's the function of manners: that no one will not know what to do.

I rescued Merlin by asking him how long they were going to work today. "Oh, late! Late!" cried Merlin cordially. "And thanks so much for putting us up"—looking to Jacoby to echo thanks but Jacoby only nodded vaguely. I escaped and went out through the back, the office of the librarian.

Raine and Lucy and Miss Maude, the librarian, were there. Raine kissed me with every appearance of pleasure —what is she? actress? flirt? wanton? nice affectionate girl? Lucy followed suit somewhat absentmindedly. She was so frantic in her crush on Raine that she hardly noticed me.

"Isn't it exciting!" said Raine, putting her hands on my

shoulders, rocking me a little, brushing knees. One knee came between my knees.

"What?"

"The hurricane!"

"I don't think it'll get here."

"But the light! Haven't you noticed the peculiar yellow light and the sinister quietness about things? Isn't this usually true of hurricanes?"

"I suppose. I hadn't really noticed."

"I was telling Lucy that there is more than coincidence involved here."

"How's that?"

"How could such a coincidence happen, that at the very time we are making a film about a hurricane, a real hurricane should come?"

"Well, it could. This is hurricane season."

"What are the mathematical chances involved? One in a million? There is more than weather involved. There is more than light involved. I feel the convergence of all our separate lines of force. Can't you feel something changed in the air between all of us?"

"Well—"

"I do, Raine!" cried Lucy, hugging Raine's arm.

Raine, color high in her cheek, spoke to me with her head ducked, as flirtatiously as Siobhan. Was this her way of being shy about her mystical convictions?

"There's a force field around all of us, waxing and waning," said Raine absently, suddenly waning herself, losing interest. She spoke a little more, but inattentively.

"Maybe you're right, Raine." I could never figure out the enthusiasm of movie folk. It was as if they were possessed fitfully by demons, but demons of a very low order to whom one needn't pay strict attention.

Miss Maude, like Lucy, fixed on Raine, eyes glistening.

Dana came moseying in, thumbs hooked in his jeans. Miss Maude's eyes bulged. He *was* something to see. Maybe he *was* the new sunlit god come to save this sad town. But when, ignoring us, he began to talk to Raine, it was about his—investments! Bad news from London, where he had bought a pub which made money but the government took 90 percent of it! "Christ, if I had just listened to Bob about Cayman," and so forth—fretting! eyes crossed with worry about alimony and taxes, and all at once you saw that he was an optical illusion, a trick, that his beauty was not only accidental and that he had no part in it but that he didn't even credit himself with it. He was like a hound dog wearing a diamond necklace.

Miss Maude was suddenly possessed by a demon all her own. Imploringly, almost tearfully, eyes glistening, she offered Raine her house for the scene between Lipscomb the decadent planter and his aunt, a strong aristocratic type ("Christ, can't you see Ouspenskaya doing her!" said Merlin), who tells him his true strength comes from the land. "You always have the land! The land is eternal!" and so forth. Miss Maude seemed to know all about the movie.

"Thank you, Maude," said Raine, giving her a hug. "I'll tell Jan and Bob." Raine, I saw, was in a kind of ecstasy of benevolence. It pleased her to be nice to Miss Maude. Raine's face shone like a saint's or like Ingrid Bergman's. Was it the hurricane which excited her or the exaltation of being a movie star and confirming her stardom in the faces of ordinary folk?

I blinked. All at once Miss Maude, whom I had known all my life or thought I knew, went off her rocker. Or she had been off her rocker for forty years and now at last came to herself. In fact she said so.

Her face suddenly wrinkled up like a prune, her eyes glittered with tears. At first I thought she was crying, but it was not grief, it was happiness, gratitude. She twisted a handkerchief in her hands.

"I just can't tell you what it means to me," said Miss Maude, pumping her tired hands back and forth.

"Raine got Jan to give Miss Maude a walk-on in the library scene," explained Lucy.

"Is there any way I can tell you?" implored Miss Maude, coming ever closer to Raine, wringing her hands, frantic with an emotion not even she could name.

"You did a good job," said Raine, backing off, getting a little more than she had bargained for. "You're a beautiful person, Maude."

"Oh, Raine, Raine, Raine," said Maude and actually threw back her head and closed her eyes.

I looked at Maude in astonishment. Had everybody in this town gone nuts or was I missing something? The special nuttiness of the movie people I was used to, but the town had gone nuts. Town folk, not just Maude, acted as if they lived out their entire lives in a dim charade, a shadow-play in which they were the shadows, and now all at once to have appear miraculously in their midst these resplendent larger-than-life beings. She, Maude, couldn't get over it: not only had they turned up in *her* library, burnishing the dim shelves with their golden light; she had for a moment been one of them!

Presently Mrs. Robichaux, a dentist's wife, whom all these years I had taken to be a mild comely content little body, showed up from nowhere and told Raine she would do anything, *anything*, for the company: "even carry klieg lights!"

The world had gone crazy, said the crazy man in his cell. What was nutty was that the movie folk were trafficking in illusions in a real world but the real world thought that its reality could only be found in the illusions. Two sets of maniacs.

Somehow they had dropped the ball between them.

Lionel came in close with the Arriflex camera saddled on his shoulder. Again Dana moved against Margot. He looked straight into her eyes, lazily and with no difficulty. Margot looked back with difficulty. Three lights were reflected in her pupil.

Jacoby held both of them, his bent hands on their shoulders, eyes fixed on the floor, like a referee talking to boxers.

"Dear," he said to Margot, "this time let's try it this way. I want your legs wrapped around him."

He's not from Poland, I thought. He'd lost his accent again.

"How?" asked Margot faintly.

"How? Christ, just do it. He'll help. He's going to grab your ass and hold you off the floor. Don't worry."

"All right."

"And when you say your one line: 'You will be gentle with me, won't you?' I want to hear both fear and tenderness. Can you manage that, dear?"

"I'll try."

"Yeah, all right. You ready? Remember, Dana, I want to hear the zipper. It's important."

"Yeah. Right."

"Merlin," I asked, "what happens to, ah, Lipscomb in the end?"

Merlin shrugged. "Just what you might suppose. He is almost reached, first by the stranger, then by his own aunt. But in the end he slips away from both. He gently subsides into booze and Chopin. Sarah opts for life, he for death.

The stranger is immolated by a town mob who think they hate him but really hate the life forces in themselves that he stirs. He is the new Christ, of course."

I walked back to Belle Isle on the levee. Sure enough, the air had got heavy and still. Yet far above, black clouds were racing, fleeing north of their own accord like the blackbirds which rose from the swamp disquieted. A yellow light filled the space between earth and clouds as if the Christmas bonfires were already burning.

I couldn't stand it. I still can't stand it. I can't stand the way things are. I cannot tolerate this age. What is more, I won't. That was my discovery: that I didn't have to.

If you were right, I could stand it. If your Christ were king and all that stuff you believe—Christ, do you still believe it?—were true, I could stand it. But you don't even believe it yourself, do you? All you can think about is that girl on the levee. No wonder you don't have time to pray for the dead. All you can think about is getting that girl over the levee into the willows.

No? But if what you once believed were true, I could stand the way things are.

Or if my great-great-grandfather were right, I could live with that. Do you know what he did? He had a duel! Not a gentlemanly *affaire d'honneur* under the Audubon oaks in New Orleans, but a fight to the death with fists and knives just like Jim Bowie, in fact on the same sand bar. He had won a lot of money in a poker game in Alexandria. The heavy loser took it hard and began muttering about cheating. That was bad enough. But he made a mistake. He mentioned my kinsman's mother's name. She was a d'Arbouche from New Roads. Now my kinsman was a swarthy man; he looked like Jean Lafitte. "What's that you said?"

inference
of Adultery?

he asked the fellow, who then said something like, "You got the right name all right." "And how is that?" asked my ancestor pleasantly. "Well, it's d'Arbouche, isn't it, or is it Tarbrouche?" Which was to say that my ancestor had a touch of the tarbrush which was in turn to say that his mother, a very white Creole lady, had had sexual relations with a Negro, and offhand it is harder to say which was the deadlier insult: that she had had sexual relations with a man other than her husband, or that the man was a Negro. "I see," said my ancestor. "Well, I'll tell you what I propose. You and I will meet in four hours, which is dawn, on the Vidalia sand bar, which is outside the jurisdiction of both Louisiana and Mississippi. With one Bowie knife apiece. No seconds." They met. Seconds did come but were scared and hid in the willows. They fought. My ancestor killed his man, was badly cut on the arms and face, but managed to grab the fellow, turn him around, and cut his throat from ear to ear. Then he sent for an ax, beheaded, dismembered, and quartered the body, and fed it to the catfishes. He washed himself in the river, bound his wounds, and he and his friends rowed over to Natchez-under-the-Hill and ate a hearty breakfast.

I could live that way, crude as it was, though I do not think men should butcher each other like animals. But it is at least a way to live. One knows where one stands and what one can do. Even defeat is better than not knowing.

Or I could live your way if it were true.

What I can't stand is the way things are now. Furthermore, I will not stand for it.

Stand for what, you ask? Well, for that, to give an insignificant example. What you're looking at. You see the movie poster across the street? *The 69ers?* Man and woman yinyanged, fellatioed, cunninged on the corner of

141

Felicity and Annunciation Streets? What would I do about it? Quite simply it would be removed.

Come here, Percival, I want to tell you something. It is not a confession but a secret. It is not a sin because I do not know what a sin is. I understand that before you can sin, you must know what sin is—Bless me, Father, for I have done something which I don't understand. I know what a trespass or an injury or an insult is—something to be set right. So I'm telling you this and, confession or not, I consider you bound by the seal of friendship if not the confessional.

Come over here. Never mind the window. Look at me. We've been through a great deal together: school, war, talk, whoring, football, nice girls, hot girls, so since you understand me and my past—if you don't, nobody does—I'm going to tell you my plans for the future. There is going to be a new order of things and I shall be part of it. Don't confuse it with anything you've heard of before. Certainly not with your Holy Name Society or Concerned Christians Against Smut. This has nothing to do with Christ or boycotts. Don't confuse it with the Nazis. They were stupid. If in fact there was a need to clean up the Weimar Republic and if in fact they did in part, they screwed everything up by getting off on the Jews. What stupidity! The Jews were not to blame. The Nazis were clods, thugs. What they should have done was invite the Jews. Half the Jews would have joined them—just as half the Catholics did. Don't confuse it with the Klan, those poor ignorant bastards. Blacks, Jews, Catholics—they are all irrelevant; blaming them only confuses the issue. We'll invite them and you. Don't confuse it with Southern white trash Wallace politics. It's got nothing to do with politics.

It is none of these things. What is it then?

It is simply this: a conviction and a freedom. The conviction: I will not tolerate this age. The freedom: the freedom to act on my conviction. And I will act. No one else has both the conviction and the freedom. Many agree with me, have the conviction, but will not act. Some act, assassinate, bomb, burn, etc., but they are the crazies. Crazy acts by crazy people. But what if one, sober, reasonable, and honorable man should act, and act with perfect sobriety, reason, and honor? Then you have the beginning of a new age. We shall start a new order of things.

We? Who are we? We will not even be a secret society as you know such things. Its members will know each other without signs or passwords. No speeches, rallies, political parties. There will be no need of such things. One man will act. Another man will act. We will know each other as gentlemen used to know each other—no, not gentlemen in the old sense—I'm not talking about social classes. I'm talking about something held in common by men, Gentile, Jew, Greek, Roman, slave, freeman, black, white, and so recognized between them: a stern code, a gentleness toward women and an intolerance of swinishness, a counsel kept, and above all a readiness to act, and act alone if necessary—there's the essential ingredient—because as of this moment not one in 200 million Americans is ready to act from perfect sobriety and freedom. If one man is free to act alone, you don't need a society. How will we know each other? The same way General Lee and General Forrest would know each other at a convention of used-car dealers on Bourbon Street: Lee a gentleman in the old sense. Forrest not, but in this generation of vipers they would recognize each other instantly.

You have your Sacred Heart. We have Lee. We are the Third Revolution. The First Revolution in 1776 against the stupid British succeeded. The Second Revolution in 1861 against the money-grubbing North failed—as it should have because we got stuck with the Negro thing and it was our fault. The Third Revolution will succeed. What is the Third Revolution? You'll see.

I cannot tolerate this age. And I will not. I might have tolerated you and your Catholic Church, and even joined it, if you had remained true to yourself. Now you're part of the age. You've the same fleas as the dogs you've lain down with. I would have felt at home at Mont-Saint-Michel, the Mount of the Archangel with the flaming sword, or with Richard Coeur de Lion at Acre. They believed in a God who said he came not to bring peace but the sword. Make love not war? I'll take war rather than what this age calls love. Which is a better world, this cocksucking cuntlapping assholelicking fornicating Happyland U.S.A. or a Roman legion under Marcus Aurelius Antoninus? Which is worse, to die with T. J. Jackson at Chancellorsville or live with Johnny Carson in Burbank?

Yes, I'll be out of here in a month or two. What do we intend to do, you ask? We? I can only speak for me. Others will then do likewise. But let me give you an example from my future life. Yes! I may be uncertain about the past, about what happened—it's all confused, I'd rather not think about it—but I know what the future and the new order and my life will be like. The new order will not be based on Catholicism or Communism or fascism or liberalism or capitalism or any ism at all, but simply on that stern rectitude valued by the new breed and marked by the violence which will attend its breach. We will not tolerate this age. Don't speak to me of Christian love. Whatever came of it? I'll tell you what came of it. It got mouthed off on the radio and TV from the pulpit and that was the end of it. The Jews knew better. Billy Graham lay down with Nixon and got up with a different set of fleas, but the Jewish prophets lived in deserts and wildernesses and had no part with corrupt kings. I'll prophesy: This country is going to turn into a desert and it won't be a bad thing. Thirst and hunger are better than jungle rot. We will begin in the Wilderness where Lee lost. Deserts are clean places. Corpses turn quickly into simply pure chemicals.

Then how shall we live if not with Christian love? One will work and take care of one's own, live and let live, and behave with a decent respect toward others. If there cannot be love—you call that love out there?—there will be a tight-lipped courtesy between men. And chivalry toward women. Women must be saved from the whoredom they've chosen. Women will once again be strong and modest. Children will be merry because they will know what they are to do.

Oh, you wish to know what my own life will be like? (Look at you, all at once abstract and understanding and leading me on, all ears like one of these psychologists: why can't you priests stick to being priests for a change?) Very well, I will tell you. I plan to marry Anna here in the next room. I think she'll have me. You can marry us if you like. I shall love and protect her. I can make her well. I know that I can just as I know I can do what I choose to do. She is much better already. Yesterday we watched the clouds flying along and she smiled. She is the first woman of the new order. For she has, so to speak, endured the worst of the age and survived it, undergone the ultimate violation and come out of it not only intact but somehow purged, innocent. Who else might the new Virgin be but a gang-raped social worker? I do not joke. Her ordeal has made her like a ten-year-old.

We shall live in this neighborhood. I like it here. New Orleans is a shabby gentle benign place. We shall buy a small Victorian cottage under the levee and live a simple life.

But we will not tolerate this age. It is not enough to destroy it. We shall build a new order.

Actually, you don't have to worry. Killings will not be necessary. I have discovered something. I've discovered that even in this madhouse if you tell someone something, face to face, with perfect seriousness, without emotion, gazing directly at him, he will believe you. One need only speak with authority. Was not that the new trait that people noticed about your Lord, that he spoke with authority?

The point is, I will not tolerate this age. Millions agree with me and know that this age is not tolerable, but no one will act except the crazies and they are part of the age. The mad Mansons are nothing more than the ultimate spasm-orgasm of a dying world. We are only here to give it the *coup de grâce*. We shall not wait for it to fester and rot any longer. We will kill it.

You are looking at me for a change. Good. At least you are not smiling at me. Yes, I am a patient in a mental hospital, more than that, a prisoner. Yes, I am aware that you are accustomed to the ravings of madmen. Yes, I see you are aware that I give myself a certain license to talk crazy, so to speak. I might even be joking. But I am also aware from a certain wariness in your eyes that you are not absolutely certain I am not serious. You must decide that for yourself.

Why do I tell you this? As a warning. You can issue the warning if you like. There is only a little time. Perhaps a matter of months. *The 69ers* poster had better come down. But of course it will not.

We will not tolerate the way things are.

What's the matter? You look stricken for the first time since you've been coming here. Ha ha, so at last I've gotten a rise out of you.

What did you say? What happened to me?

146

What do you mean? Do you mean what happened at Belle Isle?

That's in the past. I don't see what difference it makes.

You want to know what happened?

Hm. It's hard to remember. Jesus, let me think. My head aches. I feel lousy. Let me lie down for a while. You don't look so hot either. You're pale as a ghost.

Come back tomorrow.

VII

HOW COME YOU'RE WEARING YOUR PRIEST UNIFORM today? Are you girding for battle or dressed up like Lee for the surrender?

Never mind. I wasn't thinking about you anyway but about Margot.

"You men flatter yourselves," I remember Margot telling me. "You are not that important to us."

You men? Us? Classes? Categories? Was that what we had come to?

Christ, what were we talking about? Oh yes, Percival, you wanted to know what happened? Jesus, what difference does it make? It is the future that matters. Yes, you're right. I did say there was something that still bothered me. What? Sin? The uncertainty that there is such a thing? I don't remember. Anyhow, it doesn't seem very interesting.

What a gloomy day. The winter rains have set in. I understand there is a depression in the Gulf. It's a bit late for hurricanes, isn't it? Isn't it November?

But it would be appropriate, would it not? A hurricane coming now while I tell you about Hurricane Marie a year ago which came while an artificial movie hurricane was blowing down Belle Isle!

Really I should be feeling good if another hurricane is on the way. I used to enjoy hurricanes. Most people do, though they won't admit it, everybody does in fact, except a few sane people, for after all hurricanes are by any sane standard very unpleasant affairs. But what does that prove except that most people today are crazy? I am supposed to be crazy but one sign of my returning sanity is that I don't in the least look forward to hurricanes. I knew a married couple once who were bored with life, disliked each other, hated their own lives, and were generally miserable—except during hurricanes. Then they sat in their house at Pass Christian, put a bottle of whiskey between them, felt a surge of happiness, were able to speak frankly and cheerfully to each other, laugh and joke, drink, even make love. But that is crazy. Why should people be miserable in good weather and happy in bad? Surely not because they are sinners in good weather and saints in bad. True, people help each other in catastrophes. But they don't feel good because they help each other. They help each other because they feel good. No, it's because something has happened to us which is so bad that we don't even have a word for it. Sin isn't the word. Your Christ didn't exactly foresee anything like this, did he? Hurricanes, which are very bad things, somehow neutralize the other bad thing which has no name, so that one can breathe easy, become free once again to sin or not to sin. The couple I spoke of became free and happy only during the passage of the eye of the hurricane, that is, capable of both love and hate (ordinarily they were numb, moved like ghosts), of honesty and lying. It became possible for the husband to say: "Often I secretly wish you were dead. In fact, an hour ago, before the hurricane struck, I was thinking it wouldn't be a bad idea if the hurricane blew away the belvedere and you with it—I'd take my chances." (Is that a sin?) "In fact I was contemplating my new life as a widower. Not such a bad prospect. Think of the women I could have here in Pass Christian without you around." A window crashed before the wind, showering them with glass splinters. He looked at the blood. "But now I can honestly say it is good we are together. If you blew away, I'd come after you." To which the wife replied: "The truth is, I'm bloody tired of cooking and housekeeping for you. If we live through this, I think I'll go out and get a job. Perhaps move out altogether. Then it will be nice to see you in the evenings. We used to have a good time. I liked you. I feel much better in fact. Let's bandage the cuts and have a drink." They had several drinks. The wind howled and they laughed like children. The house shook like a leaf. They made love in a 160-mile-per-hour gust.

To tell you the truth, it didn't work out for them after all. Or maybe it did. Anyhow, after the hurricane they took a good hard look at each other on a sunny Monday morning and got a divorce.

I found Margot in the belvedere atop Belle Isle battening down the house for Hurricane Marie. She looked surprised to see me, squinting at me during the lightning flashes as if she couldn't place me. It came as a shock to her to see me leave my customary niche in place and time. It makes people nervous for one to step out of one's role. I had become for her part of the furniture of Belle Isle, like the console with the petticoat mirror.

"What are you doing here?" she asked, then again

looked puzzled to have asked such a strange question. Why shouldn't I be here in my own house?

"What are you doing here?"

"I can't get this dern window down." The belvedere with its widow's walk outside looked like the passenger cabin of a small ferry. Benches and windows lined the four sides.

Helping her with the window, I found myself thinking how, despite her several transformations, she still had a lot of Texas country girl in her. Even after she became a Southern belle, Mardi Gras matron, chatelaine of Belle Isle, she'd forget and curse like a cowboy—it only took pain, finger caught in station-wagon door: "Shee-it fire!" Or impatience with blacks: "What the hail you think you're doing, boy," she'd holler at Fluker gaping and goofing off at his sweeping, snatch the broom, and sweep like a frontier wife. Sharp of eye and quick to observe and imitate, she lapsed only in her swear words and her way of disposing of her mucus. Now and then she'd hawk and spit. One time when we were leaving Le Début des Jeunes Filles de Nouvelle Orléans, clear of the door and safe in the dark, she leaned out over the gutter on Royal Street and blew her nose with her fingers, slinging snot expertly. I could imagine her in her senility, dropping all her latter-day guises and cursing and hawking in a nursing home.

She was as quick to pick up the bad manners of the film folk as the good manners of the gentry, yet she did it good-humoredly as if these transformations might be necessary but were not to be taken too seriously. What was surprising was how quickly she got onto the nutty nuances of actors and such. In a matter of weeks she had shed her Texas drawl and picked up the round deracinated bell tone of Raine Robinette, who like June Allyson (Merlin said) came from Washington Heights, even the plaintive up-pitched grace note at the end of each sentence, Raine's trademark, so Merlin had to correct her—she dropped it as quickly—and the actors' way of droning away in their mock enthusiasm for mock projects. Jacoby would go on and on about moving to Louisiana and starting a crawfish farm, going into great detail about the marketing and distribution of this remarkable shellfish, yet do it with a slight gap of inattention even to himself as if he were listening to his voice. What was surprising was how good she was at acting like one of them and how lousy she was at acting the second the cameras rolled.

In the lightning flashes I was looking at her and thinking how much I loved her. "Loved" her? Being "in love." What does that mean? It means that I lived for love. "Lived for love." What does that mean? It means simply that she was my happiness and that without her I was not happy. As the saying goes, I didn't know what happiness was until I met her. Do you notice that it is impossible to speak of love without sounding like Tin Pan Alley? But it's the truth nevertheless. I can't live without you. Jesus, is there any other way to say it? I might have been content in my unhappiness if I had not met her, like one of those cave fish that don't have eyes and don't miss the sun.

But if I loved her, why did the discovery of her infidelity cause a pang of pleasure within me?

Before we were married she would drive by my office mid-afternoons and pick me up. She wouldn't take no for an answer.

"But, Margot, I'm bushed"—I, a mole, a creaky, seersuckered, liberal mole droning out the days with title search, estate succession, and integrating the schools of Feliciana Parish. Perhaps this was what I thought happiness was: keeping the River Road estates intact for the white gentry and evening things up by helping the Negroes.

Off we'd go, up or down the River Road, she driving her little $20,000 Mercedes, top down, I still blinking like a mole in the October sunlight beside her, dusty from the Annotated Louisiana Code, sniffing the German leather warm and fragrant in the sun.

Strange: It was almost as if she were the man, I the woman, so much did she take the lead, work the radio, drive the car like a man, drum her nails on the wheel, gauge the traffic, look swiftly back past me to change lanes, cast ahead in her mind for destination and route, I lumpish and docile in the seat beside her, hands in my lap, like a big dumb coed.

Like a man she was, I said, except that she would tilt her head and cut her eyes over to me, lids narrowed, lips thinned, seriously yet unseriously, as no man ever did. Or, to make herself comfortable in the hot afternoon sun, in a quick second's motion lift her ass off the seat (she could dress in thirty seconds: she told me when she was a child she used to walk to town on Saturday in school clothes and change in the filling station restroom), hike her skirt up exposing her legs. Thought I, goofy from work and drunk on October pine-winey sunlight, catching sight of the sweet heavy convergence of her inner thighs: that is where I want to live, make my habitation.

"Well?" she'd say, driving up on the levee, stopping and leaning over the wheel cradled in her arms (like a man), gaze sideways at me, diamonds of sweat glittering on her upper lip.

Aha! She's parked. What next? I felt a tingling running up the backs of my legs. Is this the way a woman feels, I wondered, when the man parks? Hm. We're parked! What next?

"You know what you are?" she'd ask.

"No, what?"

"A big raunchy Sterling Hayden."

"Who's he?"

"Sterling Hayden tending bar in Macao, in seer-suckers."

"Is that good?"

They were beautiful October days. Do you know that I made one of the biggest discoveries of my life? It is the simplest of all discoveries but do you know that to this good day I don't know whether I was the last man on earth to make it or whether I was the only man. Was I the dumbest man in the world or the luckiest? It is this: There is a life to be lived and a joy in living it and the joy has nothing to do with our crazy college carryings-on or with my crazy romantic dream of love with Lucy at Highlands. No, it was so much simpler than that. It was simply that there is such a thing as a beautiful day to go out into, a road to travel, good food to eat when you're hungry, wine to drink when you're thirsty, and most of all, 99 percent of all, no: *all* of all: a woman to love.

What else is there really in life, dear Percival, than love, an October day, a slope of levee, warm lips to kiss, and this droll man-woman creature lying beside me who was mostly man driving the car until the moment I kissed her, when all at once she became all woman and I could feel her neck giving way in that sweet flection-extension no man's vertebrae ever managed, and her body of itself and in all its lovely breadth turn toward me on its axis to greet, salute me.

Yes, she loved me then. How do I know? Because at last I woke from my stupor and, remembering what courting was, courted her. In love, I drove to New Orleans to get her out of a Colonial Dames convention (for some reason it was important to her to be a Dame and damned if she didn't haul me to South Carolina to find and photograph the tombstone of her only WASP ancestor (no Reilly in that war! a Johnson—sure enough, a Private Aaron Johnson killed in the Battle of Cowpens!). Into the ballroom of the St. Charles I walked, and up and down the aisle until I spied her in the crowd of two thousand lily-white Dames listening to another Dame talking about preserving U.S. ideals and so forth and, spotting her, signaled her out with a peremptory angling off of head and she came out, at first fearful: Was somebody dead?—then clapped her hands with joy, hugged and kissed me: "Oh, I'm so glad to see you! You came to see me! to get me? Oh oh—"

Being "in love" means that my heart leaped at the sight of her. I felt like clapping my hands too. Why her and no other woman? She had two eyes, a nose, mouth, legs like a billion other women—like a million other good-looking women, yet she acquired for me a priceless value. Elizabeth Taylor, as beautiful as she was then, could have walked by and I wouldn't have looked at her twice. It was almost religious. Things she owned were like saints' relics. The place where she lived with Tex, the big Garden District house, became a shrine—I could drive around and around the block and feel the tingle in my legs when I caught sight of the house—a Taj Mahal which held my live princess.

Was it possible that a man could be so happy on one afternoon and that there were so many afternoons? It was all so simple. We'd drive until we found a pretty place, a stretch of levee, a meadow off the Natchez Trace. We'd walk till we got tired, drink, eat, kiss, *neck!*

A confession: She took the lead the first time. No, not the first. The second. The first was my crude way with her the first time I saw her, barefoot and muddy, at Belle Isle, getting under her hoopskirt and so forth.

That day we had eaten crawfish étouffé and gumbo and drunk two bottles of wine and were full and happy and zooming up the River Road in the October twilight and I was thinking of a place to go to park, maybe even a meadow to lie in. But she just said: "Let's go to bed." I swallowed hard and felt like saying *gollee* or something like, a thirty-five-year-old man: gollee. Nowadays any eighteen-year-old would laugh at me. Yes, but I notice that young men are not as happy with their girls, at least not as happy as I was. "Do you know a place?" she asked. Happily, I did, in Asphodel, a little tourist cottage in a glen off the Trace. My hand trembled as I registered. She undressed without bothering to turn out the light (as quickly as in the Texaco restroom in Odessa: zip! zip! naked!). She stood naked before the mirror, hands at her hair, one knee bent, pelvis aslant. She turned to me and put her hands under my coat and in her funny way took hold of a big pinch of my flank on each side. Gollee. Could any woman have been as lovely? She was like a feast. She was a feast. I wanted to eat her. I ate her.

That was my communion, Father—no offense intended, that sweet dark sanctuary guarded by the heavy gold columns of her thighs, the ark of her covenant.

I helped her with the windows in the belvedere. It was not a hurricane yet but an ordinary thunderstorm. From this height one could see in the lightning white caps in the river and the far bank. It was like the sea.

She sat on the bench eyes straight ahead like a seasick passenger.

"Margot, let's leave."

"What?" The storm made a racket.

"Let's get in the car and drive to North Carolina. Right now. The colors are at their height. Siobhan is with Tex, Lucy's going back to school tomorrow."

She was silent.

"Think of it. We could drive clear of the hurricane, make it to Atlanta by two o'clock." I was thinking about the moment of entering a motel with her, the moment she always paused at the mirror and raised her hands to her hair. I was also trying to remember the last time I slept with her. How had it happened that we were not sleeping together? What was I doing living in an outhouse? I tried to remember.

"No." I had to sit close to her to hear for she spoke without raising her voice, eyes staring unfocused and un-blinking. "The company is leaving day after tomorrow. We —they—can't afford to lose two or three days to a hurricane. And there's no need really. The two or three interior Belle Isle scenes can be shot anywhere."

"I know. That's why you can leave."

"No." Her *noes* tolled like a bell. Then she said in the same voice, eyes not moving: "Jan needs me to work with him on his screen treatment of *A Doll's House*."

"A Doll's House?"

"It'll be Jan's first big film—the first he can do exactly as he wants."

"And you? What's your part in this?"

She misunderstood me. I meant her part with Jacoby. What was he to her, she to him?

"I'm Nora, Lance." She looked at me for the first time. The storm was closer and the lightning flickered like a strobe light. Her eyes seemed to dart.

"Nora?"

"The lead, remember?"

"Yes, I remember."

She clapped her hands. "I'm good, Lance! I'm really good. I'm so happy. I've never known what it is to have a talent and to develop it. To function! To function like—a fine watch. Like Olivier or Hepburn."

"You're putting up the money."

"Yes, and I'll never make a better investment. Jan's ideas are so exciting. For him cinema is not just another medium. You have to understand communication theory. Cinema is the medium par excellence for our times."

Cinema. Five years ago she'd have said, Let's go to the movies. And we'd go see Steve McQueen. We'd eat popcorn and when I finished I'd put my buttery fingers between her legs.

"Why do you and Jacoby need to do a script? Isn't Ibsen good enough?"

"You don't understand. We're not primarily interested in ideas as Ibsen was. It is Nora as a person and the narrative. Jan believes—"

"Let's leave right now, Margot. We could drive all night. Do you remember doing that and sleeping in a meadow by the Shenandoah River?"

"No. I owe this to myself. But let me explain. Jan's theory is that by the very nature of the medium cinema should have nothing to do with ideas. The meaning of a film derives from the narrative itself. Narrative and person are everything. What's more, the treatment has to be done before England."

"England?"

"That's where we're going to shoot it."

"You mean you're going to England?"

"That's where he's going to shoot it. It will cut costs by half."

"Then you're going to England?"

"Do you think I'd miss the chance to play Nora?"

"Are you sure you're going to?"

"I just told you— Oh. You mean Jan's going to take my money and kick me out."

"How does Tex feel about it?" Surely that stupid-shrewd old man could see through this.

"Tex and Siobhan are beside themselves."

"They're going?"

"Can you see Tex not going?"

"I think you might have told me."

"Honey, I was going to. We only decided last night." I was silent for a while. She said: "Don't worry about me being cheated, Lance. You don't know Jan. He's so—"

"Do you?"

"I know him. I know him like a—" She paused.

"A lover?"

"Lover. Of course I love him dearly. I love Bob Merlin. I love you. I love Siobhan. I love Tex. But it's all different."

"That's not what I mean."

"Oh boy oh boy oh boy. It's not all that important, you know."

"What's not?"

"Sex. You men set so much store by it. Well, you flatter yourselves. It's not all that important."

Why couldn't I ask her what I wanted to know?

"Did you—?"

"What?"

"Nothing." I couldn't ask.

"I don't mess with anybody and you know it. Believe it

or not, I've found something more important than the almighty penis."

I think I blushed. I wished she wouldn't say penis. It sounded white and bent off. But what would I have her say? dick? pecker? prick? tallywhacker?

Can I explain to you how relieved I was? Relieved to hear her say so easily that she had no lovers? Such offhandedness was worth a hundred oaths. It was true! But what about Siobhan's father? Even science can make mistakes.

But here's the real question. Did I want her guilty or innocent? And if she were guilty and I knew it—and I knew it as surely as I know that my blood type A plus B does not equal Siobhan's 0—why did I want to hear her say it? Why did I believe her denial? Which is better, to have a pain and find no cause or to locate the abscess, loose the pus?

The storm was worse. The belvedere rattled and rocked like the *Tennessee Belle*. Lightning was almost constant. A bolt hit the lightning rod. A blue light rolled along the widow's walk like a ball of yarn.

Margot was frightened. She grabbed me. "Jesus, Lance, we're going to be killed."

She was scared to death. She wanted to be held. I held her.

"Let's lie down here."

As suddenly she let go of me. "The bench is too narrow."

"On the floor."

"It's wet."

"Standing up then. I'll hold you up like Dana."

"That fag."

"Well—"

"I have to go. I'm dead. Would you believe that acting is more exhausting than ditchdigging?"

Would I believe? I didn't know. But I meant to find out.

Do you think I'm crazy? Look at me.

Do you hear the bluejays and the children crying in the street? The very sound and soul of late after-school afternoons in the fall. Listen. They are singing skip-rope songs.

> *Charlie Chaplin went to France*
> *To teach the girlies how to dance*
> *And this is the way he taught them:*
> *Hoola hoola*
> *Ponchatoola*
> *Salute to the captain*
> *Bow to the queen*
> *Turn your back on the submarine*
> *Charlie Chaplin sat on a pin*
> *How many inches did it go in?*
> *One, two, three . . .*

They're counting. That's called doing "hots."

The innocence of children. Didn't your God say that unless you become as innocent as one of those, you shall not enter the kingdom of heaven?

Yes, but what does that mean?

It is obvious he made a mistake or else played a very bad trick on us. Yes, I remember the innocence of childhood. Very good! But then after a while one makes a discovery. One discovers there is a little secret that God didn't let us in on. One discovers your Christ never did tell us about it. Yet God himself so arranged it that you wake up one fine morning with a great thundering hard-on and wanting nothing more in life than a sweet hot cunt to put it in, drive some girl, any girl, into the ground, and where is the innocence of that? Is that part of the innocence? If so, he should have said so. From child to assailant through no doing of one's own—is that God's plan for us? Damn you and your God. Between the two of you, you should have got it straight and had it one way or the other. Either it's good or it's bad, but whichever it is, goddamn say so. Only you don't. You fuck off somewhere in between. You want to have it both ways: good, but—bad only if—and so forth. Well, you fucked up good and proper, fucked us all up, for sure fucked me up. I'll take the Romans or the old Israelites who didn't worry about women. David had three hundred women but wanted another one. God didn't hold it against him.

There are only three ways to go. One is their way out there, the great whorehouse and fagdom of America. I won't have it. The second way is sweet Baptist Jesus and I won't have that. Christ, if heaven is full of Southern Baptists, I'd rather rot in hell with Saladin and Achilles. There is only one way and we could have had it if you Catholics hadn't blown it: the old Catholic way. I Lancelot and you Percival, the only two to see the Grail if you recall. Did you find the Grail? You don't look like it. Then we knew what a woman should be like, your Lady, and what a man should be like, your Lord. I'd have fought for your Lady, because Christ had the broadsword. Now you've gotten rid of your Lady and taken the sword from Christ.

I won't have it. I won't have it your way or their way. I won't have it your way with your God-bless-everything-because-it's-good-only-don't-but-if-you-do-it's-not-so-bad. Just say whether a sweet hot cunt is good or not. I won't have it your way and I won't have it their way, the new way. A generation stoned and pussy free and de-valued, pricks after pussy, pricks after pricks, pussy after pussy. But most of all pussy after pricks. Christ what a country! A nation of 100 million voracious cunts. I will not have my son or my daughter grow up in such a world. When I say I won't have it, I'm serious. I won't have it. I won't have my son . . . Very well, I will make another confession: My son is a homosexual now and I can understand why. He told me he was terrified of all the pussy after him. All the girls want to fuck and it scared him. Think of it: all those hot little cunts waiting to see if he was up to servicing them. Well, he couldn't, he was too scared. He found it easier, the scared little prick, to be with other scared little pricks. And I can't say I blame him. Now there are four of them, four nice scared young men living happily together in the French Quarter needlepointing Louis Quinze chairs.

So you fucked it up good and we're going to have to pull it out for you. We? Who are we? You will find out soon enough. It is enough for you to know how it is going to be, for we are the new Reformation, which is to say we are going to tell you something and show you something you should have known all along.

We are going to set it out for you, what is good and what is bad, and no Jew-Christian waffling bullshit about it. What we are is the last of the West. What we are is the best of you, Percival, and the best of me, Lancelot, and of Lee and Richard and Saladin and Leonidas and Hector and Agamemnon and Richthofen and Charlemagne and Clovis and Martel. Like them we might even accept your Christ but this time you will not emasculate him or us. We'll take the Grail you didn't find but we'll keep the broadsword and the great warrior Archangel of Mont-Saint-Michel and our Christ will be the stern Christ of the Sistine. And as for your sweet Jesus and your guitar-banging and ass-wiggling nuns, and your love feasts and peace kisses: there is no peace.

If I were a Jew, I'd know what to do. It's easy. I'd be in Israel with the sabras. They're my kind. The only difference between them and the Crusaders is that the Crusaders lost. Ha, isn't that a switch, come to think of it—that the only Crusaders left in the entire Western world are the Israelis, the very Jews who huddled and shrank and grinned and nodded for two thousand years? The Jews are lucky. They know who they are and they have Israel. We have to make our own Israel, but we know who we are.

We know who we are and where we stand. There will be leaders and there will be followers. There are now, only neither knows which is which. There will be men who are strong and pure of heart, not for Christ's sake but for their own sake. There will be virtuous women who are proud of their virtue and there will be women of the street who are there to be fucked and everyone will know which is which. You can't tell a whore from a lady now, but you will then. You will do right, not because of Jew-Christian commandments but because we say it is right. There will be honorable men and there will be thieves, just as now, but the difference is one will know which is which and there will be no confusion, no nice thieves, no honorable Mafia. There are not many of us but since we are ready to die and no one else is, we shall prevail.

Women? What about women? You heard me. A man, a youth, a boy will know which women are to be fucked and which to be honored and one will know who to fuck and who to honor.

Freedom? The New Woman will have perfect freedom. She will be free to be a lady or a whore.

Don't women have any say in this? Of course. And we will value them exactly as much as they value themselves.

They won't like it much, you say? The hell with them. They won't have anything to say about it. Not only are they not strong enough. They don't care enough. Guinevere didn't think twice about adultery. It was Lancelot, poor bastard, who went off and brooded in the woods.

No more fuck-up about who fucks and who gets fucked. The best of women will be what we used to call ladies, like your Virgin. Our Lady. The men? The best of them will be strong and brave and pure of heart, not for Christ's sake, but like an Apache youth or a Lacedemonian who denies himself to be strong. The others can whoremonger and screw whom they choose. But we will prevail.

No, it is not you who are offering me something, salvation, a choice, whatever. I am offering you a choice. Do you want to become one of us? You can without giving up a single thing you believe in except milksoppery. I repeat, it was your Lord who said he came to bring not peace but a sword. We may even save your church for you.

You are pale as a ghost. What did you whisper? Love? That I am full of hatred, anger? Don't talk to me of love until we shovel out the shit.

What? What happened then? Don't look so fearful. Nothing. I saw a dirty movie, that's all.

Friday afternoon at the movies. That's what I should call my own little film or videotape, which Elgin, my cinematographer, made of our little film company resting from their labors.

It was all very simple. Elgin came to my pigeonnier after lunch, entered as briskly as a vacuum-cleaner salesman, too briskly, with a large valise-like box and a case of reels and, without looking at me, set his suitcase on my desk, opened it, plugged it in, clipped two wires to the back of my TV, showed me how to put the reels in, and, without once having raised his eyes, made as if to leave.

"Elgin. Wait."

He stood in the doorway, freeze-framed, waiting for me to push a button and set him going.

"Elgin, the film company is pulling out tomorrow. So you might be able to pull your equipment out today. I'll let you know after I've seen these."

"I done already pulled it out," said Elgin not briskly at all but sullenly, as if I had violated some unspoken agreement. What agreement?

"Then you—"

"You won't need to do any more taping."

I looked at him.

"I see. That'll be all. Go put your tour-guide coat on."

He looked at me strangely, at first I thought sullenly, then I saw he was ashamed. I felt a sudden anger. Later, to my astonishment, it came over me why I was angry. Again a confession which does me little credit but it is important I tell you the truth. I had to admit I was angry because he had *looked*. Looked at the videotape. Then it was I discovered in myself what I had so often despised in others. For I had expected Elgin to do what I told him, to be a technological eavesdropper and spy for me but not listen or look. More than that: I had expected that somehow he *could not* look—just as the hicks I despised believed that through some magical or at least providential dispensation the Negro bellboy cannot see the naked white woman in the same hotel room. Cannot even if he wanted to: she is somehow invisible.

There is nothing like a liberal gone sour.

But I was wrong. He was ashamed, not of what he had seen, but of what he took to be his failure. A *technical* failure. I should have known.

"I'm sorry," he said, hanging his head.

"I am too." I still thought he meant he was sorry he had looked.

"It's a negative effect I can't explain."

"Negative effect?"

"Did you ever hold a magnet against a TV screen?"

"No."

"It pulls the images out of shape—the images being nothing but electrons, of course."

"Yes, electrons."

"I only watched enough to see that the effect is a little weird— But I think you may still have what you want."

"Thank you." Ha. Then he was my nigger after all, and if he could look, wouldn't, didn't. Or better, he looked for technical reasons but forbore to see. He was the perfect nigger.

He closed the door softly but presently opened it again. Again it was a Buell who still had the power to set things straight.

Elgin still didn't look at me. All he said, face courteously inclined in the cracked door, as courteous as a Montgomery bellboy, you see, I'm not looking—was: "Mr. Lance, let me know if there is anything you need."

"Okay."

Note the exquisite courtesy of "anything you need." He didn't say: Let me know if you need any help, I'll help you. He could have been understood as offering to bring a glass of water, a bourbon. It was for me to fathom the rest.

He looked now. He looked at me as sorrowfully as you —to hell with him.

One night at supper during a lull in the conversation Lucy, my daughter, who had said little or nothing and, feeling the accumulating necessity of saying something suitable, saw her chance and piped up, frowning and ducking her dark-brown head and saying it seriously: "It just occurred to me last night: here I am an adult human being, a person, and I have never seen my own cervix."

There was a silence. I found myself worrying more about her worrying about her halting conversational entry than about her not seeing her cervix. But Raine and Dana nodded thoughtfully and even, I could see, with a certain courtesy and kindliness as if to encourage her timid foray into their lively talk. Raine put her arm around Lucy, gave her a hug, and said to me:

"Think of it! A mature woman who has never seen her own cervix!"

I thought about it.

Merlin, who did not like Raine, said not to Lucy but to Raine: "So what? I've never seen my own asshole. What's the big deal?"

But it was Lucy who blushed and ducked her head even lower.

VIII

FRIDAY AFTERNOON AT THE MOVIES:
A DOUBLE FEATURE

What I mainly remember of the tapes is not the tapes themselves but the day outside. The videotapes, which came out as a movie on my tiny Trinitron and which I watched as gravely as I used to watch afternoon reruns of *Gunsmoke*, I think of now as a tiny theater set down in a great skyey afternoon loud with the rattle of blackbirds. The thunderstorm was gone, the hurricane was still a great Catherine wheel spinning slowly in the Gulf casting its pall of wind and rain two hundred miles ahead to the northeast while its northwestern quadrant sucked in the northern fall, the deep clear Canadian air funneling down, cirrus-flecked five miles high. There was no sign of a hurricane except a sense of urgency and a high commotion in the air. Restive blackbirds took alarm, rose in clouds from the marshes, settled, and rose again.

Something was indeed wrong with Elgin's camera. The figures, tiny figurines, were reddish, like people in a film darkroom, and seemed to meet, merge, and flow through

169

each other. Lights and darks were reversed like a negative, mouths opened on light, eyes were white sockets. The actors looked naked clothed, clothed naked. The figures seemed to be blown in an electronic wind. Bodies bent, pieces blew off. Hair danced atop heads like a candle flame. I stared. Didn't Elgin say the figures were nothing but electrons?

FIRST FEATURE: MISS MARGOT'S ROOM

Who were these two dim rosy figures moving silently in a red sea?

I rewound the reel and examined the reel case. The label was neatly printed, MISS MARGOT'S ROOM, exactly like the chaste and formal museum signs mounted on the brass posts supporting velvet ropes in Belle Isle.

Two figures were standing, talking. They were not naked. Their clothes were light and their faces dark. It was Merlin and Margot. I recognized the shape of Merlin's rooster shock of hair even though it flickered on his head like Pentecostal flame. Margot I knew instantly from the bright earmuff fluffs of hair at her ears and her mannish yet womanish way of setting her fist on her hip.

When they talked, their mouths opened on light.

They embraced.

The sound was not much better than the video. The voices were scratchy and seemed to come not from the room but from the sky like the blackbirds rattling and rising and falling. When they turned, their voices went away. Half sentences blew away like their bodies.

They embraced again. Merlin held her off, their bodies flowing apart like a Y.

MERLIN: You know that I always—(*pause*)—wish you every—

(You know that I always will love you? I wish you every happiness?)

MARGOT: (*An assentive murmur.*)

MERLIN: But what an ire—Oh, Christ—end—of a phizz infirm—

(But what an irony! Oh, Christ that it should end because of a physical infirmity?)

MARGOT: It did—

(It didn't?)

MERLIN: —a disproportion like Lee losing Gettysburg because of di—

(Diarrhea?)

MARGOT: Don't be

MERLIN: It's flat-out god—unax—Jesus.

(It's flat-out goddamn unacceptable, Jesus?)

MARGOT: Jesus, men. You are all so—

(Jesus what?)

Were they talking about me?

No.

They embrace again. Blobs like breasts swell on Merlin's shoulder and blow off toward Margot.

MERLIN: I fear for— But I wish you both ever—

(I fear for you. But I wish you both every happiness.)

You both? Me? No.

MARGOT: (*A deprecative murmur.*)

MERLIN: I love you so f (?)—v (?)—much.

(I love you so fucking much? so very much? probably the former considering the two-syllable beat.)

MARGOT: I love you—oh s—(?)—oh sh—(?)

(I love you too. Oh so much. Or: I love you too. Oh shit, or sheet? or she-it. Probably the last, two beats, two syllables, and knowing Margot.)

MERLIN: Do you believe I love—enough—truth?

(? ? ?)

MARGOT: (*A wary murmur.*)

MERLIN: Why—wonder—

(? ? ?)

MERLIN: —could be exploit—

(He could be exploiting you?)

MARGOT: (*Turning away: they come apart, Y becoming II.*)

MERLIN: (*An expostulation.*)

MARGOT: !

MERLIN: —mon—

(? ? ?) (Money?)

MARGOT: No.

MERLIN: Christ—not—even sure—part.

(Christ, you're not even sure you have the part?)

MARGOT: You bas—

(You bastard.)

MERLIN: Well—?

MARGOT: Up—oars, oo bas—

(Up yours, you bastard.)

MERLIN: Oh, Jesus—I'd kike—oars.

(Oh, Jesus how I'd like to be up yours?)

MARGOT: (*An indifferent murmur.*)

MERLIN: Besides that—a basic incap—intimace—

(Besides that he has a basic incapacity for intimacy?)

MARGOT: I don't care.

MERLIN: What a lousy trucking fire engine.

(What a lousy fucking triangle? I am reasonably sure of this reading: that it was not Elgin's equipment but Merlin himself who scrambled "fucking triangle" to "trucking fiangle" (fire engine). A joke. Yes, I am 99 percent sure.)

MARGOT: Do you believe I still—you?

(Do you believe I still love you?)

MERLIN: Oh, Chr—

MARGOT: Sh—sh—sh!

(Shush shush shush? or: shit shit shit? shit shit shit.)

The tiny figurines embrace again, sectors of their trunks blowing out like pseudopods of amoebae. Their bodies seem to have magnetic properties.

MERLIN: —wish you—all happ—

(I wish y'all happiness? I wish you all happiness? The latter? Merlin wouldn't say "y'all.")

Merlin vanishes. Margot droops and is still, like a puppet hung from its string.

It is a triangle. At first I thought I was part of the triangle, the losing angle, so:

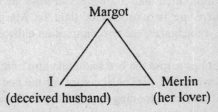

Margot

I   Merlin
(deceived husband)   (her lover)

Then I see they are not talking about me at all, that it is a different triangle:

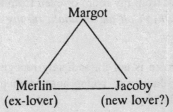

Margot

Merlin   Jacoby
(ex-lover)   (new lover?)

Another figure materializes (they don't seem to use doors). It is Jacoby. There is no way of recognizing him except by his shortness and stockiness and his big head, which he carries confidently between his shoulders. Like many short men he is of a piece, body, brain, organs compacted and operating in close order. All would be well with him, one feels, except he is shorter than Margot. He makes up for this shortcoming by a kind of confident lolling back of head. It is his way of not having to look up at her; he holds her off as if to say: Well, my dear, let's have a look at you.

They make a Y connected as far as the waist.

They do not speak but their mouths and eyes open on light. Are they whispering?

They dress, putting dark on light. No, it is undressing, for dark is light and light is dark. They are shedding light clothes for dark skin.

They approach each other. Sections of their bodies detach and fly off. Other sections extend pseudopods.

They turn, their hair blowing sideways in an electric wind. There are two sockets of light on Margot's back. They are, I recognize, the two dimples on either side of her sacrum.

Margot lies across the bed and pulls him onto her. He is gazing down at her. Her head comes off the bed and bends back until her face is looking upside down at the camera. Her eyes close on light, but her mouth opens letting out light.

Still there is no conversation but presently a voice says, at first I think from my room or even from the sky with the blackbirds: *Oh oh oh ah ah aaah, oh my Jesus oh ah ah sh—sh—sh—*

? ? ?

But the voice is not immediately recognizable as either Margot's or Jacoby's, being hoarser than Margot's and higher than Jacoby's.

A prayer?

INTERMISSION

I switch off the machine and walk out into the skyey day. There is the blinded dazzled headachy sensation of coming

174

out of a movie in the afternoon. The blackbirds are rising and settling, the wind has picked up but is fitful, blowing sycamore leaves back and forth across my tiny pigeon porch.

I sit on my porch and watch the blackbirds rising and settling and the clouds hurrying toward the hurricane like latecomers to the kickoff.

The blackbirds fall silent. The clouds straighten out and form a line. The sky becomes flat and yellow. The view from the porch is very simple. There are six parallel horizontal lines, the bottom rail of the iron fence, the top rail, the near edge of the River Road, the far edge, the top of the levee, the straight bottom line of the clouds. There are many short vertical lines, the iron spikes of the fence. There is a single oblique line, a gravel road leading from the River Road over the levee. Atop the levee are the triangles of the bonfires. The slanting boom of a ship intersects with the triangle of the bonfires, making trapezoids and smaller triangles.

The hurricane machine cranks up. The live oaks blow inside out. It is necessary to use the hurricane machine even though a real hurricane is coming, not just because the real hurricane is not yet here, but because even if it were it wouldn't be as suitable for film purposes as an artificial hurricane.

SECOND FEATURE: MISS RAINE'S ROOM

There are three red figures on the pink bed. Pieces of bodies, ribs, thighs, torsos, fly off one body and join another body. Hair blows in a magnetic wind. Mouths and eyes open on light. Light pubic triangles turn like mobiles, now narrowing, now widening, changing from equilateral triangles to isosceles triangles to lines of light. The posters of the bed make a frame.

Lucy is lying lengthwise in the middle of the bed. She is recognizable by the flame-curl of hair under her ears, by her big breasts, and by the still slightly immature not wholly incurved line between calf and knee. Lucy is like a patient. Certain operations are being performed on her. The other two figures handle her as efficiently as nurses. Raine is slim and swift, moving so fast her body leaves ectoplasm behind. Dana stands naked and musing beside the bed, one hand browsing over his shoulder like an athlete in a locker room.

The three lie together. Their bodies fuse but their arms move like a six-arm Shiva.

Now they are doing something else. Dana kneels in a horizontal plane, takes Lucy's head in both hands, and guides it toward him. Raine moves much more quickly. Her sleek head flies off and burrows into Lucy's stomach.

The figures make a rough swastikaed triangle:

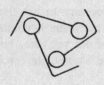

Elgin is right. The sound track is poor. No words are audible except near the end an unrecognizable voice which is neither clearly male or female seems to come from nowhere and everywhere—and only fragments at that: *Oh Christ dear sweet Jesus oh oh—*

Another prayer?

Crows begin to fly north against the wind. It is unusual to see crows in such numbers, flocking like blackbirds. Then they straggle out for a mile. Ellis Buell says crows are the smartest of all birds. This is probably true. At least I know for a fact they know the range of a shotgun (Fluker claims they can distinguish a twenty gauge from a twelve, then move just out of range). The only time I ever killed a crow was by pure luck and a .22 rifle. He was flying at least five hundred feet high. Without expectation I led him by three feet and shot him through the head. Surprised, he fell at my feet with a thump. A ruby drop of blood hung from his black bill.

Still I had to watch the 5:30 news!

Unhooking the videotape, I turned on the TV. The hurricane watch had been changed to a hurricane warning. Marie, two hundred miles due south, was headed due north. She filled the whole Gulf. It became necessary to make preparations.

Everyone became serious and happy.

Storekeepers seriously-happily boarded up their windows. Volunteers seriously-happily sandbagged the levee. Shoppers seriously-happily shopped for battery radios, batteries, flashlights, Coleman lamps, kerosene lamps, kerosene, candles, canned goods, powdered milk, dried apricots, Hershey bars, raisins.

Happiest and most serious of all were owners of fallout shelters dug out during the A-bomb scare many years ago and never used. Happy families huddled underground around TV sets showing Marie spinning ever closer.

Happy drinkers sat in friendly bars under the levee drinking Dixie beer and reminiscing about other hurricanes. Even householders of low-lying houses left home happily, headed for motels in the Mississippi hills. Ordinarily bored police rode happily up and down country roads and bayous warning people to evacuate.

I too made certain preparations. I made a shopping list but, unlike other shoppers, I first discarded certain objects before purchasing others. Assembling the video cameras, tape deck, tapes, recorder, amplifier—some $4,500 worth —I packed the lot in a Gladstone bag and at nightfall hauled it over the levee to a skiff locked to a cypress in the batture, rowed out two hundred yards, and dropped the bag in the channel. When I regained the batture I was half a mile downstream but it was easy rowing back in dead water.

Only then did I make my shopping list. Besides the usual hurricane items it contained:

1 18″ Stillson wrench
4 10′ sections Gerona plastic pipe, 3″ diameter
4 3″ sleeves
1 90° elbow
1 45° elbow
1 3″ nipple (foot long)
1 3″ to 1″ reducer
1 lb. sealing PBC cmpd
1 roll duct tape
2 kerosene lamps
1 gal. kerosene

During the filming and before I went to the hardware store, I visited Tex and Siobhan. They were getting on each other's nerves worse than ever. They both got on my nerves. Siobhan clung to me and beat me in the ribs with her fist. It was necessary to do something about Siobhan. It had been necessary for some time. The difference was that now it was possible to do something.

Siobhan loved music and took lessons on the old French spinet. Tex promised to buy her a new "pinana."

"I'm going to buy you the biggest Steinway grand pinana in New Orleans. You gon play the new pinana for Tex?"

"No," she said, not looking at Tex but clinging to my thigh with a fierce scissors grip of her thin legs and beating me fretfully. "Is he really going to buy me a piano?"

"Absotively, posalutely!" cried Tex.

Then I had a piece of luck. In his boring, repetitive way he began to come at me, jabbing me the way Siobhan beat me with her fist, jabbing with things he had said so often before he didn't even listen himself.

"I'm telling you, boy, you better change that old black pipe under the house. That stuff rots like wood. I smelled a gas leak yesterday."

"How could you smell it? There's no captan in it. Methane has no smell."

"I smelled it!"

He didn't smell it. He wasn't listening to himself. He didn't even know he said he smelled it.

"I'm going to the hardware store now. Now listen to me, Tex. Here's what I want you to do."

For the first time he was startled to attention by my tone, as if somebody had jostled him and he had waked from a long boring dream. He was listening! I was going to tell him what to do. He knew this and knew he was going to do it.

"What?"

"For a long time you've wanted to take Siobhan to Odessa to visit your folks."

"Sho," he said, listening.

"I want her out of here tonight. This is a bad storm. Both of you get going now. I mean now. You can either drive to New Orleans and fly to Texas or drive all the way, but leave within the hour."

It was the best I could do: Siobhan, I do believe the old bastard meant well, I only hope he didn't drive you crazy or bore you to death.

"We'd rather drive, wouldn't we, Siobhan? We'll play count animals. I'll count moocows and minnie cats and you count down hogs and twobit horses."

"No fair!" said Siobhan, but she did let go of me and go to Tex. She liked the idea of a trip. "There are more cats and cows than hound dogs and quarter horses."

They were going and that was that. Here is an incidental discovery: If you tell somebody what to do, they will do it. All you have to do is know what to do. Because nobody else knows.

The film company was shooting the last scene before the hurricane. The set was the front gallery of Belle Isle. It was the only remaining scene which could not be shot in Burbank. Following the scene, the crew planned to pack up their station wagons and go home.

It was not a long scene but it required many takes. In the scene the sharecropper, played by Elgin, and the sheriff, played by the actor who looked like Pat Hingle, come to Belle Isle accompanied by the Christlike hippy stranger, played by Dana, who has reconciled poor white sharecroppers, poor black sharecroppers, overseers, sheriffs, blacks, whites, and the half-caste girl, who was accepted by neither race. They have come to rescue the planter, played by Merlin, and his daughter the librarian, played by Margot, from the hurricane. The planter, however, fixed in his ancient prejudices and secretly liking the apocalyptic fury of the hurricane, decides to remain. He also expects his daughter to stay with him. The daughter decides to leave her father and go with the stranger. It is the farewell scene between father and daughter. After the farewell, the planter, who is not so much prejudiced as indifferent, caught up by aesthetic rather than social concerns, returns to the house alone, to his organ. Crashing chords of a Chopin polonaise fuse with the mounting fury of the hurricane.

"I want more of a Lear-like effect, Bob," said Jacoby, turning off the hurricane machine after one of many takes. "You know, mad king raging on the heath, wild-eyed, hair blowing."

"Yeah, right, Lear, okay," said Merlin ironically, but Jacoby missed the irony.

Before the shooting began, I went to the bank and withdrew $75,000 from Margot's and my checking account.

"What the hail, Lance?" said Macklin Maury Lamar, my cousin, who was president of the bank.

"We're giving it to the American Negro College Fund."

"Ah."

I told him this for two reasons. One was that it was the only reason he would believe, believing as he did that I was still a liberal and therefore capable of any madness. (Yet curiously it was for him an understandable madness: you know how old Lance is, etc., etc.)

The other reason was that my explanation was, in a sense, true.

"Yeah," said Macklin. "A wonderful cause. In fact I agree with you, that's what they need."

What was worrying Macklin was not this particular withdrawal but the likelihood of losing Margot's and my half-million-dollar *checking* account. Or my asking him to pay interest.

"How do you want it, Lance?"

"In cash. Any denominations."

"Why the cash, Lance?" asked Macklin, laughing heartily, eyes worried.

"I'm afraid your bank will blow down tonight. The money will be safer at Belle Isle."

"There you go! Ha ha." Macklin laughed and slapped his side, all the while keeping a sharp eye on me, trying to parse out craziness and horsiness, wondering whether I was ordinarily crazy as he always held me to be or possessed by some new craziness.

He gave me the $75,000 in hundreds in a locked canvas bag, handing me the little brass key separately.

After the shooting was finished at Belle Isle and the crew was busy dismantling the hurricane machine and packing their station wagons, I summoned Elgin to the pigeonnier and gave him the $75,000. He unlocked the bag with the little brass key. He looked at the money.

"How much money is this?"

"Seventy-five thousand dollars."

"What's it for?"

"It's very simple. I have a great deal of money, more than I can use, and there are two things you want."

"Yes?"

"One is to finish your education at M.I.T. despite the fact that your scholarship has run out."

"Yes."

"The other is you want to marry your classmate Ethel Shapiro and buy a house in Woodale, a subdivision of Concord, which though a cradle of American liberty is unwilling to sell houses to blacks or Jews especially blacks married to Jews. Yet you are determined to buy a house there despite all obstacles."

"Not despite. Because." Elgin looked down at the money. "Okay. But you don't owe me anything. I'd have done it for you anyway. It was an interesting problem. Sorry about the tape quality. The color was defective."

"I liked it that way."

"The sound was rotten, too. Jesus, I felt bad about that."

"Don't worry about it. It was okay."

"Well—" said Elgin, standing in the doorway. He was always standing in the doorway.

"Yes?"

"I have a feeling there is something else. Perhaps a condition."

"A condition?"

"Something you want me to do."

"Only two things."

"What?"

"Leave now."

"Now?"

"Now. In the next hour."

"The other is, don't come back?"

"Right."

"Okay." We might have been discussing his chores for the day.

"Oh yes. Something else. Take Ellis and Suellen to Magnolia, Mississippi, where y'all have kinfolks. It's on I-55, on your way north. They can return after the storm. You won't have any trouble persuading them. They're both scared to death. They are the only people around here who have any sense."

"Okay. Is that all?"

"That's all."

"What are you going to do?"

"Me? I'm fine, Elgin."

"Don't you need me to help you move all those folks out of here?"

"No."

"Okay. Well—"

We shake hands. He gives me a level-eyed look. He's seen too many movies. Or maybe it's being in one. The level-eyed look means we understand each other and have been reconciled, perhaps by the Christlike stranger played by Dana. When the truth is, nobody understands anyone else, and nobody is reconciled because nobody knows what there is to be reconciled. Or if there is something to be reconciled, the way it is done in the movies, by handshakes, level-eyed looks, expressions of mute understanding, doesn't work.

Don't you agree? No? Do you really believe people can be reconciled?

"One more thing, Elgin."

"Yes?" He was standing in the doorway in a way he learned from Jacoby. It was an actor's way of standing in a doorway at a moment of farewell, eyes fine, face slanted.

"When you shake hands with somebody, squeeze."

"Okay," he said frowning. He left slightly offended.

Did it ever occur to you in considering those instances of blacks who decide they want to act like whites and are very observant and successful in doing so (they are even better than the Japanese in imitating us—so much so that Elgin can act more like Mannix than Mannix) that no matter how observant one is, one cannot by observation alone assess the degree of squeeze in a handshake or even be sure there is a squeeze at all?

I was wrong about one thing. Merlin too had good sense and no taste for hurricanes. He was leaving.

For once I astonished myself: I wanted him to leave! I wanted him to get away, escape, the man who had made love to my wife in the Roundtowner Motor Lodge in Arlington, Texas, on or about July 15, 1968, and begot my daughter Siobhan.

Why?

Because he, poor old man, had come to as bad a place as a man can come to. Going back to Africa to find his youth. To see leopard. It was as if I had lit out for Asheville looking for dead Lucy. An old man should find new things. Shooting was too good for him. Anyhow I liked him and he liked me.

I caught him fidgeting up and down the gallery after the rest of the crew had gone.

"I was working on the causeway in the Keys when that son of a bitch (they had no women's names for hurricanes then) hit in 1928. They're no joke and I'd as soon not see another one."

"Didn't some people get killed?"

"About five hundred. Christ, what I haven't seen in my life. What I haven't done. Three things I've loved—women, life, and art."

"In that order?"

"In that order."

"Well, you've got plenty of life left."

He looked at me, then looked at me again.

"Right!" he said. "And I'm in good shape. I've got a good body. Feel that, Lance," he said, making a bicep.

"Okay. Very good."

"That's the arm of a young man. Feel my gut."

"Flat and hard."

"Hit me."

"That's not necessary."

"Go ahead, hit me. You can't hurt me."

"I believe you."

"I can beat the shit out of anybody here—except you, Lance. I believe you could take me."

"I doubt it. I'm in rotten shape."

"You want to arm wrestle?"

"No."

"You've got a good body. You know what you ought to do?"

"No."

"Kung Fu. You'd be great at it. You're a natural athlete, with an athlete's grace and strength. It would be good for you."

"You may be right, Merlin. You know what you ought to do?"

"What?"

"Get out of here."

"We're leaving the first thing tomorrow morning. Those other nuts want to spend the night."

"Marie is arriving tonight. You may not be able to leave tomorrow."

"I know. But those bastards want to make a party out of it. Margot ought to have better sense."

"If I were you, I would leave now. It's all the same to me." It was.

He paced the gallery, frowning, cocked an eye at the yellow sky.

"Or is Jacoby still the director?"

"Jacoby! That son of a bitch couldn't direct traffic in Boutee, Louisiana."

"Well?"

He snapped his finger. "By God I will leave!" His spinning white-fibered eye looked past me into the future. He snapped his finger again. "You know what I'm going to do?"

"No."

"I'm going to head north right out of this swamp. I'm going to drive straight to Virginia, up the Shenandoah Valley, and pick up Frances, who has a horse farm near Lexington. I'll say to her: Let's go back to Tanzania. We were there once. We lived in a Land Rover. We saw leopard. She's a soldier, a good girl. She might even— She's always been my love. I took her once to Spain and showed her the Ebro River, where I fought. Yes, Christ, I did that too. Can you believe it? She's a good girl, a comrade. She's a comrade, brother, daughter, lover to me. All I have to do is say, Honey, let's go back to the high country, and she'll go. Jesus, what an idea you've given me! I might even do a film. What do you think of a film about a man and woman who are good comrades, go on a hunt, and then have good sex together?"

"It sounds fine."

"If it is fine, why do I feel so rotten? I've always been a man with a great longing and lust for life and love, Lance. Do you understand that?"

"Yes."

"I know it could be good between me and Frances again."

"It might be."

"Tell me honestly."

"It's possible."

"It would be good even if—"

"Yes, it would."

"I feel rotten now but it could be good between us. What do you think?"

"I think it might be good between you."

"Frances knows me better than any other woman."

"I'm sure of it."

"She and I were always good together."

"That's good."

"We could be good together again."

"I'm sure of that."

"I might do something, a story, something, about the dying out of the wildebeest and the death too of human love and then a renewal and a greening, a greening and a turning back of the goddamn advancing Sahara. You understand?"

"Yes."

"The Sahara of the *soul* too."

"Yes, but right now you ought to think of leaving."

"I'm leaving. I'll speak to the others."

"What about the others?" I asked with a slight constriction of anxiety in the throat.

"To say goodbye. Christ, they wouldn't dream of leaving. Do you know what they're doing now?"

"No."

"Raine is taking sandwiches and champagne up to your belvedere. They're going to have a party named Goodbye movie, hello Marie."

I must have looked blank for he explained: "Goodbye movie hurricane, hello the real thing."

"That's a good place to get killed up there. Too much glass."

"Just try to tell them that."

"I intend to speak to Margot."

"On second thought why don't you tell her goodbye for me. As for the others, I'd as soon Marie blew their asses in the river. Do you know what those batbrains are doing?"

"No."

"They're popping pills and hauling anisette and tequila up to the belvedere. They're going to have a party."

188

"I know."

Merlin gave me a long firm handshake with two hands and a long level-eyed stare clouded with hidden meanings. He'd been in the movies too long.

"Lucy, jump in your Porsche and take off for school. You've got thirty minutes."

"Papaaauh!" She trailed off in a musical downbeat-upbeat, an exact rendering of Raine's famous mannerism.

"You heard me."

"I want to stay with Raine through the hurricane."

"No goddamn it. Now get going."

Lucy looked surprised. Everyone acted as if I were an ancestor who had wandered out of his portrait and begun giving orders. Everyone obeyed from sheer surprise.

Later I heard Lucy ask Suellen, who was packing her metal candy boxes in Elgin's Plymouth Charger: "What's got into Papa?"

"Mr. Lance know what he doing, girl," said Suellen conventionally but in truth relieved that somebody, anybody, was taking charge.

"What's the hurry, Papa?" asked Lucy, thinking of Raine again.

"Well, for one thing, they need you at the Tri-Phi house. I just talked to Mrs. Davaux. The freshmen are getting panicky even though the storm is only going to sideswipe them. Mrs. Davaux thinks you're the one to calm them. She says you have real leadership qualities. Otherwise you're going to lose half your pledges to the Chi O's— whose seniors are all back." (I did talk to Mrs. Davaux and she did say something like that.)

Ah, that was a different story. A hard choice between Raine and Troy and the hurricane, and shoring up wavering

Tri-Phi pledges. Her Tri-Phi loyalties would have won out, I think, even without my orders.

"Anyhow, Raine's not leaving. She'll be around for a while."

It was true in a sense.

"Okay, Papa. To tell you the truth, I'm a little scared."

"Good. Now get going."

"Okay, Papa."

Putting her hands on my shoulders, she held me off, setting her head to one side Rainelike. Jesus Christ, the movies.

"Papa, I love you."

"I love you too."

The wind was picking up. Now it was sustained between gusts. I went out on the galleries and closed the shutters, shot the heavy bolts. They locked from the outside.

Afterwards I met Raine in the hall on her way to the belvedere with a tray.

"What's the matter with you, Lance?"

"What do you mean?"

"You look awful."

"I'm tired."

"Here. I've got drinks right here."

"No thanks."

"Then try a couple of these. One now and one later." She gave me two capsules. "They're the best of all downers. They leave you relaxed but euphoric. You feel absolutely free to choose, to plan and act. You can choose to sleep or not to sleep. You become your true self."

I looked at her. "Very well."

The truth was, I needed something. There was a cold

190

numbing sensation spreading from the pit of my stomach. What I really wanted was a drink.

She set down the tray and poured me a drink of water. I swallowed both pills. She looked at me. "Why don't we meet later tonight?"

"Very well."

She started up the attic steps.

"I wouldn't stay up there too long, Raine. The wind is expected to reach over a hundred. The glass may not hold."

"We won't. We're just enjoying the lovely sky and clouds and lightning. Did you ever see such a sky? Why don't you join us?"

"Not right now. Send Margot down though. I want to speak to her."

Margot came down. She stood in the dark hall at right angles to me, arms crossed, foot cocked on heel.

"Margot, will you leave with me now? We can go anywhere you like."

"No."

"Then will you come and stay with me tonight?"

"No."

"That's it?"

"That's it."

"What do you mean, that's it?"

"I do love you, Lance."

"But—"

"No buts. I love you as I've always loved you, with the old me. But there are other me's. One grows."

"Then love me with the old me."

"What can I do?" She shrugged. She was not too attentive. Her head was slightly atilt as if she were listening for a new overtone in the storm. "The feeling is not there. One can't help one's feelings."

191

She hollowed her mouth and cocked her head. I could not hear over the uproar of the storm, but I knew her tongue went *tock tock* against the roof of her mouth.

Something worked in the pit of my stomach. It took hold and caught. I realized it was the drug catching on, meshing into my body like a gear.

She swung around to face me, hands on her hips. Holding herself erect, she set one foot forward and turned slightly out. Her face was severe, unpainted, Scandinavian. Christ, she was already Nora Helmer in *A Doll's House*.

"What are you going to do, Margot?" I asked dreamily.

"What am I going to do?" *Tock tock*. "Well, I'll tell you one thing I can't do. I can't just sit here year in and year out waxing furniture and watching the camellias bloom. You can understand that."

"Sure. Then let's go to—ah, Virginia."

"Virginia?" Her face strayed two degrees toward me.

"I don't know why I said Virginia," I said, feeling an odd not unpleasant distance opening in my head. "If not Virginia, then anywhere you please."

"No, I'm sorry, sweetie." She kissed and hugged me absentmindedly. In the hug I could feel that her diaphragm was held high. She was breathing in a certain way. She was being Nora.

The drug was acting. A certain distance set in between me and myself. Here's what I hoped for from the pills: a little space between me and the pain. I understood what Margot said but I couldn't stand it. But how do you live with something you can't stand? How do you get comfortable with a sword through your guts? I didn't expect a solution or even relief. I only wanted a little distance: how does one live with it—the way a drunk lives with being a drunk, or a crook lives with being a crook? No problem! I envied both. But this! How do you live with this: being stuck onto pain like a cockroach impaled on a pin? The drug did this: before, I was part of the pain, there was no getting away from it. Now I had some distance. The pain was still there, but I stood off a ways. It became a problem to be solved. Hm, what to do about the pain? Who knows, there might even be a solution. Perhaps there's something you can do to ease it. Let's see.

"Why don't you come up to the belvedere with us? It is absolutely spectacular."

"No. There're some things I have to do."

"Very well." She kissed me distractedly with a loud kinfolks kiss, smack. *Tock tock.*

When I finished locking the shutters, I returned to the pigeonnier. One had to lean into the south wind. There was wind between the gusts. The storm was like a man who can't get his breath.

The space between me and myself widened. I was sitting in my plantation rocker feeling a widening in my head.

The next thing I knew I was still sitting in my rocker. It was moonlight outside. The moonlight was coming in. I got up and opened the door. It was still. An orange moon rose behind the English Coast. A great yellow rampart of cloud filled the western sky beyond the levee. It looked as solid as the Andes and had peaks and valleys and glaciers and crevasses.

Leaving the door open, I went inside and sat in the rocker and thought of nothing. I breathed. My eye followed the line between the moonlight and the shadow of the doorjamb which ran across the floor of St. Joseph bricks set in a herringbone pattern.

OUR LADY OF THE CAMELLIAS

I must have dozed off because the next thing I remember
was the certain sense that there was someone in the room
with me. No mystery: I was looking straight at her. Therefore I must have dozed or I would have seen this person
come in. But the interval must have been very short because the angle of moonlight lying across the bricks had
not changed.

There in the straight chair across the desk from me sat a
woman I seemed to know, or at least seemed to be expected to know. She knew me. I started guiltily, smiled,
and nodded to cover my lapse of manners. Christ, you
remember, Percival; there must have been forty women in
that parish of a certain age who look more or less alike,
who have a certain connection with one's family, but
whose names one never gets straight. They are neither old
nor young. They could be thirty-five or fifty-five. They
look the same for thirty years. Was this Miss Irma or
Cousin Callie or Mrs. Jenny James? They are dark-
complexioned, have full figures and a certain reputation
from the past. Something had happened to them but we did
not speak of it—one's father had got them out of trouble.
Oh, you remember what happened to Callie. Perhaps she
had run off with an older married man. For the next forty
years they do well enough. Often they hold down a small
political job at the courthouse, or sell Tupperware—perhaps Cousin Callie has been Judge Jones's mistress for
twenty years. At any rate, they outlive everybody. They are
healthy. They show up at funerals, weddings, and New
Year open houses. One can't imagine what they do between times.

The only thing I could be certain of was that this person seemed to have every right to be there in my pigeon-

nier. And that she knew me and I was expected to know her. She smiled at me with perfect familiarity. No doubt she had come to seek shelter from the hurricane at Belle Isle, the strongest building hereabouts.

She sat bolt upright yet gracefully, smoothing down her dress into her waist, showing her figure to good effect. It was a knit dress which perfectly fitted her full breasts and hips.

Now she arched her back and sat even more bolt upright. It would never have occurred to me to ask: "Who are you and what do you want?"

Her hair was dark, perhaps a bit gray, heavy, long, and looped around her head in a not unattractive way. It had not been recently washed. I caught a whiff, not unpleasant, of unwashed woman's hair.

I looked at her. She smiled at me, a winning smile, but her eyes glittered. She was the sort of woman, Percival, you remember from childhood, who was extraordinarily nice to you, who spoke well of your parents, who said how nice they were, how handsome you were. Yet at the mention of her name your parents exchanged glances and fell silent.

She was also the sort you might well remember if you remember how a voluptuous forty-year-old woman attracted a fifteen-year-old youth, how if we were playing football and lounging on the grass at a time-out, sweaty, tired, and cheerfully obscene, and she passed by in the street, erect, heavy in the thigh and small in the waist, we'd fall silent until the inevitable: How would you like some of that?

Then I noticed the camellia pinned at her shoulder— and at the same moment it came to me that this was not yet the season for camellias—a large open flesh-colored bloom with a sheaf of stalks sprouting from the center bearing stamens, pistils, pollen, pods, ovules.

She was real enough, I think, though I cannot explain the camellia. The slight embarrassment of not being able to remember her name was all too familiar and not like a dream. She'd come for shelter, she said (doesn't this prove she was real, in dreams explanations are not required), but she'd changed her mind. She didn't want to impose on us. Maybe she'd better stay with a relative in town, Cousin Maybelle.

But where did she get the camellia?

She still spoke well of everyone. "Your father was such a perfect gentleman. What perfect tact and understanding!"

"Understanding?"

"Of Lily. Your mother. Oh, Lily. What a lovely delicate creature. Like a little dove. Not like me. I'm more a sparrow. Plain but tough."

"A dove?"

"Maybe more like a lovebird. She lived for love. Literally. Unless she was loved, she withered and died. Maury understood that. God, what understanding he had! And he also understood his own limitations and accepted them. He understood her relationship with Harry and accepted that. That man was a saint."

"What was her relationship with Harry?"

"You're joking. La, it was not secret."

"They were lovers?"

"For years. Everybody knew. So romantic! They were like Camille and Robert Taylor."

Everybody but me. Does everybody know everything but me?

"That was after my father's—uh—indictment?"

"Yes. Poor Maury was crushed, even though it was all just dirty politics and nothing was proved. I've always thought his illness had something to do with what he thought of as his disgrace. Pooh, men are ridiculous. And he was too—tenderhearted. But so aristocratic!"

I was looking in my father's sock drawer for the small change he kept in the fitted scoops for collar buttons and caught sight of something under the argyle socks. There it was, the ten thousand dollars, dusky new green bills in a powdered rubber band neat and squared away like a book, and there it was, the sweet heart pang of horror. I counted it. The bills felt like stiff petals, not like paper, like leaves covered by pollen. My heart beats slowly and strongly. Strange: I was aware that my eyes were doing more than seeing, that they were unblinking and staring and slightly bulging. They were "taking it in," that is, devouring. For here was the sweet shameful heart of something, the secret. For minutes there was an awareness of my eyes devouring the money under the socks, making little scanning motions to and fro, the way the eye takes in a great painting. Dishonor is sweeter and more mysterious than honor. It holds a secret. There is no secret in honor. If one could but discover the secret at the heart of dishonor. . . .

Harry Wills was undressing, taking off his duke's costume in the auditorium locker room after the ball. There was the usual drinking and horsing and laughing. No Robert Taylor, he was oldish, blue-jowled, big-nosed, hairy-chested, strong-bellied, thin-shanked, not a Realsilk salesman any more but a Schenley distributor: a traveling salesman! Wet rings from the glass of whiskey shimmered on the bench beside him. Except for his green satin helmet, sword sash, and red leatherette hip boots, he was naked. His genital was retracted, a large button over a great veined ball. As he caught sight of me, I watched him, gazed into his eyes, and saw his brain make two sluggish connections. One was: Here I was, a young Comus knight, the very one who had run 110 yards against Alabama. The other: here was I also, the son of Lily. (Jesus, was I also his son?) The two revelations fused in a single great rosy Four Roses whiskey glow of fondness, perhaps love. (A father's love?) Rising unsteadily, he grabbed me around the neck and announced to the krewe: "You know who this is! This is Lancelot Lamar and you know what he did!" They knew and their knowing confirmed the terrible emotion swelling within him. He told them anyway. "This boy not only ran back that punt 110 yards. He was hit at least once by every man on the Alabama team—twice by some. Haven't y'all seen the film?" The other dukes nodded solemnly. They had. They drank and gave me a drink and shook my hand. Hugging my neck, Harry sat down, pulling me down into a heavy air of lung-breathed bourbon, cigarette smoke, and genital musk.

"Jesus," he said, shaking his head at the wonder of it and cursed from the very inchoateness of the terrible unnamed feeling. "Have a drink! Goddamn . . . !"

Do you remember my mother? I never thought of her as "beautiful" or "good-looking" but rather as too pale, with wide winged unplucked eyebrows which gave her a boy's look. You thought she was beautiful? Perhaps I don't remember her after she began to drink. Later she became sly and even a little voluptuous. After years of secret drinking, there came to be a tightness and glossiness about her face. Her chin receded a little. Her eyes became brilliant and opaque and mischievous as if she knew a joke on everybody. You know, I've since known several genteel lady drunks who develop this same glossy chinless look. Is that a facial syndrome of woman alcoholics? Or a certain kind of unhappy Southern lady? Or both?

I remember her earlier not as "beautiful" but as thin-boned, quick, and sporty. There was a kind of nervous joking aggressiveness about her. She liked to "get" me. On cold mornings when everyone was solemn and depressed about getting up and going off to work or school, she would say, "I'm going to get you," and come at me with her sharp little fist boring away into my ribs. There was something past joking, an insistence, about the boring. She wouldn't stop.

Uncle Harry, jovial Schenley salesman and third cousin once removed, family friend and benefactor who brought me presents—even presents on ordinary weekdays, imagine a glass pistol loaded with candy on an ordinary Tuesday afternoon or a Swiss army knife with twenty-two blades—who was not only nice to me but took Lily, who was delicate then and had to rest a lot, for "joyrides" to False River—"Get her out of the house, Harry!" my father said—leaving him, my father, to his beloved quiet. Once he, my father, painted a mystical painting of our alley of live oaks showing the perpetual twilight filling them even at noon, and above, great domed spaces shot through by a single stray shaft of sunlight, a picture he entitled "O sola beatitudo! O beata solitudo!" He wrote a poem with the same title. Poet Laureate he was of Feliciana Parish, so designated by the local Kiwanis, lying on his recliner on the deep shaded upper gallery dreaming over his history manuscript, dreaming not so much of a real past as what ought to have been and should be now and might be yet: a lovely golden sunlit Louisiana of bayous and live oaks and misty green savannahs, Feliciana, a happy land of decent folk and droll folkways and quiet backwaters, the whole suffused by gentle Episcopal rectitude.

Uncle Harry then and Lily entering a tourist cabin on False River of a sunny wintry afternoon, the frost-bleached levee outside, the raw soughing gas heat striking at leg and eyes, the gracious cold still trapped in Lily's fur, the sheets slick-cold and sour.

But now, in the pigeonnier and in the eye of the storm, the sense at last of coming close to it, the sweet secret of evil, the dread exhilaration, the sure slight heart-quickening sense of coming onto something, the dear darling heart of darkness—ah, this was where it was all right.

You always got it backward: you don't set out looking for clues to God's existence, nobody's ever found anything that way, least of all God. From the beginning you and I were different. You were obsessed with God. I was obsessed with—what? dusky new graygreen money under interwoven argyle socks? Uncle Harry and Lily in the linoleum-cold gas-heat-hot tourist cabin?

The rising moon grew brighter and smaller. The great bastion of cloud wheeled slowly. Andes peaks and mesas and glaciers revolved slowly past my window. My mouth was open. I became aware of a difficulty in breathing as if I had asthma. I don't have asthma. I looked at my Abercrombie & Fitch desk weatherstation, Christmas present from Margot. The barometer read 28.96. I went to the open door. Children and youths in their teens were playing in the bright moonlight on the levee. They were exhilarated by the stillness of the great wheeling storm. Some worked seriously on the bonfires, adding willow logs and rubber tires to make smoke. Some somersaulted or lay flat and rolled down the levee. A young girl in a long white dress danced alone a French version of the square dance, a *Fais do-do*, mincing forward and backward, holding her head first to one side then to the other, curtsying, her hands spreading wide the folds of her skirt. Their cries came to me through the thin dead air, muffled and faraway. I became aware that it was the girl's voice. She was singing. Her voice carried in the hushed air. It was an old Cajun tune I used to hear at Breaux Bridge.

> *Mouton, mouton—et où vas tu?*
> *A l'abatoire.*
> *Quand tu reviens?*
> *Jamais—Baa!*

That was curious. There were no Cajun families here on the English Coast, only a few light-colored Negroes with French names, whom we called freejacks because they were said to have been freed by General Jackson for services rendered in the Battle of New Orleans.

Where did she come from?

In 1862 my great-great-grandfather Manson Maury Lamar, infantry captain with the 14th Virginia, struck up the Shenandoah Valley in A. P. Hill's corps, which invested Harper's Ferry, took thirteen thousand prisoners, got news of McClellan's assault on Lee at Sharpsburg seventeen miles away, hit a jog for the seventeen miles, and arrived just as Lee's right was giving way, took his company into battle at a dead run. It was the bloodiest day of the war. He would never talk about it, they said. But he would also never talk about anything else. He said nothing. My uncle fought in the Argonne. He said it was too horrible. But he also said he never again felt real for the next forty years.

My son refused to go to Vietnam, went underground instead in New Orleans, lived in an old streetcar, wrote poetry, and made various sorts of love. Was he right, or was I right, or are you right?

I went to see Anna this morning. We spoke. She sat in a chair. She's going to be all right. She speaks slowly and in a monotone, choosing her words carefully like someone recovering from a stroke. But she's going to be all right. She had combed her hair and wore a skirt and sat on her foot and pulled her skirt over her knee like a proper Georgia girl. I told her I would be leaving the hospital soon and asked her to come with me.

"Where are you going?"

"I don't know."

"I see."

After a while she said: "And you want me to come with you."

"Yes."

"Why?"

"Isn't that enough? I want you to come with me."

"Do you love me?"

"I'm not sure what that means. But I need you and you need me. I will have Siobhan with me."

"I see." She seemed to know all about Siobhan. Did you tell her? She nodded. "A new family. A new life."

That's all she said. She kept on nodding. But I wasn't sure she was listening. Do you think she meant she would come?

Do you hear the sound of music faraway? No? Perhaps I only imagined it, no doubt it is the echo of a dream or rather a vision which has come to me of late. But I swear I could hear the sound of young men marching and singing, a joyful cadenced marching song. A Mardi Gras marching band over on St. Charles? No. You're right, it's November, nowhere near Mardi Gras. Besides, it wasn't like a high-school band. It was young men singing and marching. It was both a great deal more serious and joyful than a high-school band.

Anna got bad news today. Her father died of a heart attack. Now she like me is alone in the world. He left her nothing but a cabin and a barn and fifty acres in the Blue Ridge not far from Lexington, Virginia. Well, that settles it. No Big Sur after all and perhaps it's just as well. In fact it is a kind of sign. It is Virginia where we're supposed to be. I see that clearly now.

Virginia?

Yes, don't you see? Virginia is where it will begin. And it is where there are men who will do it. Just as it was Virginia where it all began in the beginning, or at least where the men were to conceive it, the great Revolution, fought it, won it, and saw it on its way. They began the Second Revolution and we lost it. Perhaps the Third Revolution will end differently.

It won't be California after all. It will be settled in Virginia, where it started.

Virginia!

Don't you see? Virginia is neither North nor South but both and neither. Betwixt and between. An island between two disasters. Facing both; both the defunct befouled and collapsing North and the corrupt thriving and Jesus-hollering South. The Northerner is at heart a pornographer. He is an abstract mind with a genital attached. His soul is at Harvard, a large abstract locked-in sterile university whose motto is truth but which has not discovered an important truth in a hundred years. His body lives on Forty-second Street. Do you think there is no relation between Harvard and Forty-second Street? One is the backside of the other. The Southerner? The Southerner started out a skeptical Jeffersonian and became a crooked Christian. That is to say, he is approaching and has almost reached his essence, which is to be more crooked and Christian than ever before. Do you want a portrait of the New Southerner? He is Billy Graham on Sunday and Richard Nixon the rest of the week. He calls on Jesus and steals, he's in business, he's in politics. Everybody in Louisiana steals from everybody else. That is why the Mafia moved South: because the Mafia is happier with stealing than with pornography. The Mafia and the Teamsters will end by owning the South, the pornographers will own the North, movies, books, plays, the works, and everybody will live happily ever after.

California? The West? That's where the two intersect: Billy Graham, Richard Nixon, Las Vegas, drugs, pornography, and every abstract discarnate idea ever hit upon by man roaming the wilderness in search of habitation.

Washington, the country, is down the drain. Everyone knows it. The people have lost it to the politicians, bureaucrats, drunk Congressmen, lying Presidents, White House preachers, C.I.A., F.B.I., Mafia, Pentagon, pornographers, muggers, buggers, bribers, bribe takers, rich crooked cowboys, sclerotic Southerners, rich crooked Yankees, dirty books, dirty movies, dirty plays, dirty talk shows, dirty soap operas, fags, lesbians, abortionists, Jesus shouters, anti-Jesus shouters, dying cities, dying schools, courses in how to fuck for schoolchildren.

The Virginian? He may not realize it yet, but he is the last hope of the Third Revolution. The First Revolution was won at Yorktown. The Second Revolution was lost at

Appomattox. The Third Revolution will begin there, in the Shenandoah Valley.

Now I remember where I heard the music. Do you believe in dreams? That is, do you believe that a dream can be prophetic? You smile. Christ, don't you believe anything any more? You smile. Your God used to send messages in dreams, didn't he? No, this was not a message sent to me by God but my own certain vision of what is going to happen. I know what is going to happen. I dreamed it, but it is also going to happen.

A young man is standing in a mountain pass above the Shenandoah Valley. A rifle is slung across his back. He is very tan. Clearly he has been living in the forest. Though the day is very hot, he stands perfectly still under a sourwood tree as the sun sets in the west. He is waiting and watching for something. What? A sign? Who, what is he? WASP Virginian? New England Irish? Louisiana Creole? Jew? Black? Where does he live? It is impossible to say. He is dark, burned black as an Indian. He could be a Sabra from a kibbutz. All one can say for certain is that he is careful, that he has something in mind, and that he is watching and waiting. For what? For this: presently he sees something, a mirror flash from the last sun rays from the mountain across the North Fork. Still he waits. The sun goes down. Quickly it grows dark. He faces northeast watching the faint green luminescence from the great dying cities of the North, Washington to Boston.

As quickly as he appeared, he vanishes.

Presently there comes a sound from faraway of young men singing. There is a cadence and a dying away to the sound. Are they marching?

Oh Shenandoah, we long to see you
How we love your sparkling waters

And we love your lovely daughters
From these green hills to far away
Across the wide Missouri

Oh, Columbia, our blessed mother
You know we wait until you guide us
Give us a sign and march beside us
From these green hills to far away
Across the wide Missouri.

What? What about the women?

Women? How will it be for women?

In order to understand that, you must first understand the strange thing that happened to the human race. It is an event which you people had an inkling of but then turned upside down and inside out for your own purposes.

It is the secret of life, the most astounding and best-kept secret of the ages, yet it is as plain as the nose on your face, there for all to see.

You were onto it with your doctrine of Original Sin. But you got it exactly backwards. Original Sin is not something man did to God but something God did to man, so monstrous that to this day man cannot understand what happened to him. He shakes his head groggily and rubs his eyes in disbelief.

The great secret of the ages is that man has evolved, is born, lives, and dies for one end and one end only: to commit a sexual assault on another human or to submit to such an assault.

Everything else man does is so much bushwa and you know it and I know it and everybody knows it.

Women have only just now discovered the secret, or part of it, the monstrous absurdity of it. Can you blame them for being outraged? Yet even more absurd are their pathetic attempts, once having made the discovery which men are too dumb to make, to pretend it isn't so, to cover it up, or to blame it on men.

What the poor dears discovered is the monstrous truth lying at the very center of life: that their happiness and the meaning of life is to be assaulted by a man.

Ah, sweet mystery of life indeed, indeed yes, exactly, yes indeed that is what it is: to be rammed, jammed, stuck, stabbed, pinned, impaled, run through, in a word:

Raped.

The meaning and goal and omega point of evolution is at last clear. It was obscured in past ages by the servitude of man. The poor bastard was so busy surviving and mainly not surviving, starving and dying, that only recently has it dawned on him what an extraordinary apparatus he is. He was decent because he was overworked.

Pascal told only half the story. He said man was a thinking reed. What man is, is a thinking reed and a walking genital.

Why do you look at me like that? After all, the facts are elementary. They are as every biology student knows: of the three million species on earth the human female is the only one capable of living in a state of constant estrus; of having an orgasm; of making love face to face with her mate.

Ha, it's funny in a way, women liberated and educated, free at last to learn the truth, and the truth? That she is the only creature on earth in perpetual heat. What a discovery! That she is good for only one thing.

Eye to eye, face to face, belly to belly, breast to breast, day in and day out, in heat the year round—there is the omega point of evolution! A comedy isn't it, women trying to escape that? That's like a hen wanting to be a hawk. A lioness, yes, a lioness can do it, for she is a lion most of the time, fighter and hunter, and only periodically hikes her tail.

But a woman? She is your omega point. Take such a species, the human, give it a two-hour work week and a life expectancy of a hundred years and it doesn't take a genius to see what God has in mind for man.

What hath God wrought? Hm yes.

Suddenly things became clear. The pornography of American life is not the work of evil men. No, it is the sensible work of clever men who have at last fathomed God's design for man.

By the way, it is not true that Americans are by nature the most pornographic people on earth. The Russians and the Chinese are simply behind times, busy catching up. Ha, wait till those buggers get the forty-hour week.

THE GREAT SECRET OF LIFE

God's secret design for man is that man's happiness lies for men in men practicing violence upon women and that woman's happiness lies in submitting to it.

The secret of life is violence and rape, and its gospel is pornography. The question is, Can we bear to discover the secret?

Do we have to accept the verdict of evolution, that the omega point is sexual aggression, the giving of it or the taking of it?

The Jews in the Old Testament knew the secret: that man is conceived in sin.

Then what shall we do about it?

You say we are redeemed. Look out there. Does it look like we are redeemed?

The storm? You don't like my theology. I see. Oh, you want to know what happened that night. Yes. Well, I can tell you that quickly. It doesn't really matter now.

When I woke, the eye had passed and the south wall slammed in with what must have been a line of tornadoes. Under the rising keening of the wind came a new sound as of a thousand diesel towboats rumbling down the river. Wind whistled through the holes of the pigeonnier like an organ loft. In a flash of lightning I saw Belle Isle. The oaks were turned inside out, white as birches, but Belle Isle stood steady and serene. I thought of the heavy old fourteen-inch attic timbers straining and creaking against their iron straps and bolts.

The woman was still there. She stood up. I noticed without much interest that she looked different. Now she looked less like an obscure relative, a voluptuous middle-aged aunt who has survived some forgotten disgrace, than—my mother! Or rather a photograph of my mother which I remember studying as a child. She gazed at me with a mild, equable, even a slightly puckish expression. The snapshot showed some V.M.I. cadets and their dates grouped around, sitting in, leaning on, a 1925 Franklin touring car. It was after graduation and a military wedding. The bride and groom are facing the photographer. She wears a loose-fitting dress which comes exactly to her kneecaps and a wide lace collar. Her hair falls to her shoulders, where it curls up. The other girls' mouths are painted in bows but my mother's mouth is pale. Her wide brows are unplucked. In her prankish way she is proferring an unsheathed sword (her date's? the groom's?) to the photographer. The sword is upright, the blade held in her hands, the hand guard making a cross. Is she doing an imitation of Joan of Arc leading her army, cross borne aloft? Whenever my mother's friends spoke of her, they used words like "wonderful sense of humor," the "class clown," "imp," and so on. She had two close friends. They called themselves the three Musketeers.

The woman stood. It was the same woman. She was saying something, her lips were moving, but in the storm I could not hear her. Her expression meant something routine and self-deprecating like: Thank you so much, but I don't want to be a bother. She turned and tried to open the door, but it wouldn't open. It was then she gave me the sword—

The sword? Ha ha. It was the Bowie knife.

Then she looked like my mother again, and when she gave me the Bowie knife, she picked it up from the desk and thrust it at me point first in the same insistent joking way my mother would bore her sharp fist into my ribs.

Again she tried to open the door. It must be the wind, I thought, holding it shut. But when I tried to open it, I saw that an oak limb, a thicket of leaves and branches, had blown against it.

Ah, she gave me the knife to cut the branches and free the door.

You can't go now, I yelled above the shriek of the wind and the roar of the diesels on the river. Her shrug and nod I took to mean: Very well, I'll stay at Belle Isle.

Very well, I'll take you over. But then I thought of something. No, you stay here, it's safer, there are fewer trees and it's safer here under the levee.

Yet all the while I was doing what she asked me to do, in the obliging way, you know, that you do something when Miss So-and-So asks you to, trying to open the door, my face down and getting my shoulder into it.

I'm sorry, I said, but—

But when I stood up, she was gone. Not wanting to be a bother, she must have stepped past me.

I was standing, thinking, and looking down at the knife in my hand. It was three o'clock. There was an orange cannonade of lightning in the southern sky but you couldn't hear the thunder. As I watched, the last bonfire blew away, a very strong symmetrical one built of heavy notched willows like a log cabin, tapering to a point, the four corners secured by thirty-foot tree trunks as straight as telephone poles. It blew away, exploded silently and slowly, the timber springing apart like a toothpick toy.

I was sitting at my desk fiddling with the knife. My head felt light and there was the feeling of freedom you have when you recover from a high fever. It is possible, one realizes, to stand up, walk in any direction, and do anything. Did the sensation have something to do with the low pressure? The barometer Margot gave me now read 27.65 inches. That's very low, I thought, as I fiddled with the pencil. No wonder I felt queer.

Presently I got up and found a hunting coat with big side pockets and a pouch in the back for game. I put a flashlight in the side pocket. By opening the door a few inches, it was possible to use the knife as a machete and hack through the oak branch sprung against the door. How did the woman get out? The knife flashed gold in the lightning. I felt its edge. It was sharp as a razor. Who had sharpened it? I looked at the knife and put it in the game pouch of the hunting coat, the point of the blade stuck down in a corner, and tied the drawstring tight across the flat of the blade.

I stepped outside. The noise was bad but the wind was not bad until I reached the corner of the pigeonnier. Then it blew my mouth open, hollowed out my cheek, and made a sound across my mouth as if I were shouting. I fell down. Above me I could hear the organ sounds of the wind in the holes of the loft. The glazing must have blown out. After several tries at getting up, I discovered it was possible to walk by turning sideways to the wind and planting a foot forward. It was like walking down a steep mountain. Something was cutting my cheek. It must have been rain because it was not cold. My mouth blew open and again I fell down but managed to crawl into the lee of a big oak stump. I didn't remember the stump. The keening and roaring was not a sound any more. It had turned into a lack of pressure, a vacuum, a silence. I sat in the roaring silence for a while. The stump was tall. I didn't remember the tree. It must have been one of the oaks in the alley. It looked as if it had been sheared off fifteen feet above the ground by an artillery shell. I turned on my flashlight and looked at the sign in the tourist parking area. ADMISSION $5.00. A pine needle had blown through it. I sat for some seconds trying to understand the physics of it, how a limber pine needle can blow through a board.

The doors to the cellar were on the north lee side of the house, so it was possible to open one. I went down into the darkness, not using the flashlight at first. The two-foot brick walls were like earthworks. The storm died suddenly to a muted uproar, a long steady exhalation. But there was another sound, a creaking and groaning, like the timbers of a ship in a heavy sea. I realized it was the fourteen-by-fourteens in the attic far above.

Walking slowly toward the Christmas tree, I felt with my foot for the recess. When I reached it, I sat on the edge of the concrete and waited, hoping that dark as it was I might still be able to see something. After a while it became possible to make out a glimmer of pipes against the dark. Standing, I felt for the top pressure gauge and held the flashlight close to it. It read 38 PSI. I closed the valve below it watching the needle fall to zero. I propped the flashlight, slanted up, in the wheel of the bypass valve. The big Stillson wrench wouldn't move the gauge at first. I was afraid of breaking it off but finally I was able to get a purchase on the fitting below the gauge. It took all I had to start it. When it came off, I tried the three-inch Gerona nipple. That was the trouble. Naturally the plastic nipple didn't fit the threaded metal sleeve but simply abutted it. The Gerona pipe could not be threaded so there was nothing to do but make a crude abutted joint and seal it as best I could with PBC compound and many wrappings of duct tape. A bad job but it should hold against the low pressure.

The rest was simple: a ninety-degree elbow and three ten-foot sections of the Gerona which reached to within a foot of the main intake duct of the new fifteen-ton Carrier. Using the Bowie knife, I sliced off fiberglass insulation until metal showed. Then, using it like a chisel and the Stillson as a hammer, I made an X in the sheet metal and bent the corners in. Then drive a nipple into the opening—take care not to lose it!—and connect it with the Gerona system with a sleeve and another nipple. Slice off more fiberglass, pack it into the crude joint, seal with compound, and wrap the whole with the rest of the duct tape, perhaps fifty feet or so. The difficulty was propping the flashlight at the right angle.

How strange memory is! Do you know what my memory records as the most unpleasant experience of that night? The damn fiberglass. Particles of it worked under my sleeve and collar. It makes my neck and arms itch just to think of it. Death's banal, but fiberglass in the neck is serious business.

I switched off the light and sat leaning back against the chimney gazing up into the darkness and waited for the compound to set.

Then I opened the valve. The gas made no sound in the pipe. At least I could not hear it, but I fancied I could feel a slight shudder in the ten-foot sections of Gerona. Naturally there was no smell because the captan which gives house gas its characteristic odor had not been added.

Sticking the knife and flashlight back in my hunting coat, I picked up the two kerosene lamps and went upstairs in the dark.

At the top of the hanging staircase in the upper hall it was pitch black. But I knew every inch. A foot or so (I reckoned) from the cathedral chair I set down the kerosene lamps and put out my hand—yes, it was there, the chair. I listened. There was no sound but the murmur of the storm and the creak and pop of the timbers in the attic, as if Belle Isle were laboring through heavy seas. Somewhere a window glass broke. There was no sound from the bedrooms.

I went to each door, Troy's Margot's, Raine's. At Raine's door there was a different kind of murmuring, an overtone to the storm. A weak watery light flowed through the crack in the door.

I felt along the wall until I touched the air-conditioning register. My hand felt nothing, but when I put my face against it, there was a cool breath against my cheek. There was no odor. It could have been air.

For a long time I stood at Raine's door. I can't remember whether I was listening or thinking or doing nothing. What I remember is that it was possible to stand there at least twenty minutes, hands at my sides, without fatigue, registering the sensations of my body. My heart was beating slowly, my breathing was deeper than usual—was it the low pressure of the storm? The storm roared softly like a conch shell over my ear. The fiberglass was beginning to bother my neck.

Then, taking some thirty seconds to do so, I opened the door. So well did I know every inch and quirk of Belle Isle that without thinking I put a slight strain upwards on the silver doorknob while turning it because the heavy door had settled on its hinges and the latch did not move easily.

The door opened at the rate perhaps of an inch every five seconds. The first thing that came into view was the curio cabinet next to the iron fireplace, then a corner of the bed. The light probably came from an electric camp lantern set on the floor. The weak light seemed to radiate in rays, like a child's drawing of light.

Once several years ago, passing in the hall, I heard Elgin in this bedroom conducting a tour, eight or ten Michiganers. "This cabinet was sealed up before the Civil War." There was a marvel about it which Elgin saw and the tourists liked and I hadn't thought of, this small volume of 1850 air trapped and sealed in glass. Elgin had a sense of the legendary. "These little bilbos you see still have General Beauregard's fingerprints on them." Bilbos? Where did he get that? He must have meant bibelots, the little bric-a-brac figures.

The door was opening without a noise. Or if there was a noise, it could not be heard. The storm beyond the shuttered widow was like a heavy surf.

There was the Ray-O-Vac lantern, not on the floor but on the bedtable, shedding a small cone of rayed light.

Troy Dana was lying prone on the far edge of the bed, naked, his face buried in the pillow.

Raine was standing at the window, even though the shutters were closed and locked. Lightning made yellow stripes through the slots. She wore a short hip-length nightgown—shift?—which left her legs bare. Her legs were short but well developed. She looked like a fourteen-year-old girl who had spent twelve years dancing.

Appearing silently beside her, I thought to startle her, but she turned to me as if I had always been there.

"Isn't it beautiful?"

"What?"

"The hurricane."

"Yes." All one could see through the shutters were the heaving and whitened oaks.

"Look at that faggot. Passed out. OD'd. In this lovely hurricane."

"Will he be all right?"

"Oh sure, unfortunately."

I saw too that she was drunk with something not alcohol. Her face was close under mine and her breath had a sweet chemical smell. Her voice was not slurred but low and bell-like. Her eyes winked gold in the lightning. The only sign of intoxication was her incapacity for surprise. Whatever happened was the occasion of a mild disconnected wonder, my appearing—or General Beauregard appearing.

"You didn't know that I went for you?"

"What?" I said, cocking my ear away from the storm.

"You know, like going for somebody."

"You did?"

"You're so dumb! And with all that going on—" She waved vaguely toward the hall (by no means drunk or even swaying, but mainly flat and unsurprised: for her one thing was more or less like any other, and could be spoken of in her low bell-like voice).

She put her hands on my belt buckle, grabbed it with her fingers stuck inside, and gave me an odd little jostle.

"Couldn't you tell?"

"Tell what?" I gazed into her gold eyes.

Her mild gold gaze drifted indifferently from me to Troy to the hurricane.

"My God, isn't that something." Through the shutters I could see a big white socket where a limb had been ripped off one of the oaks. "Does it turn you on?"

"To what?"

"Me," she said like a drowsy little temple bell. She put her arms around my waist, locked her hands, and squeezed me with surprising strength. "You're a big mother."

I pulled her up to me. She was like a child, but broader, a broad child.

"Let's lie down," she said, tugging fretfully at my buckle. "I'm sleepy."

"Go on," I said absently. I remembered something I had to do. "I remember something I have to do."

"What are you doing?" she asked from the bed.

"I don't like this light," I said, picking up the Ray-O-Vac, which was shooting out weak white rays. The kerosene lamp was on the floor.

"Oh, a coal oil lamp!" Lying in bed, she clapped her hands slowly and without noise. "But hurry up."

Before lighting it, I checked the air-conditioning register. It was set high in the wall. My hand could reach it but I couldn't feel the gas. The cheek is more sensitive. I sat in the corner opposite the register and removed the glass chimney of the lamp and took out a match. I gazed up into the dimness of the fourteen-foot ceiling. Cold air falls. Methane rises. I struck the match. Nothing happened. I lit the wick and replaced the glass chimney and switched off the Ray-O-Vac. The soft yellow light opened like a flower and filled the room.

Raine's lips formed a word. She beckoned to me.

Time passed but it was hard to tell how slow or fast. I was standing by the bed looking down at her. She beckoned and said something. I dropped to one knee beside the bed to hear her. The pillow mashed her lips sideways like a child's.

Something occurred to me. Do you think it could be true that in our heart of hearts we *always* know what is going to happen to us? Not only does a person dying in a hospital know perfectly well he is going to die even though he may not know what he knows. Not only that but even a passenger on an airplane that is about to blow up somehow knows in a part of his being what is going to happen.

Anyhow she knew. That is, she knew something.

She was talking about her childhood. The kerosene lamp reminded her of growing up in West Virginia. Her father was a drunk ex-coal miner with black lung. Her mother took to staying out late at night with men, leaving her with the other children. She was fourteen. She thought her mother was taking money from the men. Her mother was. She hated her mother. But her mother was doing it to buy Raine her first party dress, a "basic black" with "classic opera pumps."

"Here's the funny thing," said Raine through her famous but now mashed lips, not caring how she looked, gazing at the flame in the chimney which I could see upside down in her pupil. "You would have thought I'd be grateful. Let me tell you something. Gratitude is shit. You know what I was? Happy. That's all. And that's better. I was happy to have the dress. I didn't care how she got it. But that was what she wanted: to see me happy. So all was well after all, wasn't it? I was happy and she was happy to see me happy."

Time seemed to pass both slowly and jerkily. Or maybe that's the way I remember it.

218

"Come here," said Raine.

I was standing over her. She was lying prone, bare legs apart. One hand was stretched awkwardly behind her, fumbling for me. She touched me.

I remember thinking: Why is the real so different from fantasy? Do you remember our locker-room fantasies? How would you like to have Ava Gardner here and now on this rainy day, in this gym, the gym cleared out, nobody but you and Ava on the janitor's cot in the boiler room, and so forth. But a hurricane is even better, and there was Raine Robinette herself, groping for me, her famous lips mashed against the pillow, her famous thighs under me. And alone with her, or as good as alone, maybe even better: Troy there but out of it, curled up on the very edge of Lucy's queen-size rosewood tester.

And I? I was sitting gazing down at her, my thumbnail against my teeth, thinking of the queerness of the present here-and-now moment. Other times belong to someone or something or oneself and smell of someone or something or oneself. The present is something else. To live in the past and future is easy. To live in the present is like threading a needle. It came to me: our great locker-room lust had no relation to the present. Lust is a function of the future.

Now her hand, knowledgeable even though stretched awkwardly behind her and upside down, was touching me. I was watching her, thumbnail against tooth, gazing at nothing in particular.

No, not at nothing. At something. Something winked on a finger of the groping hand. It was the blue sapphire in Lucy's ring. Raine was wearing my daughter Lucy's Tri-Phi sorority ring. It was loose on Raine's middle finger. Raine wore it the way a girl wears a boy's ring. Lucy had a big callow teen girl's hand.

As I was gazing at the ring on the groping hand, I began

to smile. My eyes focused and seemed to wink back at the ring. A little arrow of interest shot up my spine. I smiled and guided Raine's hand to me. You know why I smiled, don't you? No? Because I discovered the secret of love. It is hate. Or rather the possibility of hate. The possibility of hate rescued lust from the locker-room future and restored it to the present.

"Here now," I said smiling, and tenderly pulling her body up, reaching around the front of her until my hands felt the soft crests of her pelvis.

"What?" she asked. "Oh."

At first as her face was pressed into the pillow her lips were mashed down even more. I was alone, far above her, upright and smiling in the darkness.

Later she wanted to turn over. "Ah," she said. We watched each other, her face turned and looking back, her eyes aslit and gleaming in the soft light. We were alone and watchful, that is, each of us was alone and watchful of the other. No longer children were we but adults and watchful, which comes of being adults. What had God in store for us? So it was this. For what comes of being adult was this probing her for her secret, the secret which I had to find out and she wanted me to find out. The Jews called it knowing and now I knew why. Every time I went deeper I knew her better. Soon I would know her secret. We were watching each other. We were going to know each other but one of us would know first and therefore win. The watching was a contest. I was coming close, closer. We watched each other watching. It was a contest. She lost. When I found it out, the secret, she closed her eyes and curled around me like a burning leaf.

I left her asleep next to Troy, the two nested like spoons.

The rest of it? What? Oh. Yes. Well, I'll be brief. Do

you mind if I summarize? There is no pleasure in dwelling on it. Anyway it happened almost as an afterthought. The whole business took no more than fifteen minutes.

I didn't see what I wanted to see after all. What did I want to see? the money in my father's sock drawer? Why was it so important for me to see them, Margot and Jacoby? What new sweet-horrid revelation did I expect to gain from witnessing what I already knew? Was it a kind of voyeurism? Or was it a desire to feel the lance strike home to the heart of the abscess and let the puss out? I still didn't know. I knew only that it was necessary to know, to know only as the eyes know. The eyes have to know.

But I did not see them after all. I felt them.

I entered Margot's bedroom, mine and Margot's, that is. Somehow there seemed no great need for precautions now. Perhaps it was because the storm was at its height. There was a steady shrieking as if the hurricane were blowing through steel rigging. It was pitch dark. So I could not hear them or see them! Who was shrieking? they? the hurricane? both? Belle Isle groaned and labored. The great timbers sang and popped overhead. The lightning was less frequent now but brighter. I waited and counted during the intervals. The flashes came about eight or ten seconds apart.

The shrieking was so loud it seemed to make things invisible.

Now in the short foyer of the master bedroom I knelt and lit the second lamp, this time leaving the chimney off. I began to worry about leaving the chimney on the lamp in Raine's room. I turned the wick low.

Standing straight against the wall of the foyer, I calculated I could see the reflection of the foot of the bed in the mirror of the huge crotch mahogany armoire which stood against the inside wall of the bedroom. I waited, perfectly still, back, head, palms of hands touching the cool plaster.

When the lightning flashed, striping the room through the shutters, I could see two bedposts striped like barber poles in the mirror even though the mirror was fogged by age, its silvering moth-eaten.

It was the great Calhoun bed, built by my ancestor for his friend John C. Calhoun to sleep in in the White House in 1844. But Calhoun never slept in the White House so Royal Moultrie Lamar kept the bed. It was like a cathedral, a Gothic bed, posts as thick as trees, carved and fluted and tapering to spires and gargoyles above the canopy. The headboard was as massive and complex as an altar screen. Panels of openwork braced posts and rails like flying buttresses.

Between flashes I walked without hurrying to the cul-de-sac between the armoire and the far wall. From here one looked directly at the top half of the bed. The shrieking grew worse but the lightning was a long time coming. It came, a short bright burst like a camera flashbulb. Something moved. But my view was obstructed by the triangular bracing between the post and the side rail.

Something white gleamed on the Aubusson rug at my feet. I picked it up. A handkerchief? No, a pair of jockey shorts. I gazed at it dreamily. There was something archaic about it, an ancient artifact it was. It was like finding a toilet article, a broken clay comb in one of the houses at Pompeii. I dropped it behind me and waited.

Presently the lightning stopped but the noise was so loud, a bass roaring and soprano shrieking, that it was palpable, a thickening and curdling of the darkness. It became natural to open one's mouth to let the sound circulate, shriek into one's ears and out the mouth. I felt invisible.

Then, though I don't remember how I got there, I was

standing by the bed looking down. There was nothing to see. Kneeling I put my ear to the openwork panel of the flying buttress, an unconsecrated priest hearing an impenitent confession. But presently, in a lull there was a voice. I could not make out the words but the voice rose and fell in a prayer-like intonation.

God. Sh— God. Sh—

In my confessional I fell to musing. Why does love require the absolute polarities of divinity-obscenity? I was right about love: it is an absolute and therefore beyond all categories. Who else but God arranged that love should pitch its tent in the place of excrement? Why not then curse and call on God in an act of love?

My eyes began to make things out. No darkness is absolute. The candle glow from the foyer made the faintest glimmer on the white walls. It was possible to make out the looming shape of the bed. I was standing. There was a shape on the bed. Its skin was darker than the white sheets. Now I could see it, the strangest of all beasts, two-backed and pied, light-skinned dark-skinned, striving against itself, holding discourse with itself in prayers and curses.

Ah then, was this God's secret plan for us? (What did your Jewish Bible say about *all* men being conceived in sin?) A musing wonder filled me. I ran my thumbnail along my teeth.

My head ached, yet I felt very well, strong and light, though a bit giddy. My body seemed to float. Then I realized that the methane had come down. It had filled the high dim vault of the room and had come down close enough to breathe. At first I could not understand why my heart was beating fast and my breath labored, because I felt good. Then I understood. It was the methane. Standing, I was above them. It. I considered: it would be better to get lower and closer. It was dark.

Though I must have been leaning, I seemed to be floating over them. Jacoby's back was a darkness within the dark. Musingly I touched it, the beast.

"Oh, yes," it said.

A white thigh and knee angled out. I considered her, its, foot, the toes splayed and curled up—isn't that called a Babinski sign, Doctor, Father, whatever you are? You know, I'd seen that before, the way her toes curled out and up, and had secretly thought of it as a sign of her common Irish or country-Texas origins or both. It seemed vulgar. I could remember my mother saying a lady always points her toes when she dances. Now my hand was exploring the white thigh, searched for and found what it already knew so well, the strap of fiber along the outside which bound the deep flesh above and below it. My fingers traced the fiber toward the knee, where it had a ribbed-silk texture.

"Ah," said the beast.

Then lightly I let myself down on it, the beast. It was breathing hard and complexly, a counterpointed respiration. I was breathing hard too. The methane had reached the bed.

Suddenly it, the beast, went very quiet, all at once watchful and listening and headed up like a wildebeest catching a scent. Its succubus back, Margot's, was still arched and I could barely reach around its thick waist and clasp my hands together.

Squeezed together, the beast tried to break apart.

"What in the—?" said Janos Jacoby.

"Oh my God," said Margot, muffled, but instantly knowing everything.

Mashed together, the two were never more apart, never more themselves.

I was squeezing them, I think, and breathing hard but feeling very light and strong, so light that I imagined that if

I had not held them I would float up to the ceiling. Do you remember how we discovered "red-outs," how if you squeezed somebody from behind hard enough, first they became high, then saw red, then became unconscious. I could squeeze anybody on the team unconscious, even Fats Molydeux from Mamou, who weighed 310.

It is possible that I said something aloud. I said: "How strange it is that there are no longer any great historical events." In fact, that was what I was musing over, that it seemed of no great moment whether I squeezed them or did not squeeze them.

"How strange it is that there are no longer any great historical events," I said.

At any rate, it is certain that after a while Janos gasped, "You're not killing me, you're killing her."

"That's true," I said and let go. He was right. I had been pressing him into Margot's softness. He was as hard as a turtle and not the least compressed by the squeezing but she had passed out. But no sooner had I let go, and more quickly than I am telling you, than he had leaped up and begun doing things to me, California-kung-fu-karate tricks, knee to my groin, thumb in my eye, heel-of-hand chops to my Adam's apple, and so forth. I stood musing. There were many clever and scrappy moves against my person which I duly and even approvingly registered. "A bed is no place to fight," I said and we flew through the air until we crashed into the armoire. Janos must have found the knife in my game pouch where it had cut through the cloth and which I had forgotten, for when we broke apart at the armoire, he had it in his hand and was making wary circling movements, feinting and parrying like a scrappy movie star being put to the blood test by Apaches.

"Ah now," I said with relief, advancing on him, rejoicing in the turn events were taking. "Ah." A fight! A fight is a simple event. Getting hurt in a fight is not bad. I was backing him toward the cul-de-sac between the armoire and the corner. When he felt the wall behind him, he made a quick California move, whirled, cut my shoulder with the knife, and kicked me in the throat. I couldn't breathe but it didn't matter much because we were breathing methane anyway. After he whirled he must have also thrown the knife, for the flat of the blade hit my chest and the handle came to hand as neatly as if it were a trick we planned. Again I was embracing his back. This time I was more aware of his nakedness and his vulnerability. Here he was in my arms, a mother's boy, not really athletic despite his kung-fu skill, but somewhat pigeon-breasted and not used to being naked and smelling of underarm and Ban. So he might have appeared, an Italian boy, a Jewish boy, naked and vulnerable at the army induction center in the Bronx. He was not used to being naked. Did it ever occur to you that we spent a lot of time naked, naked in the locker room, naked in the river swimming, naked taking sunbaths on the widow's walk? Naked, he was more naked than we ever were.

We were on the floor. My thighs clasped his in a scissors grip.

"For Christ's sake, what are you doing?"

"Nothing much."

"That's something I'd like to talk about," he said panting hard yet speaking quickly and sincerely.

"What?"

"The absurdity of life. I've sensed you were into that."

"Ah."

"What?"

"Yes," I said marveling over his actor's gift of getting onto the way people talk. For I could recognize my voice in his, the flat giddy musing tone. He had observed me

226

after all. Were we both drunk on methane or was it the case that in fact there were no "great moments" in life? Or both?

"Let's talk. There's one thing I always wanted to ask you."

"Yes?"

"It has to do with something I've always desperately wanted in my life. I think you want it too."

"Yes?"

"I want—"

We'll never know what he wanted because his head was bending back and I was cutting his throat, I think. No, I'm sure. What I remember better than the cutting was the sense I had of casting about for an appropriate feeling to match the deed. Weren't we raised to believe that "great deeds" were performed with great feelings—anger, joy, revenge, and so on? I remember casting about for the feeling and not finding one. Yet I am sure the deed was committed, because his voice changed. His voice dropped a foot from his mouth to his windpipe and came out in a rush, not a word, against my hand holding the knife. He was still under me and there was no feel of the heat of blood on my hand, only the rush and bubble of air as the knife went through the cartilage. I held him for a while until the warm air stopped blowing the hairs on the back of my hand. Yes, I feel certain that is what happened.

Standing by the bed, I gazed down at Margot. I do not remember the storm. She was not dead, not even unconscious. She was watching me, I think. The kerosene light made her cheekbones look wide, an Indian's cheekbones. Her eyes were pools of darkness. They were open, I think. How could I be sure? I sat on the bed and with my arm across her put her cheek to my face. She was breathing.

When she blinked, her eyelashes stirred the air against my cheek. In the midst of the hurricane I felt this minuscule wind her eyelashes made against my cheek. She said something. I felt her diaphragm move under my arm.

"What?"

"What are we going to do?" She spoke in my ear. "Is he—?"

"Yes."

"Oh no," she said in simple dismay as if Suellen had dropped her best Sèvres vase.

Margot, unlike me, had a feeling but not a remarkable one. It was dismay that things had gotten out of hand. Perhaps the house had begun to break up under the force of the wind. We had better do something about it.

"What are we going to do?"

"We?"

"You."

"I don't know."

"Oh oh oh," she said, taking one hand in the other and actually wringing it. "Is there anything I can do? Oh my God."

"You could have."

"Me. Just me?"

"Yes."

"Why me?"

"Because I loved you." That was true enough I knew even though I couldn't remember what it was to love her.

"Loved? Love?" she asked.

"Because you were the only person who knew how to turn it all into love."

"Love?"

"Sweetness dearness innocence singing laughing. 'Love.'"

"Laughing?"

"That may have been your secret. You had a way of laughing."

"Yes, I know. I'll tell you what."

"What?"

"Take your weight off me a little. I can't breathe."

"Neither can I. I'm not on you. It's not the weight."

"Oh, God. What is wrong? I can't breathe."

"Don't worry about that. It's the storm."

"I tell you what, Lance."

"What?"

"Let's go away."

"Where?"

"Anywhere. We can start a new life. I'm the only one who can make you happy." It is strange but she spoke offhandedly now, as if nothing mattered a great deal. She too knew that there are no longer any "great historical moments." She even took hold of the fabric of my hunting jacket and in her old way plucked a loose thread from it.

"That's true."

"I know that I know how to and you know that I know how to."

"Yes."

It was true.

We must have been poisoned by the methane because the roaring of the storm was inside my head and I could hardly hear her. She was delirious. She was talking again, but not even to me any longer, about being a child in the Texas countryside and walking to town Saturdays and taking her good shoes along in a paper bag. She would change shoes at the bridge and hide the old shoes in a culvert.

"I'm nothing—" she began. "What's the matter with me?"

"What?"

"That's what you never knew. With you I had to be

either—or—but never a—uh—woman. It was good for a while. Oooh. Everything's gone black. I'm dying."

"No. The lamp went out."

I sat on the bed thinking: How could the lamp go out? To this day I don't know. Perhaps the wick was too low.

"Wait," I told her and crawled on all fours to get it. Why did I say that to her? Wait. Because I wanted her to tell me how we could do it, start all over again? But not in a serious way. Yes. I was delirious too. I had forgotten about the methane and was thinking of planning a trip with her.

Before I lit the lamp, I sat on the floor, the lamp between me and the bed, my back against the outer wall.

"Do you really think—" I said, turning up the wick, and struck the match. For a tenth of a second I could see her in the flaring, lying on her side like Anna, knees drawn up, cheek against her hands pressed palms together, dark eyes gazing

Without a sound the room flowered. All was light and air and color and movement but not a sound. I was moved. That is to say, for the first time in thirty years I was moved off the dead center of my life. Ah then, I was thinking as I moved, there are still great moments. I was wheeling slowly up into the night like Lucifer blown out of hell, great wings spread against the starlight.

I knew everything. I even knew what had happened. Belle Isle had blown up. Why, I wondered, wheeling, hadn't Raine's room blown first? Was it because the duct was much smaller there or because I had left the chimney on the lamp?

I must have been blown through the wall, with the wall, because I came down on the outer sloping thicket of the great oak where the limb swept to the ground, touched, and came up again. When I came to myself, the fire was hot against my cheek. But there was no great inferno. The roof and upper floors were gone and what flame there was was blown flat and in places separate from the building like the flame of a Bunsen burner. The south wind of the hurricane blew the heat away from me. I felt myself. Nothing was broken. I looked at myself. My hand and shoulder were bloody. I did not feel bad. I stood up, for some reason put my hands in my pockets, and walked up the front steps as I had done ten thousand times before. The heat, carried away by the wind, was not great. Perhaps I had been unconscious a long time. Most of the walls of the ground floor were down. There was no second floor.

What did you say? How did I get burned?

I had to go back to find the knife.

IX

What a beautiful day! Don't you think so? The last day of the hurricane season. All danger of hurricanes past. The morning sun bright and high refracted through the clear crystal prism of northern air with that special moderation, the promise of warmth, of fine November days in New Orleans. Everything is mild and unexceptional here, isn't it? even the weather. By eleven o'clock the winos on Camp Street will be creeping out of their holes and stretching out or curling up like cats in sunny doorways to take a little nap. Not a bad life.

Stop pacing up and down. I'm the prisoner, not you. Why the long race, the frowning preoccupation? Look at the street. Even the cemetery, especially the cemetery, looks cheerful. The mums are still fresh and yellow. The tombs spick-and-span, the rain trees bright as new copper pennies. Yesterday young people were singing in the old section. Some of them even sleep in the oven crypts, shove the bones aside and unroll their sleeping bags, a perfect fit. An odd thing about New Orleans: the cemeteries here are more cheerful than the hotels and the French Quarter. Tell me why that should be, why two thousand dead Creoles should be more alive than two thousand Buick dealers?

Ah, I forgot to tell you my good news. I'm leaving today. They're discharging me. Psychiatrically fit and legally innocent. I can prove I am sane. Can you? Why do you look at me like that? You don't think they should? Well, in any case, my lawyer got a writ of habeas corpus and my psychiatrist says I'm fit as a fiddle, saner in fact than he—the poor man is overworked, depressed, and lives on Librium.

Just think of it! At noon I shall walk through the front door of this building for the first time in a year, stroll down that block of Annunciation Street I've studied so minutely, turn the corner of Tchoupitoulas, and read that sign there.

Free &
Ma
B

At last I shall know what it says.

Then I shall turn around and look back at this window, reversing the direction of a million looks the opposite way.

It is not a small thing to look back at the place where one has spent a year of one's life.

Then I shall cross the street to La Branche's (formerly Zweig's) Bar and Grill, enter the cool ammoniac gloom where Zweig, La Branche, is mopping the floor of small hexagonal bathroom tile, sit at the bar, and order a Dixie draught and an oyster po' boy.

Then I shall pick up my little suitcase, which contains my worldly possessions, a change of underwear, one suit, socks, sweater, Bowie knife, and boots, walk to St. Charles, catch the streetcar to Canal Street, close out my bank account at the Whitney (about $4,000), walk to the Union Terminal, and catch the Southerner to Richmond. Think of that. Rocking along through the lonesome pine barrens of Mississippi in this two hundredth anniversary year of the first Revolution into the old red clay cuts of Alabama, gliding into Peachtree Station in Atlanta in the evening, order a few drinks in the club car while the train rambles north in the Georgia twilight. Then off at Richmond in the cold dawn hours and catch a Greyhound for the mountains.

Siobhan? Yes, now that I'm legally sane and competent, I can have her. And I intend to get her from Tex as soon as I'm settled in Virginia. We'll do fine, if Tex has not bored her to death or driven her out of her mind with his horsh pistols and coinkidinkies. I suppose I should be grateful to him. At least he took care of her. But I wish now I had let her stay with Suellen. Some black people are still sane.

Anna? Oh, she's well. But she's not going with me after all. I'm going alone. She's been kind enough to lend me her place in the Blue Ridge until I can find my own little half acre.

What happened to Anna? Really it's incredible. I shall never understand women. We were going to have a new life together. I thought we were suited to each other—each stripped of the past, each aware that an end had come and that there had to be a new beginning, just like a man and woman striking out for the territory through the Cumberland Gap in the old days. Then, to my astonishment, I mortally offended her. I suggested that she had suffered the ultimate indignity, the worst violation a woman can suffer, rape at the hands of several men, forced fellatio, and so on, that I too had suffered my own catastrophe, and that since we had both suffered the worst that could happen to us and come through, not merely survived but prevailed, we were qualified as the new Adam and Eve of the new world. If we couldn't invent a new world and a new dignity between man and woman, surely nobody could.

Do you know that she took offense? In fact she flew into a rage. "Are you suggesting," she said to me, "that I, myself, me, my person, can be violated by a *man*? You goddamn men. Don't you know that there are more important things in this world? Next you'll be telling me that despite myself I liked it."

There is something to what she says. The other day I opened St. Augustine's *The City of God* thinking to find what some of your best people had to say about the great questions, God and man and so on. And what do you think I found? The good saint devoting page after page soothing the consciences of nuns, virgins who had been raped by Visigoths and enjoyed it despite themselves. No doubt howled with delight.

So Anna told me to shove off. Very well. I did. Perhaps it is better that way.

I expected too much from her. I expected her to have made the same discovery I made, to have found the great secret of life, the old life that is, the ignominious joy of rape and being raped. We, I thought, she and I, were going to discover something better. And in her heart she knows the secret as well as I but she can't bear to admit it. Can you blame her? But we would have made good pioneers in the new life because neither one of us could tolerate the old. Someday women will admit the truth, will refuse to accept it, and then they will be my best recruits.

Oh, one last thing she said. She held my hand for a while after shaking hands goodbye. "When you get up there in Virginia," she told me, "you'll find a fallen-down house but a small solid-two-hundred-year-old barn. One side is a corn crib and a tack room with a loft. It would make a lovely cozy place to live in the winter and big enough for three." Christ, do you think this is another woman trying to fix me up in a pigeonnier? Why is it that shelters for animals now seem more habitable than ordinary houses? Hm. A done-over corn crib. But she said *big enough for three*. I had the feeling that if she could take her revenge, shoot enough men to even the score, not only for herself but for the bad trick played on her and her sisters by God or biology or evolution or whatever, she then might settle down with me in a barn, and we could hold each other as lovers should do, cling to each other like children, while Siobhan frolicked in the loft. Do you think she'll come?

You look at me strangely. I don't think I ever thanked you for listening to me. You know that I could not have told anyone else. Yes, I'm quite all right now. No, no confession forthcoming, Father, as you well know. But there is one thing . . . There is a coldness . . . You know the feeling of numbness and coldness, no, not a feeling, but a lack of feeling, that I spoke of during the events at Belle Isle? I told you it might have been the effect of the hurricane, the low pressure, methane, whatever. But I still feel it. That is, today, I don't feel it. I don't feel anything—except a slight curiosity about walking down that street out there. What do you think of it, that there is a certain coldness . . . Do you feel it?

The truth is that during all the terrible events that night at Belle Isle, I felt nothing at all. Nothing good, nothing bad, not even a sense of discovery. I feel nothing now except a certain coldness.

I feel so cold, Percival.

Tell me the truth. Is everyone cold now or is it only I?

What? You remind me that I said in the beginning that there was something I wanted to ask you. Ah yes. Well, it doesn't seem important now. Because there is no answer to the question. The question? Very well. The question is: Why did I discover nothing at the heart of evil? There was no "secret" after all, no discovery, no flickering of interest, nothing at all, not even any evil. There was no sense of coming close to the "answer" as there had been when I discovered the stolen money in my father's sock drawer. As I held that wretched Jacoby by the throat, I felt nothing except the itch of fiberglass particles under my collar. So I have nothing to ask you after all because there is no answer. There is no question. There is no unholy grail just as there was no Holy Grail.

Not even the knife at his throat seemed to make any difference. All it came down to was steel molecules entering skin molecules, artery molecules, blood cells.

You gaze at me with such—what? Sadness? Love? What about love? Do I think I can ever love anyone? Explain the question.

But that is beside the point. The point is, I know what I need to know and what I must do. Shall I tell you? Christ, you of all people should understand. Come here and stand with me at the window. I want to show you something, some insignificant things you may not have noticed. Why so wary? You act as if I were Satan showing you the kingdoms of the world from the pinnacle of the temple.

Listen. Do you hear them? Young people singing and laughing, enjoying themselves in the city of the dead. Perhaps they know something we don't know.

I'm like that old lady at the window across the street. I don't miss much. For example, I saw you earlier down there. In the cemetery. Surprised? I saw what you did, even though you did it very quickly. You stopped at a tomb and said a prayer. A relative? A friend? A request? So you pray for the dead. You know, something has changed in you. I have the feeling that while I was talking and changing, you were listening and changing. Am I wrong or have you reached a decision of sorts? No? You're waiting for me to finish?

Just take a look. What do you see? The same friendly little scene I first showed you the other day. The same street, the same junked 1958 Cadillac, the same movie, the same neat little Volkswagen with the MAKE LOVE NOT WAR sticker pulling in this very moment with the same mousy little coed at the wheel, the same two homosexuals holding hands next door, a quiet decent couple actually, much like any other couple, raper and rapee, with needs like yours and mine plus an occasional tube of K-Y jelly.

Look closely, you'll see that one or two insignificant items are different out there in the street. Notice the new bumper sticker on the VW: IF IT FEELS GOOD DO IT. Notice the poster near the old colored entrance of the movie. It's new. *Deep Throat* where once we saw *Henry V* and *Key Largo*.

Yes, insignificant changes, I'll admit. In fact, not really a change at all, but only more of the same. You shrug. What of it? Yes, you're right. What of it?

You say you wish to know what I'm going to do. Very well. I'll gladly tell you because when I woke this morning I knew for the first time exactly what I was going to do. Really it's simple. I can't imagine why I had to go to such lengths to discover it. There it was under my nose all along.

Yes, it dawned on me that suddenly, the solution is as clear and simple as an arithmetic problem. As a matter of fact, that is what it is: a matter of logic as simple as two plus two. I saw exactly how things are and what I must do. For your benefit I can even state it as a simple scholastic syllogism.

1. We are living in Sodom.

2. I do not propose to live in Sodom or to raise my son and daughters in Sodom.

3. Either your God exists or he does not.

4. If he exists, he will not tolerate Sodom much longer. He will either destroy it or let the Russians or the Chinese destroy it just as he turned the Assyrians loose on the Jews, and Sparta on Athens. How many Spartans would be needed to take these 200 million Athenians? Ten thousand? A thousand? A hundred? Twelve? One?

5. If God does not exist, then it will be I not God who will not tolerate it. I, one person. I will start a new world single-handedly or with those like me who will not tolerate it. But the difference between me and God is that I won't tolerate the Russians or the Chinese either. God uses instruments. I am my own instrument. No Russkies or Chinks in the Shenandoah Valley. We won't tolerate either. We won't tolerate that out there and we won't tolerate the Russians. We know what we want. And we'll have it. If it takes the sword, we'll use the sword.

6. I'll wait and give your God time.

You are silent. Your eyes are vacant.

So you plan to take a little church in Alabama, Father, preach the gospel, turn bread into flesh, forgive the sins of Buick dealers, administer communion to suburban housewives?

At last you're looking straight at me, but how strangely! Ah, all at once I understand you. I read you as instantly as I used to when we were so close. All of a sudden we understand each other perfectly, don't we?

Tell me if I'm right or wrong.

You know something you think I don't know, and you want to tell me but you hesitate.

Yes.

You speak! Loud and clear! And looking straight at me!

But I can see in your eyes it doesn't make any difference any more, as far as what is going to happen next is concerned, that what is going to happen is going to happen whether you or I believe or not and whether your belief is true or not. Right?

Yes.

We are not going to make it this way, are we?

No.

It's all over, isn't it? I can see it in your eyes. We agree after all.

Yes.

Yes, but? But what? There must be a new beginning, right?

Yes—

But? You don't like the new beginning I propose?

You are silent. So you are going to go to your little church in Alabama and that's it?

Yes.

So what's the new beginning in that? Isn't that just more of the same?

You are silent.

Very well. But you know this! One of us is wrong. It will be your way or it will be my way.

Yes.

All we can agree on is that it will not be their way. Out there.

Yes.

There is no other way than yours or mine, true?

Yes.

One last question—and somehow I know you know the answer. Do you know Anna?

Yes.

Do you know her well?

Yes.

Will she join me in Virginia and will she and I and Siobhan begin a new life there?

Yes.

Very well. I've finished. Is there anything you wish to tell me before I leave?

Yes.

About the Author

WALKER PERCY went to medical school and interned at Bellevue, intending to be a psychiatrist. After a bout with tuberculosis, he married and converted to Catholicism. He became a writer and his first novel, THE MOVIEGOER, won the National Book Award and has never been out of print since its publication in 1961. Mr. Percy died in 1990.